Copyright © 2016 Helen Jones

Photography and cover design copyright © 2016 Helen Jones

All rights reserved.

ISBN:1539010724
ISBN-13:9781539010722

A Thousand Rooms

Helen Jones

A Thousand Rooms

To my family, now and forever

CONTENTS

1.	New Red Shoes	1
2.	Is That All There Is?	11
3.	The World's Worst Date Ever	26
4.	Riding The Carousel Of Disappointment	43
5.	Death Is A Bitch And So Am I	66
6.	If You Go, Can I Come Too?	81
7.	Door People Are The Worst	101
8.	Chandrani's Heaven	112
9.	A Thousand Rooms	131
10.	A Meeting Of Souls	143
11.	This Has Got To Be Heaven, Right?	158
12.	Goddamn City Boys	183
13.	The Magic Pool	199
14.	What Comes After All	224
15.	Waiting…	233
16.	Time To Go	243
17.	Reborn	254
	Acknowledgements	258

Helen Jones

New Red Shoes

You don't wake up expecting to die.

I didn't, anyway.

    But now here I stand, looking down at what used to be me. Lying on the pavement covered with a white cotton blanket, a small blot of blood near my nose. My new red shoes have been neatly placed in a pair next to my head, as though waiting for me to sit up and put them back on. Guess the impact must have knocked them off. I can see the car a little way further up the street, the distraught driver sitting on the curb, head in hands, being comforted by a police officer crouched next to him, hand on his back. It was my fault, really. I move closer, seeing the pattern on the windscreen radiating out from the point of impact, my final moment preserved in sparkling crackles of glass, bright in the Sydney sunshine.

    I wander back to my body and notice that the strap has

broken on one of my shoes. My *new* shoes. Honestly. I've only had them a couple of weeks, only worn them a handful of times. They were so whimsical, so bright and shiny as they sat on their little stand in the shop I couldn't resist.

I've a good mind to take them back.

Boom! Just like that, I'm in the shoe store. What the hell? I think, looking around. How did I…? Oh, yeah, I'm dead. Then I see my shoes, my beautiful red shiny shoes, sitting on a table. Marked down. 25% off.

Today is definitely not turning out well.

All at once, as if the thought has pulled me back, I'm with my body again. Things have moved on. An ambulance has arrived, two paramedics lifting me gently onto a stretcher. I watch them curiously, taken by the fact that their hands are touching me but I can't feel it. The still-distraught driver is now sitting in the back of a police car, blue lights flashing on top, while a tow truck winches his battered vehicle into position, ready to tow away.

So now what? None of this seems real. Which is why, I guess, that I'm not freaking out. Because I mean, normally, you would, right? But I don't really remember it happening and I just feel that freaking out isn't going to help things, anyhow.

A strange sense of calm descends on me, as though I'm on the outside of it all. The ambulance leaves, then the police car. The tow truck driver starts his engine and then he's gone as well, a small scatter of broken glass near the curb the only evidence that something happened here. People are starting to stroll along the sidewalk once more, the day resuming its routine. My shoes are gone too. Everything is gone except for me.

Seriously, now what?

I look around again, in case I've missed something. What about that bright light, the one everyone talks about? *Don't go into the light.* Ha, I remember that from Poltergeist, watching it with friends when we were younger and scaring ourselves silly, shrieking like loons at the rattle of trees in the garden, possums banging in the roof space, convinced the ghosts had come to haunt us as well. But I never believed in anything specific, you know? As I grew older I vacillated between thinking that when we died that was it, show's over, and the suspicion that there was something, I wasn't sure what, but definitely *something* on the other side.

And now here I am on the other side and the show isn't over, not by a long shot but there doesn't appear to be a whole lot of anything here, at least that I can see. What about all those people, the loved ones already passed away, that you're supposed to see? Where is my guardian angel? Why isn't anyone here to meet me? I mean, all right, like I say, I never really *believed* in all that stuff. At least I said I didn't. But maybe a very small part of me, the part that used to lie awake alone in the early hours of morning and wonder is this *it*, is this my life? Maybe that part of me believed.

I look up. It's a beautiful day, or at least it's shaping up to be. A blue sky dotted with white drifting clouds, the sun shining and the temperature hovering around the mid-twenties. Not so warm for Sydney, but it is autumn, after all. I watch the clouds for a moment and think to myself, perhaps I'm supposed to go up? You know, ascend to Heaven like they say in the Bible. I guess Heaven is where I'm supposed to be going, anyway. Or somewhere.

As I think it up I go, light as a balloon, floating over the houses, red tile roofs and patchwork gardens like a child's drawing as I pass overhead. I squeak in surprise, waving my arms around as I try to steady myself, rolling in the air like a fish in water until I get myself in line. I'm out over the harbour now, the big iron coat hanger of the Bridge below me, cream coloured sails of the Opera House sitting on its point. I can see the ferries, yellow and green, trails of white foam on the dark blue water, getting smaller and smaller like toys as I get higher and higher. I hold myself straight, trying not to wobble as I go up, feeling a little more in control. Yep, I can do this. Don't know where I'm going, but I can do this. Then I notice my feet.

I'm still wearing my red shoes. But I guess I'm wearing everything I was wearing when I, um, well, you know. Anyway, it just looks so weird, them dangling below me like that, and then I realise how high I am, clouds like white wreaths around me, the blue sparkling harbour curving out towards the distant heads and I panic. I completely lose it and start to plummet like a stone, the boats and Bridge and water coming up to meet me as I close my eyes and scream, bracing myself.

You can't die twice in one day, can you?

A Thousand Rooms

But instead of a splash there's only a sort of thump and I open my eyes to find I'm back at the scene of the accident. I'm shaking all over, my breath short and gasping. Staggering over to a nearby low wall I sit down, biting my lip as I stare at the traffic whizzing past, one hand to my heart as I wait for it to stop pounding. I consider the fact that I'm supposed to be dead and so how can my heart feel as though it's jumping out of my chest? Then I wonder if any of this is happening at all.

Rubbing my hands over my face, I smooth back my hair and get to my feet. I check the back of my skirt for dust, but it all seems fine. I take another deep breath as I decide what to do next. This is always how I handle a crisis. At least at work, anyway, where tight deadlines and demanding accounts mean I spend my days putting out fires all over the office, whether talking down a frantic creative or making the impossible possible for a client who always wants things done a week ago last Tuesday. I stop, take a breath and step back, and think what's best to do next. It usually serves me well, so this time I hope it won't be any different.

But everything seems to be completely normal. There's no pain. There's no blood on me, at least none that I can see as I look down my front, turning to see if there's anything on my back. But no, the black A-line skirt and cardigan I put on this morning seem as fresh as ever. I put my hand to my head, gingerly feeling the spot where I'd hit the car windscreen, but all I feel is my own soft hair under my hand, no blood, no (ugh) grating bone or anything you might expect after going through what I've just been through. So this is all completely weird and normal at the same time. I walk along the street a little way and it's as though nothing has happened to me at all. My feet touch the ground, the sun is bright above me and I wonder if perhaps I've hallucinated the whole thing, had some sort of episode on my way to the office. But then it happens.

A woman is coming towards me and I smile at her, as I usually do when I'm walking to work, but there's nothing. No answering smile, no indication she's even seen me. Which is not unusual, in a big city. Not everyone wants to be friendly. But she keeps coming towards me and I stop like some sort of rabbit stuck in headlights because I can see she isn't going to stop and it's too late to get out of her way so I brace myself for impact and, ugh, I am *inside* her. Oh God, it's terrible. In fact, it's the most horrible thing I've ever experienced (except for dying, I guess). It's like being enclosed in a red pulsing mass and I scream in horror and then, thankfully, it's over and she's moving on down the street as though nothing has happened and I sink to the ground, sitting cross-legged on the pavement and shaking all over because

    a)   that was gross and
    b)   I am definitely dead.

There are more people coming now and I get up as quick as I can, not wanting to experience anything like that again, ever ever *ever*. I turn to one side to avoid a man in a suit and realise I'm outside a shop with a big plate glass window and I can see… nothing. I mean, I can see the street and the people and the traffic and all that's usual along here, but where I'm standing there's nothing. I have no reflection any more.

I grimace and stick out my tongue and waggle my hands near my ears. I leer and skip and do a little dance, wondering if I've lost my mind. But I haven't. The only thing I seem to have lost is my reflection. And my life. My mind keeps shying away from that fact, despite the repeated digs and niggles and horrible happenings that would seem to indicate that yes, something has happened, Katie. You are no longer the girl you were.

Except I am. I *am*. I feel exactly the same. I just can't see myself anymore. The panting breaths return and I back away from the window, except I can't see myself doing it so I turn away and walk quickly along the pavement, dodging passers-by (and oh my God, why are there so many people here today? Is it always like this?). My chest is hurting and I put my hand to it again as I turn down a side street and keep walking until I can't anymore and I come to a stop, reaching for a nearby fence to steady myself as I try to catch my breath.

It's quieter away from the main road, birds chirping and squawking overhead. The trees are pleasant and shady and I gradually relax as I hang onto my bit of fence. The houses along here are small and perfect, originally built as workers' cottages over a hundred years ago, now lovingly restored and extended by a new generation of inner city office workers. And they are worth an absolute bomb. I know, because I always wanted to buy one, but the prices just kept going up and up and up until I had to settle for my little apartment. Don't get me wrong, I love my place; it's in a small quiet block and walking distance to the water, but it's not like these gems. I look over the fence at the one nearest to me, taking in the white timber cladding, the sash windows and lacy ironwork on the small verandah, two small pots of lavender by the old front door. It's gorgeous, and a wave of envy hits me anew. A dense spray of roses tumbles over the front fence, thorny vines tangling with the cream painted pickets, velvet red and pink petals everywhere. They are old fashioned roses, my favourite, the ones that look as though whoever designed them squished as many petals as humanly possible into each bloom, like pink pinwheels dripping with scent. I lean forward and bury my nose in the nearest one, not caring about spiders or bees, just wanting to have something normal in my day but... nothing. Again.

I can't smell a thing.

I frown, wondering if the knock on my head has affected my sense of smell, and then I remember. It has. It's affected everything. I'm dead. And, now that I think about it, everything seems slightly muffled. I can see as well as ever, but everything sounds a bit distant, as though my ears are blocked from swimming too long. Across the road, someone is trimming their hedge using one of those electric trimmers, but the buzzing roar of the machine is muted, as though it's coming from further away. I shake my head from side to side, wondering if it will help, but it doesn't. I try to touch the rose, but realise I can only feel it faintly through my fingertips, and I can't move it at all, no matter how I try. My other hand, the one holding onto the fence, feels sweaty and slippery and I let go as though I've been stung, realising I can't feel the wood under my fingers, only the vague shape of it instead. It's as though I'm trapped behind a transparent veil, cutting me off from the rest of the world. I get that spinny heart-pounding feeling again, the screaming panic I've been keeping at bay by sheer force of will since the accident bubbling up inside me. I look around, wondering if anyone, anything, can help me, but there's nothing I can see. All at once I want desperately to be at home, sitting on my sofa, cup of tea in hand.

And I am there.

I'm standing in my living room. Sliding doors look out to jacaranda and bottlebrush trees, and the small balcony where I grow potted herbs. I'm home. I exhale a breath I hadn't realised I was holding. I love my home. It's not big, nor is it particularly new, but it's mine and I don't have to share it with anyone. Just one bedroom, a small kitchen and bathroom, and a large sunny lounge with a little alcove where I have my home office tucked away. There's a large bookshelf filled with books against the wall and a small table and chairs out on the balcony where I eat most days. Just being here makes me feel better, as though I can start to make sense of what's happened to me, try to restore some sort of normalcy to my day. I head into the kitchen and, out of habit, reach for the kettle. But I can't pick it up, the handle slipping through my fingers.

And then I break.

I just start crying and wailing and I bend double in the middle of my kitchen, making noises like I've never heard before. I just want a goddamn cup of tea! Is it too much to ask? But no, I have to be dead and there's no-one here and I'm screaming as loudly as I can, but I know that I could scream my throat into shreds and nothing will change. No one can hear me. This goes on for a while. I sink to my knees, eventually, hiccupping and sobbing, my hands flat on the floor as I lean forward, my hair in my face. Then I sit back on my heels and heave a huge sigh, wiping my face with both hands, pushing my hair back. I don't feel much better, but I don't feel worse, either. I get up and wander back into the living room where I sit down on my couch, holding my weight carefully as I do so just in case I go through it. But I don't, the strange veil that seems to be separating me from the world holding me just above it. So I sit there, watching light flicker through the long feathers of jacaranda leaves.

And I wait.

Is That All There Is?

The flickering light through the leaves is soothing and I drift away, feeling as though I'm dissolving, the patterns against the sky starting to change. Maybe this is it, I think. Maybe after you die you just sort of hang around for a while, then you fade away. I want to care but can't find it in me, just wanting the whole thing to be over.

A ringing sound startles me out of my strange stupor, but I still don't want to move. I manage to turn my head and look over at the phone, which is on a little table next to the couch. It's a landline. I know, those went out with the dinosaurs, right? But I still have one. I do use it from time to time – it's good as a backup if my mobile runs out of juice. Plus my mother likes them – she has this thing about mobile phones, not liking all the features and doodads you get with them. 'They should just be for making calls. That's it. That's all I want.' The guys at the phone store *love* her. But somehow it's stuck with me too, the idea that I should have a landline. I have an answering machine as well and, as I don't want to move and can't answer the phone anyway, it clicks into life. An angry voice sounds in the room. It's my boss, Darryl.

'Are you coming in today? I've tried your mobile and there's no answer. I need you in here, dammit, the client's going mental! Call me as soon as you get this.' There's a loud click and the machine turns off, the little red light blinking.

Yeah, Darryl. He's the head of our account division at the ad agency. He's handsome, a silver fox with one of those loud deep voices and, when he's in the boardroom pitching to clients, he is a genius. He can sell anything. Too bad he seems to have had a complete personality bypass in every other way. I mean, I get that you can't babysit people, that you have to work under your own initiative, but a little constructive praise once in a while goes a long way. He's one of those people you only seem to hear from when something goes wrong. I sigh. Well, he's going to have to ask someone else what's going on today – I won't be there for him to milk for information. He's so fucking annoying, the way he always does that, and as I think about it I feel as though coils of wire are tightening inside me, making me fully present once more. The phone rings again and I frown. Who's calling now? It had better not be Darryl again. The machine takes over once more and the voice this time is female and sounds panicked.

'Katie? Oh God, I hope it isn't true. Katie, call me and

tell me you're having a sickie, please?' It's Sarah. I should try and call her back, I think. But I can't. I don't know where my mobile is. Then I remember.

It was the text that did it.

I'd had a date on Saturday, nothing super special, but I kind of liked the guy and he'd promised to text me. But then nothing for three days. So I'd been on super sensitive text tenterhooks, grabbing my phone from my bag each time it buzzed, let down each time, no message from him. And that's what had happened this morning. I'd been going to cross the road when my phone buzzed and I paused to grab it before stepping off the curb. Paused long enough for the car to come around the corner, long enough not to notice until it was too late and I was flying through the air, victim to forces out of my control, my phone flying from my hand to bounce and shatter before I did the same on the windscreen of the car.

The phone clicks back to silence and I sit some more. There's a niggle of worry about Sarah, but it's a pretty small niggle and, if I don't think about it too much, it goes away, the calm descending once more. I mean, what can she do? What can anyone do? It's as though there's a weight pressing down on me, holding me in place. I don't need anything. I don't need to eat or drink or go to the bathroom or scratch or even breathe, if I don't think about it. And I don't know what else to do now, so I just sit. The thought crosses my mind that maybe I might be in shock. Some sort of Spirit Shock. Ghost Trauma. Phantom Phreak Out. I turn the phrases through my mind, imagining them as a tagline for an ad campaign. But I can't imagine what sort of client would need such a thing, so I just keep sitting, staring at nothing, waiting for I don't know what.

Time has passed. I don't know how much, really. It's another thing I seem to have lost, as though all the things connecting me to the earth are letting go, one by one. There's the faint sound of a key in the lock and I turn my head, but it's a huge effort. I hear the door to the apartment open, footsteps in the little hallway, and Sarah comes into the room.

Sarah is my best friend. She just is. We've been friends since we were children, our friendship growing as we did. She is short and curvy, her hair blonde and shiny. Her blue eyes are wide and staring as she rushes in, calling my name, my spare key in one hand, her phone in the other. I see her look in the kitchen, then she disappears and I know she's gone back down the little hall into my bedroom – I can hear her in there – and then she reappears, going out to the balcony even though it's obvious I'm not here (although I am) and my heart sinks. She knows. She's heard what happened. Coming back into the lounge she drops the key on the small table in front of the couch, the little gold fish key ring rattling against the glass top. Her hand goes to her mouth and she looks around as though she thinks she's missed something, like I might be hiding in a cupboard or wedged into the bookcase.

'I'm here,' I want to say, but I can't, the coil pulling tight in me once more. She moves towards me and I jump up in horror because I've realised what she's about to do and, no matter how much I love her (and believe me, I do), there is no way I'm letting her sit on me. I move to the side just in time, as she sits pretty much where I just was. Her face crumples and she sobs, wiping her eyes, the diamond on her left hand catching the light as she rubs her face and takes a breath, tucking her hair behind her ear as she starts scrolling through her phone with the other hand. She taps at the screen, holding the phone in front of her. I can just hear the faint sound of it ringing, then a voice answering.

'Wendy, it's Sarah. No, no, she's not here.'

Wendy is my mum. And just like that guilt comes crashing over me, the guilt of a single girl living in the city who doesn't call or see her family enough. What the hell am I thinking, just sitting here? Oh my God. I had meant to call Mum today, but I hadn't. And I haven't spoken to my sister for a week. Shit. And now I can't do *anything*. Sarah is still talking to my mum and I can hear her voice faintly over the speaker. It sounds higher than normal, and Sarah is nodding her head, her face twisting again, tears running down her cheeks.

'Okay, I'll come and meet you there, and then I'll go back with you,' I hear her say. 'I'll lock up here. Um, d'you need me to bring anything from here?' She nods again. 'Okay, you take care, okay? I'll be there soon.' Her voice is all croaky with sobs and my heart clenches to hear it, to know she's crying for me. I miss her so much already, even though she's sitting right there.

I still remember meeting Sarah. We were in primary

school together and just hit it off the first day in the playground, both of us hanging from the monkey bars, legs flailing as we both tried to move across at the same time, falling onto the leaves in a fit of giggles, instant friends. And it never changed. All through the turmoil of adolescence we were there for each other, a shoulder to cry on, an ear to listen, through crushes and mean girls and the inevitable changes. God, I was so jealous of Sarah's boobs. I mean, they were huge, early on, and I could never catch up. She hates them, still does, saying she envies my ability to wear little tops and nice jackets, but I would love, just for one day, to experience having a lush bosom like that. Guess you always want what you don't have.

I look down at my chest, momentarily distracted. Can I imagine them bigger now? I mean, in this new existence if I think about being somewhere, I'm there, so if I think about having double D's will they appear? I concentrate, staring hard at my chest but… nothing happens. Crap. Well, so much for that idea, I guess.

Oh. Shit. Sarah's leaving. Damn. I hear the door closing behind her, the key in the lock and I feel such a sense of loss it leaves me breathless for a moment. Sarah would understand. She'd be able to help me, would listen to me pour out all my fear and sorrow and confusion. But I can't even talk to her. And that's just about the shittiest thing yet.

But it's about to get worse. I know what I have to do now. I take a breath and I check my hair is tidy, my clothes neat. Then I wonder what the hell I'm doing as no-one can see me anyway. I think about my parents' house, and I am there.

But no one is here.

That's weird. I mean, both my parents are retired, so one or both of them should be here. And then I remember the conversation I'd heard Sarah having with my mum. She said she would 'meet her there.' And there would have to be where I am. Where what's left of me is. Oh God, they're having to identify me.

That is the most horrible thought. I close my eyes and grit my teeth, not wanting to be called to wherever they are, to have to watch them go through that. It's pretty selfish of me, I know, but I'm just not ready for this. So I fight it and the tugging sensation passes and I open my eyes and find I'm still standing alone in my parents' living room, staring out at the sea.

It's a nice house, this one. It's where we grew up, my sister Ellie and I, in the days when you could get a decent sized house with a sea view for not too much, at least not out of the reach of the average working wage. The house is timber, single level, with big glass windows at the front looking across the road to the sea. I love this view. I used to sit for hours, wrapped in a blanket, watching the colours change and the sky moving, the picture never staying the same.

I wander slowly around the room, my hand trailing along the polished wood of Mum's big wall cabinet, the shelves groaning with pictures and keepsakes. There's the misshapen dolphin I made for her in Grade 5 and, next to it, a slightly squashed looking starfish made by Ellie, five years later. The photos are so familiar, but I stop and look at them, realising with a sick feeling that's all there's ever going to be, at least as far as I'm concerned. I touch the frames, barely able to feel them, my eyes tearing up. Pictures of me and Ellie as smiling toddlers, high school photos with tragic hair and make-up. And Ellie's wedding day. She only wanted me for her bridesmaid and so there we are, the four of us, Ellie in her gorgeous floaty gown, me in mint green, Mum and Dad in their smart outfits, all of us grinning, so happy for her. I smile at the next photo, Sarah and Pete close together, grinning up at each other, confetti petals sprinkled in their hair. So much love that it shines out of the photo. She was lucky, I guess. Huh.

Next to that photo is a baby one, little scrunched up face under a white hat, pastel checked blanket tucked around him. My nephew, David. He's nearly two now, a rambunctious bundle of giggles, and I adore him to bits. Ellie and Pete live not far from Mum and Dad, so they get to see him a lot. Much more than I do, anyway.

I turn away, looking around the living room at the familiar couches, the slightly dated décor, floral borders around the walls and it's as though those tight coils inside me start to loosen, as though being here is helping in some way. I still don't know why I'm hanging around, or where Heaven is or even how to get there, but these familiar rooms full of memories are something for me to hold onto for now, to help me push the panic away. Maybe this is where I'm supposed to come back to, the place where I began.

The big windows are flecked with salt spray, pale

against the glass and I pass through them onto the wooden balcony without even thinking about it. My favourite chair is still there, an ancient wicker basket type thing and I sit down on it, tucking my legs under me as I watch the sea, letting my thoughts drift with the waves. I start to relax, the world growing dim around me.

Bang! The sound of a door slamming wakes me. I know, I know, I'm dead, so how is it that I'm sleeping? But that's what it feels like I've been doing, curled up in my old chair listening to the sea. It's just been, an absence of everything. Which is weird again, and I panic, in case it's the start of me being snuffed out. Maybe it happens gradually; you know, you visit your family and friends and life, one last look before the long dark, and then you go. Shit fuck bugger, I wish I knew how this worked! I wish someone could help me. The panic starts again and it's all I can do not to scream for a moment, then I see the light go on in the house and hear my dad's voice and know that they're home and I have to go and see them, no matter what. I stand up from my chair and waft through into the living room and there they are.

Mum and Dad are sitting together on the couch, Dad with his arms around Mum as she cries on his shoulder, his own face dark with strain and grief. Ellie is red-eyed and clutching a sleeping David as though he's a lifebelt, Pete sitting on the arm of the chair next to her, his hand on her arm. He looks around at everyone before standing up and rubbing a hand over his face, his jaw dark with stubble, brown eyes suspiciously bright.

"Righto, I'll put the kettle on then.' He doesn't wait for an answer, moving away towards the kitchen, Ellie watching him go. And all at once it's as though I can see a dense swirl of grey mist surrounding my family, linking them together, dotted with small sparkles that wink in and out, loose ends swirling as though in a wind, or as though looking for something. I blink and it's gone and I take a step back, wondering what the hell I've just seen. But then I get it, all at once, the knowledge coming from somewhere deep inside. It's their sorrow I can see and the loose ends are looking for me. My little family is broken, and it's all because of me.

'Ellie.' This is my dad speaking, his voice rough as though he has a sore throat. My sister looks at him, her cheek resting on little David's head as he snuggles against her. Dad goes on, 'Can you, would you mind, um, calling the er, funeral home? It's just, your mum…' He trails off as Mum lets loose with another flood of tears, soaking the shoulder of his good shirt. I can hear Pete banging around in the kitchen, the faint hiss of the kettle coming to a boil, and I see Ellie nod, her mouth working.

'I already did,' she replies, her voice all shaky and rough like Dad's. 'While you and Mum were um, with her. And they said Monday was fine.' Dad nods. He looks so tired, his hands old and gnarled on Mum's back and my eyes well up at seeing my parents like this. I mean, it's not like I'd been dwelling on it or anything, but I'd kind of expected them to go first. That it would be me and Ellie going through the house, sorting through their possessions, the detritus of a life spent together. And my sister, my little sister – I remember her toddling around, always wanting to follow me. Borrowing my clothes without asking, fights and laughter and dancing at her wedding. And now she's planning my funeral. Shitty. Double shitty with an extra dose of super fucked. I can't take any more of this. I want to go home.

And then I'm gone, back to the couch in my little apartment. I sit staring into space, the place where my heart should be a twisted spiral of agony. I just want it to be over now. I don't want to have to see this any more, to see their pain and not be able to do anything. I just want to be gone to wherever I'm supposed to go. I sit and I stare some more, the last light of day fading to night, and then it all goes dark for me again.

I wake with a start. I'm sprawled sideways on my sofa and, from the bright sunlight streaming in the window I can tell it's morning. What the hell? Did I fall asleep on the couch?

Wait.

Was this all a terrible dream?

Oh, oh, oh, hope starts to flare in me as I sit up, feeling disoriented in the way you do when you sleep funny. Of *course* it was a dream! My God, it has to be. I mean really, I'm *dead*? Ha ha. I need to cut back on the wine before bedtime. Glancing at the clock on the wall I see it's nearly 9am. Shit shit double shit. Standing up I head for the bathroom, wanting to have a shower and get on with the day because I'm already late for work.

And as I think about it I'm at the office, just like that.

Standing next to a cubicle just across the floor from my own. Fuck. Seems as though I'm dead after all. It wasn't a dream. All the horrible stuff that happened to me yesterday was real. I'm dead and nothing's changed. If I think about how much I want to swear I may start and never stop.

I hear footsteps coming and jump back, pressing myself against the cubicle wall, not wanting anyone to walk through me again. Then I realise I'm halfway through the cubicle wall and just, ugh, this is so fucked up. Thank God it's empty, no one at the desk. Pulling myself clear of the wall I head towards my desk because, I don't know, what else am I supposed to do?

It's pretty swish, our office. A refurbished older building near the harbour with lots of chrome and glass and polished timber floors, it was redone a few years ago at astronomical cost by a team of architects, photographed for glossy magazines, hailed as a triumph, a 'new working environment.' It looked absolutely amazing and we were all super excited about moving in and leaving our old digs behind. However, after a few days we came to realise that all the glass walls made us feel as though we were in a giant fish bowl, while the wooden floors echoed as though a herd of brumbies were galloping across the boards each time someone walked on them. The modern low rise cubicles and offices without doors meant quiet time was almost impossible to achieve, while the bright sunlight coming through from all the glass skylights dazzled as it bounced off all the chrome trim, making hot days

unbearable. But hey, at least we *looked* cool, right?
To be honest, this is the first time that the weird veil separating me from the rest of the world has come in handy, the clatter of feet lessened, the heat of the day not reaching me. So I sidle along to my desk and get there eventually, rounding the edge of the cubicle to stand behind my chair. I'm not sure why I'm bothering, really. I mean, it's not like I can do anything. I can't check my emails, update any work files, even clear out the bottom drawer where I keep a sparkly cardigan and heels, just in case I get asked out after work (this has never happened, unless it's as part of a group). So why am I here? My desk is surprisingly tidy. I mean, I keep it fairly neat, but there's usually a pile of stuff on one side, things people have left for me that I need to look at. But there's nothing there today. Well, nothing except a single flower laid across my keyboard like some sort of barrier to stop people using it, as though it's reserved just for me. It's a lovely flower, one of those pink orchid type blooms, pointed petals spotted with brown, bright yellow stamens leaving dust on the pale plastic keys. I wonder who left it there.

I know why it's there, of course. My mouth twists and I look around. But, other than the flower, the office seems normal. In fact, it looks as though everyone's heading in for some big meeting, people moving in and out of the boardroom from all corners of the office. It's one of the only rooms with solid walls, so I can't see inside, but I am miffed. I mean, I would have been at work normally, if I wasn't dead. And I hadn't heard anything about a big meeting coming up. Typical, really. I'm sure Darryl would have told me about it at the last minute, made me reschedule my day to attend. And as I think of him I'm in his office. Ooh. Standing right behind his desk, where he happens to be sitting. Yikes. I freeze, not wanting him to freak out when he sees me in his inner sanctum. But then I remember and I relax. Ha, he can't see me at all. I do a little dance, just because I can, but then I stop, because I feel kind of silly. Darryl still sits at his desk, phone to his ear. Sounds like he's giving someone hell.

'But I can't be left just hanging here! For Chrissakes, isn't that what you *do*?'

The velvet voice is in full boom and I look through the glass to the office beyond, but no-one seems to be listening, at least not obviously. To be honest, the place does seem a little subdued. Wondering if they all had a big night last night I rack my brain, trying to remember if there was anything on, but come up blank. It helps that Darryl's office has a door, one of the few that does. He complained so loudly and profusely about the noise when we moved in I think they put the door in just so we didn't have to listen to him anymore. But I have to say I saw his point, even though it rankled me to agree with him on anything. So he's booming away and I can just hear a faint voice on the other end.

'Well, get me someone! I have an account to manage here and no-one to do it, the client's screaming blue murder, damn them, and the deadline just won't wait!'

The voice on the other end comes back to him and he shakes his head, running a hand through his still thick hair. His voice comes down a notch from Full Boom to Mid Bellow with a touch of extra Velvet.

'Of course. I mean, it couldn't have happened at a worse time. It's just-'

But the rest of what he says is lost to the roaring in my ears as anger rushes through me. Is he talking about *me*? Is he talking about a *replacement*? *Already*? Is that all that matters, the stupid fucking account? I'm so insulted I don't know what to do with myself for a moment. Then I'm furious. 'I'm not even goddamn *buried* yet!' I want to scream at him. Then I do scream at him, because I can, kicking at the stupid umbrella stand he has next to his desk and of course it does nothing except make my foot feel weird for a moment, as it passes through the blue and white ceramic. But he can't hear me. No one can. So I leave, heading back to my desk where I stand, fuming, wishing I could do something, *anything*! Wishing I could pick up the stupid flower and shred it, wishing I could lift my monitor and just, I don't know, *throw* it. Fucking hell.

A shadow falls across my desk and I look up to see Jeremy standing there. Or, Dreamy, as a lot of the girls in the office call him. He looks upset, but that doesn't affect how gorgeous he is. His dark blond hair is brushed back from his face and touching his collar, honey skin that I know smells like warmth and sunshine. Oh, how do I know this? Let me tell you how I know this.

The World's Worst Date Ever

It's a big claim, I know. But bear with me.

Years ago Jeremy and I worked together at another agency, both of us on our first jobs out of school, office lackeys sent from department to department to do the grunt work, all under the guise of 'learning the ropes.' We bonded in our shared hatred of one account manager who seemed to take delight in humiliating us whenever she could; shouting at us in front of the entire office, sending us into meetings unprepared or with the wrong information, and using us as scapegoats whenever anything went wrong. We used to sit and bitch and moan and drink coffee together, vowing revenge on her as I tried not to look at his mouth while he was talking, or his piercing blue eyes, or the broad shoulders under his smart shirt. We were friends, laughing together, walking around the city, sharing cabs home when we had to work late and

I loved his company.

Then one day, he asked me out.

Oh, I was thrilled. Because it had been what I was working for, sitting close, flirting as best I could, trying to be cool and yessss! he finally asked me. For Saturday night. I mean, it was Thursday, so it was a bit short notice, but I didn't mind, not really. He didn't tell me where we were going, just that he'd pick me up at seven so I spent most of Saturday deciding what to wear, putting together a kickass outfit from my meagre (at the time) wardrobe, waiting in a welter of excitement until the buzzer went and I ran down the crumbling stone stairs of my old apartment block to meet him. He looked amazing. Tall and lean in jeans and a pale shirt, open at the neck so I could see a vee of that honey skin and I immediately wanted to touch him. He seemed happy to see me, smiling and telling me I looked nice, but underneath it all he seemed a bit preoccupied.

'So where are we going?' I asked, all excitement as we got in his car. He pulled out of my street, taking a turn that would lead us into the suburbs. Wait, we weren't going into the city? He still hadn't answered me and had that preoccupied look again as he drove along, a crease between his eyebrows.

'Um, well, we're going to a friend's Stag and Doe.'

'Oh, right, um, okay.'

A Stag and Doe? Was he freaking kidding me? I mean, I hadn't dated a lot but I knew that it was about getting to know someone better and so, what the hell? Sitting back in my seat I looked out the window, watching brown brick houses flash past, gardens bushy with eucalypts, dry summer grass curling in the heat. I could feel myself sweating under my carefully chosen strappy top and jeans, high-heeled sandals already giving me a blister.

'So, good friends of yours?' I ventured and he glanced at me, smiling again and oh, he was so dreamy I kind of forgot for a second what I'd asked.

'Yeah. I hope you don't mind, I mean, you know, I just really wanted to bring you. I know it's kind of lame, combining their hens and bucks night, but, you know...'

I nodded. 'Okay.' But he looked uncertain and so I flashed him a smile of my own, wanting to reassure him. 'Really, it'll be fun.'

It'll be fun? Who was I kidding? Huh. I tried to comfort myself with the thought that maybe, because he already knew me so well from work, he wanted to bypass all that 'getting to know you' stuff and just jump straight in, introduce me to his friends right away. 'Here she is, the girl of my dreams' flashing neon above my head, my smile bright, 'yes, ladies, he's all mine.' I drifted away in my little fantasy, feeling all warm and thrilled at the thought of it.

The car slowed and we turned into a car park. It was for one of those venues you get in the suburbs, low level, not many windows, but inside I knew would be a big room with a bar, the section with the tables carpeted and the dance floor polished wood, murder in high heels. My heart sank again and I tried not to sigh as I got out of the car, thinking about all those cool city clubs near the water, cold drinks on wrought iron terraces in leafy streets. But then he took my hand and smiled at me and I was his once more.

'C'mon, let's go in.'

I could hear music playing already, bass thudding through the walls, even though the sun was still bright outside. My stomach was rumbling. I hadn't eaten, thinking we would at least be having dinner and I hoped desperately that would still be the case – a hot night plus no food and alcohol was never a good combination for me. Holding onto hope and his hand I followed him inside. Immediately I was hit with that function centre smell - you know, carpet cleaner and laundered linens and flowers and under it all, the ghost of a thousand dinners served. The foyer was carpeted in garish swirling red and yellow, frosted glass panels dividing it from the main bar and dance areas and I tried not to sigh again, concentrating on the feel of his hand in mine.

We walked over to the sign-in book and Jeremy let go of me to put his name down, then I did mine. He took my hand again and I almost blacked out for a second because it was so warm, the calluses on his fingers rough against my skin and I imagined him touching me elsewhere, anywhere, with those hands. He smiled at me and I sort of sighed and smiled back as we went inside, him still holding my hand and me feeling as though I was lit up and glowing. The glow dissipated, a bit, when I saw what was in there.

It was a Stag and Doe, as promised, guys and girls everywhere, drinking and laughing. There seemed to be a sort of casino theme, a table set up at one side of the room with card games and a spinning wheel, a blonde girl in a sparkly waistcoat dealing the hands. There was a DJ as well, the music a pulsing beat that promised to get louder and more raucous later. It was already noisy, what with the crowd and the music and the talking plus it felt hot, the air conditioners fighting a losing battle with the outside humidity and all the hot air inside. There was a bar across the room, all polished brass and glasses. I tugged on Jeremy's hand and he looked at me.

'Shall we get a drink?'

He grinned. He was heartstoppingly handsome and I couldn't wait to get my hands on him later. 'Sure.'

As we threaded through the tables I could see people looking at us, a few waving and Jeremy nodded back, though he seemed to be looking around for someone, a frown on his perfect brow. He didn't stop, nor did he introduce me to anyone, so I smiled and waved as well, feeling my glow getting smaller. Oh well, it's early in the evening, I told myself. We hadn't even had a drink yet; I was sure I'd get to meet his friends soon.

There was a bit of a crowd around the bar and, as they parted to let us through, I saw a redhead leaning against it, talking to someone, a glass of wine in her hand. She had gorgeous hair, long and curly, and a nice figure. She was wearing jeans and a strappy top, just like me, but hers were more expensive. Still, I was with Jeremy. I turned to him and saw his face sort of, light up. The frown went and at that moment the redhead turned and saw him. Her eyebrows went way up as she noticed me, then she was all smiles, though I could tell she was checking me out. We reached the bar and Jeremy, finally, introduced me to someone. To her.

'Katie, did you say?' She drawled it like she was really amused, looking me up and down as Jeremy said her name, but I didn't hear it on account of the rage bubble blocking my ears and turning my eyes to lasers so too bad, redhead, guess we won't be besties tonight. She seemed to get it, smirking at me and I wound my hands around Jeremy's arm and smiled up at him.

'Shall we get a beer?' Jeremy signalled the barman and, like a gentleman, ordered and paid for two beers while redhead and I pretended to smile at each other. I wasn't sure why she was so up my nose, but I just knew that I had never disliked anyone the way I dislike her. Still, I made an effort because she was a friend of Jeremy's.

'So, where do you work?' I said, pretending an interest I didn't feel. She looked surprised, and said, 'At Butterwood Smith. I'm in production there.'

Butterwood Smith? Bitch. That was the best agency in Sydney. I would have loved to get a job there. In fact, I had tried, really hard, to get one and I knew Jeremy had as well. It was one of the things we used to complain about, another shared experience.

'Oh really?' I said, trying to keep the jealous wobble from my voice. 'That's cool. I'm at-'

'I know where you work,' she said, all sort of dismissive and then Jeremy was there with the beers, handing one to me with a smile. I took a long, long drink because I was so hot and thirsty, but also because it would keep me from spitting on the redhead. She was eyeing me as if I was some sort of walking social faux pas and I really didn't give a fuck. So I drank more, almost finishing the bottle. Jeremy looked a bit surprised.

'Were you thirsty?' he asked, kind of unnecessarily, as it seemed obvious that I was, but he also didn't know about the jealous spitting so I grinned at him.

'A little,' I said, trying to play it cool. 'But that's much better, thanks.'

'So, shall we sit down?' He went to take my arm and then redhead said,

'Or do you want another beer to take with you, just in case?'

I turned to glare at her and I saw Jeremy give her a look as well and it seemed to shut her down, but not all the way because goddamn her, she followed along behind us and came to sit down, sliding gracefully onto the high stool, one strappy sandalled foot balanced elegantly on the slat, her elbow on the small table as she sipped her wine, dark eyes with glittery lids fixed on me.

At this point I feel I need to tell you that I don't drink that much. I know I have a bit of a potty mouth and can be a bit loud at times, but drink and I really don't go well together. You know, we have fun at first, but there comes a point in the evening where I need to stop because it will all go horribly wrong if I don't. And now I'd necked a beer pretty quickly on an empty stomach and could already feel the effects, so I perched on my barstool and looked around to see if I could get some water anywhere.

'Are you all right?' redhead asked in her drawling way

and I knew, in that way women do, that I could, in fact, have been on fire and she would not have deigned to pour her wine on me. But Jeremy, being a man, did not pick up on this subtlety and so rewarded her with a smile before turning to me.

'Do you need another drink?'

'Um, I'd like some water, actually, please.' He was about to get up and find it when a waiter went past and redhead grabbed his arm and said something to him while flashing me a look that screamed pity. I narrowed my eyes at her, but only slightly, so Jeremy wouldn't notice again. The waiter left, coming back a few minutes later with a tray bearing a glass of water, two beers and wine.

'A round on me,' she said, smiling again and so I had to pretend to be all grateful, trying not to gulp the water down. Jeremy was trying to make conversation and I was totally pissed off now, because I could hardly hear him over the noise in the place and I didn't like having to share him. I could see people looking at the three of us and it seemed we were a topic of interest, for some reason, people looking and talking and then looking again, and I was starting to feel uncomfortable, so I picked up my second beer and started to drink it. Redhead said something to Jeremy I couldn't quite hear, then she looked at me like she was really amused about something, some joke she knew but I didn't and I immediately wanted to smack her smug amused face because I knew it was something to do with me. She turned to Jeremy again and all at once I saw it.

Oh my God. Now that I thought of it, hadn't he told me

he had a girlfriend a couple months ago? I'd been surprised when he'd asked me out, to be honest, but hadn't wanted to question it, not wanting to push my luck. But it was so obvious, as they sat there staring at each other and talking in low voices, their hands moving across the table towards each other as though magnetised, like they had to touch soon, they just couldn't help it. I watched those hands as they moved and a waiter put another beer in front of me and I drank it, too. I tried to join the conversation but it was becoming very very clear that I was, in fact, the third wheel at this table. So I drank some more and tried to hold down the anger and hurt at the fact that he had obviously just brought me here as some sort of statement to his ex, to show her that he'd moved on and found someone new though, by the way he was looking at her, it was obvious he hadn't.

The music picked up, lights flashing on the dance floor and the redhead looked up, excited. 'Oh, I love this song!' She turned to Jeremy, all lashes and smirking. 'You know I do, remember? Let's dance.' She stood up and looked at me as though realising I was at the table for the first time and I swear to God, I just wanted to smash my beer bottle and jam it in her face. Which is awful, because I'm really not like that. 'Oh, um, Kelly?'

She said it like a question and Jeremy looked at me too and there was a flash of guilt in his eyes. Well, good for you, fucker, I thought. Then he said 'Katie,' while looking up at smirky redhead and she giggled and was all,

'*Katie*, sorry, d'you want to dance too?'

Did I want to? Damn straight I did! I am an awesome

dancer. And right now, with a few beers under my belt and no dinner and a rage the size of Vesuvius burning a hole in me I am ready to Dance It Out, bitch, oh yes I am, just watch me. So I smiled at her, my best fuck you smile and I stood up.

'Oh yeah, I love this song too? Remember at work the other day...' and I turned to take possession of Jeremy, *my date*, but he'd already gone. She was dragging him to the dance floor, holding his hand and seriously, why could I not smash her with this bottle? Any jury in the land would understand, wouldn't they? So I started towards the dance floor and several things made themselves immediately apparent:

    a. I was drunk.
    b. These heels were far too high for any sort of meaningful dancing to take place.
    c. Even if I wasn't drunk. And hungry.
    d. Which I was.

But the challenge had been laid down, the gauntlet thrown and smirky redhead was acting all concerned, looking around for me. I waved as I tottered towards the dance floor which, just as I suspected, was the sort of highly polished wood that plays havoc with high heels and drunken people, usually a feature of those funniest home video wedding montages where one or more guests flail and end up taking themselves and often other people out. I was not going to be one of those people, I told myself firmly as I stepped onto the floor. Which was fine, as long as I didn't move too much.

I stood there glued to the spot, lights flashing as I shimmied awkwardly in place, unable to pull any cool dance moves, instead trying desperately to keep my balance as smirky redhead danced around me – I mean, I may as well have been a pillar on the dance floor for all the attention she and Jeremy were paying me as they danced together and I wondered whether she might actually swing from me, like some sort of demented pole dancer and I decided that if she touched me I would, in fact, rip her face off. And then the music changed to something slow and all around us couples were moving together, starting to sway. Jeremy, who, may I remind you, was my date, seemed to be in some sort of quandary. He was looking from the redhead to me and didn't seem to know what to do and she, acting all magnanimous, opened her hands and stepped back.

'Have fun,' she said, smirking at me again as she left the dance floor, glancing back over her shoulder at Jeremy, flirty bitch. But I had no more time to worry about her because he came over to me and put his arms around my waist and finally, finally I was close to him, close enough to smell the warm honey smell of him, close enough to lick the skin at his throat. To my credit, I restrained myself from doing that last bit, because I knew I was on thin ground there. So instead I twined my arms around his neck and smiled at him. But he knew and, all credit to him, tried to apologise.

'Um, Katie, I'm sorry. Maybe I shouldn't have brought you here, you know?' He glanced over to redhead and I waited for him to look at me again. When he did I smiled, even though I was dying inside.

'It's OK. I get it, I think. At least this is nice.' I looked at him, a bit flirty but the effect was ruined when my stomach decided to growl so loudly I was surprised the music didn't grind to a halt. He looked at me in horrified surprise.

'Haven't you had dinner?'

'Er, no, actually, I didn't, because I wasn't sure whether we would, um'

He pressed his lips together, looking at me with guilty eyes. 'I'm a pretty crappy date, hey?'

'No, no, ' I said. 'It's fine. I mean, you probably thought they'd serve food here.'

He looked at me for a long moment then, to my surprise, leaned in and kissed me on the cheek. Just a brush of the lips, but enough to get my heart pounding and clear some of my liquored-up stupor.

'You deserve better than this,' he said, those blue eyes looking into mine. 'C'mon, let me take you to dinner at least.'

I felt a huge wave of relief roll over me, that the evening could be saved after all.

'Sounds perfect,' I said, giving him my best smile, wanting him to know that I was the one for him, that he was making the right choice to be with me.

The song finished and we left the dance floor together, his arm around my shoulders and for the first time that evening, I could see redhead was rattled. She was still smiling, still seeming cool, but I could see the tightness in her face, the faint panic in her eyes.

'We're leaving,' said Jeremy. 'Katie needs to eat, so I'm taking her for dinner. I'll see you later, OK?'

But *I* won't, I wanted to squeal with glee. Ha ha ha ha ha. He's leaving with meeeee, and *I* never have to see you again! But as we were about to turn away redhead, and I don't think I imagined the slight desperation in her voice, said,

'But they're about to serve food. Why don't you stay and eat here?'

Fuck. Because of course Jeremy's face lit up again. He looked at me. 'Are you okay with that?' Credit to him for asking, I guess, but no, of course I wasn't fucking okay with that. But instead of standing up for myself and demanding he take me for a nice dinner instead of this excuse for a date, I smiled weakly and capitulated.

'Oh, right. Yeah, that's fine.' I could smell food, actually. Not ghost food, like when we came in, but the real thing, appetising scents drifting through the room. More waiters appeared but, instead of real food, they were carrying those trays with little canapés, you know, mini burgers and little toasts with dip on them and crappy small crab cakes, all no bigger than a mouthful.

Another point I would like to make. I like this kind of food. It's fun and tasty if done well, and this was done well. But it's not a meal. I don't care how many little trays and waiters you send out, five bites of not very much at all is not a meal, so don't try and tell me it is, that you are 'feeding me' if I come to your evening event and that's all the food that's on offer.

We went back to the table, our very own black Formica

circle of hell. The waiters whizzed past and I tried to get their attention, managing in the end to get about three prawns and one of those little burgers, which I washed down with another beer as Jeremy and redhead started talking again. After a while I was pretty bored and tired and drunk and, you know what, I'd had enough. So I slid off my stool and stood up, holding onto the table because the four bites of nothing had in no way soaked up any of the beer I'd had, and I cleared my throat loudly.

Redhead and Jeremy looked at me, and he got that guilty look again but, even though he looked, to my sozzled gaze, as though he might taste of butterscotch, I had no more fucks to give and so I shot them both a hard look and said, 'I think I might get going, I'm a bit tired.'

I gave Jeremy a smile, one of those ones where you don't show your teeth and I looked in my bag for my phone, scrolling through for the taxi number. 'Hello,' I said. 'I'd like to book a cab-' And Jeremy looked horrified again.

'Don't do that,' he said, his voice sharp. 'I'll take you home.'

'Just a sec,' I said to the cab company and I looked at him. 'Really? Sure you don't want to stay a bit longer?' I knew this was bitchy but I was tired and irritated and starving and I didn't give a shit. He looked contrite and took the phone from me and I let him, I guess because I was so surprised.

'Sorry, cancel that,' he said. 'She's fine.' He hung up and gave the phone back to me. He looked kind of pissed off for a sec, but then he smiled and said, 'Let's go.'

Redhead, meanwhile, had been watching all this with a smug amused look again, and I thought 'last chance with the bottle' as I shot her another glare, but all I wanted was to go home and make a microwave cheese sandwich and sit in bed. So instead of smashing her I took Jeremy's arm and we turned to go.

'Bye, Katie,' she said, all smirky and I stuck my finger up as we left, not bothering to look back. Jeremy said nothing as we headed to the car, and I hadn't anything to say to him either. I felt quite heartbroken, actually. I'd so looked forward to this evening, and it couldn't really have been any worse. And now I wondered how things would be between us, whether even our friendship would survive this, and that made me even sadder, for I knew I'd miss him.

My buzz started to wear off as we drove through the dark streets, street lights blurring into one as I looked out the window, seeing my reflection in the glass. I was so hungry I felt sick, and so angry I felt even sicker. Jeremy was quiet, but it wasn't a comfortable kind of quiet. I could almost hear him thinking. As we got close to my place he pulled over at the side of the road, stopping the car. I looked at him in surprise.

'Are you dropping me here?'

'No.' He looked down at his hands, then at me, his mouth, that luscious mouth, twisting. 'Um, I'm really sorry about tonight.'

I stared at him for a long moment and he looked back at me and, maybe, there could have been a moment there. But I broke the stare.

'Don't worry about it.'

'No, it was shitty of me-' he tried again and I decided like a dope to let him off the hook.

'Hey, it's okay. Just take me home, and I'll see you at work on Monday.'

'Really?' He looked hopeful then, a strand of blond hair dropping in his face and I longed to push it back, but I didn't, keeping my hands tight in my lap.

'It's fine,' I said, nodding at him. He started the car and drove me the last few streets to my place. I had one foot out the door before he even fully stopped, my seatbelt already undone.

'See ya,' I said, as I jumped out and ran for my steps, the taste of beer and sadness bitter in my mouth. I didn't look back, even though I thought I heard him call my name. When I got inside I went into my kitchen and took off those stinking heels and threw them across the room, then made myself a sandwich, hacking at the cheese, layering it on the soft bread, microwaving it so the cheese was all melty and soft. I took my sandwich and my aching feet to bed, sitting up against the pillows, all alone. And I cried and cried and cried.

I did see him at work on Monday, but things were never the same between us. He left the company three months later, moving on to bigger and better things and in time I did the same. But it's not a huge industry so it wasn't really a surprise that we ended up working together again, though at least on different accounts. No, the surprise is that he is here, standing by my desk and looking really upset.

    My mouth twists and I wish I could talk to him. But I can't. He reaches out, trailing his hand along the edge of the cubicle, his blue eyes dark. Then he leaves, heading towards the boardroom along with everyone else. I watch him go, the door closing behind him.

    I look at my desk once more, at the little award statue, a curl of silver on a square stand, at my files and books and coloured sticky notes pinned to the board and my anger fades away to be replaced by what feels like sadness. My mood drops even further as I think of Darryl in his office, so eager to replace me. I rest my hand on the back of my chair and I look around the strangely subdued office one last time, trying to tell myself that it's a good thing I don't have to come here any more and sit in the glass and sunlight and noise, be part of the stress and drama that's a daily part of what I do. Yep, I tell myself as my vision mists over, it's fine, really it is. And, you know, whoever they get to take my place, I'm sure they'll be fine too. They'll be great. And Jeremy will be fine too. I wipe my face and close my eyes so I don't have to look at it any more and I think of home.

    And there I am.

Riding The Carousel of Disappointment

So now the fuck what? I sigh deeply, sitting down on my couch and staring out at the dancing leaves. My herbs need watering, the leaves curling and starting to brown, dust gathering on my little table and chairs, but I can't do anything about it. There's a pile of new books on my bookshelf and I wish I could read one of them, but of course I fucking can't. This nothingness of an existence is starting to get really old and tired. Not knowing what else to do and wanting a different viewpoint, I get up and wander into my bedroom. The door is shut but that doesn't stop me – I go straight through it without even thinking. I suppose I could have gone through the wall from the living room if I'd wanted to, but I'm just not ready for that sort of shit yet.

My bedroom is lovely. At least, I think it is. It's a peaceful place, built-in wardrobes along one wall filled to bursting with clothes and shoes and bags, evidence of my love of shopping. I have a nice bed, king size with one of those foam mattress toppers, the quilt feather down, the pillows soft and fluffy, all in restful blues and lilacs and white. Other than that, there's a dressing table and chair, a bedside table with a lamp and a little pile of fabric covered storage boxes on the other side of the bed. My window looks out onto the gardens at the back of my apartment block, a tree shading it from the bright sunlight. Sometimes I wake to cockatoos screaming in the branches, at other times the high pitched squeaks of lorikeets, nature's alarm clock during the week but highly annoying on weekends. But that doesn't matter any more. Nothing does.

    I lie down on my bed, staring up at the white painted ceiling, crystals on the little chandelier catching the light and reflecting it around the room. What am I supposed to do now? I mean, it feels so normal, just lying here. And that's what's messing with my head, the fact that half the time things feel as though they're completely normal, while at other times, they just don't.

    Like how I just walked through my closed door as if it wasn't even there. Yet now I'm lying on my bed just like I always do. Though if I really think about it, the bed feels a little less… there and, when I look at the quilt, I'm not making any indent on it. My hands run across the covers but I can only feel them faintly, like a whisper against my palms. That weird veil again! Separating me from the world, reminding me that I am no longer part of it. My mouth turns down and I can feel a crinkle forming between my brows, my eyes prickling with tears. Shit. Katie, you've really done it this time. There is no coming back from this.

I wipe my face, then wipe my hands on my skirt. I can feel that, strangely enough. I take a deep sighing breath. And that's another thing. For someone who's dead, I'm doing a lot of breathing. The tears start again and I huff out a sob, followed by another. Then I stop myself. It's an effort, but I do it. Otherwise I might lie here crying forever.

What I need to do is figure this out myself. I'm stuck with being dead, and it looks as though I'm stuck being alone as well. Nodding to myself I start to make a mental list, a pros and cons of being dead, trying to be objective about the whole thing because if I don't, I think I may explode. Right, so…

a) If I don't pay attention, I go through things; walls, doors, *people*. Ugh. Con, definitely a con.
b) I can still sit and lie on things, but only if I think about it. Which feels kind of normal. But I can't touch or affect anything. Definitely *not* normal. So, a pro and a con there.
c) I don't need food or water or anything like that, which is OK, I guess, seeing as I can't touch anything. But I find myself longing for a sandwich or some fruit, or even an ice-cold beer. So, not a pro, really.
d) I'm stuck in this outfit, but at least it's one I like – imagine how I'd feel if I'd been in my

trackies and sweatshirt on a late night run to the supermarket when I'd died. That would not have been good. So a pro and a con again, I guess.

e) There are no visible wounds; I'm not some sort of zombie nightmare, at least as far as I can tell. So that's a pro.

f) I can also, for some reason, be anywhere I want to be just by thinking about it. And that's very cool. A definite pro.

g) No one can hear me. A definite con. As is the fact that I'm alone.

Sitting up I swing my legs over the side of the bed and run a hand through my hair. Okay, so maybe things aren't so bad. I'll just hang around here for a while, maybe go to my funeral then see what else I can do. Sounds reasonable, right? Maybe I'll think myself to India, or Paris, or somewhere I've never been before. That could be fun. I could be some sort of dead backpacker, travelling the globe whenever and wherever I want to go. No super long flights jammed like a sardine in economy class, no cripplingly expensive airfares or hotel bills – just me and my red shoes, travelling light. I smile, liking the sound of that. But, just like that, my little bubble of excitement pops and I flop back onto the bed. For there's only one place I really want to get to, and I can't find my way. Heaven, or wherever I'm supposed to go, eludes me.

Rolling over onto my side I curl up. If I could I would pull a pillow to me and cuddle it, but of course I can't.

Without warning, the room starts to rock and spin, moving faster and faster, colours whirling around me as though I'm inside a kaleidoscope and I feel horribly as though I'm falling, a sickening lurching feeling. I reach for the edge of my bed, wanting something to hold onto as my whole world spins out of control but I can't grasp it, feeling it slip through my fingers as I fall even further. I scream, wondering what the hell is happening to me. Then I land and my eyes open wide with surprise as I see where I am.

I'm back in Thompsons Point, the town where I grew up on the coast north of Sydney. I'm standing in a nightclub foyer, thumping music coming through the glass doors, muscled bouncers guarding the entrance. There's a line of people against one wall and I realise, to my horror, that one of them is me. Or a younger version of me, at least. Younger me is standing with Ben Mitchell. It's fourteen years ago and we are on a date.

Oh God! I clench my fists and close my eyes, then stare accusingly up to where I think Heaven might be, if I could just fucking get there. My face stretches in horror as I wonder if, maybe, I might actually be in Hell. That maybe, when I was looking up, I should have been looking down instead and now Hell or wherever I am has reached up and taken me and now I'm being forced to relive my life, over and over. I back up against the curving pale wall, hands flat against it. My breath pants in and out as I look around, trying to get a grip. And eventually I get one, of sorts. I mean, if this is Hell at least it's not hot.

There are no devils and pitchforks and people screaming. But it's still pretty bad.

    I fold my arms, trying to seem casual, just in case something, somewhere is watching me. There seems to be nothing else to do but watch what happens, so that's what I do, shoving the yammering panic down inside me as I wait to see what's next. Younger me is still waiting in line, smiling occasionally when Ben says something to me. I knew him from school. He was in a couple of my classes and I thought he was kind of cute, if a little quiet. So when he'd asked me out it was kind of a surprise. But I said yes, of course I did. It's only polite, if someone plucks up the guts to ask you, to say yes – at least that's what I thought back then. So there we are, Saturday night at one of the coastal hotspots, waiting to get in. Younger me looks pretty nice, I think, dressed in a knee length A-line skirt with a tight tank top, one of those Kookai ones in the cute colours, plus my new jewelled flip-flops. But my hair is a disaster. I remember I'd had it cut a few days earlier, the stylist promising me I'd look 'just like Gwen Stefani,' but instead I think I look like some sort of poodle hybrid, my hair, surprise surprise, curling when it got cut short. Nightmare. So I've done what I can, a little sparkly clip holding some of it off my face, but I'm still terribly self-conscious about it, I can see by the way I keep reaching up to rearrange it.

    I hadn't realised this club was where Ben was taking me, otherwise I would have worn different shoes. They don't normally let ladies in, you see, unless they're 'wearing a heel.' I know - tragic, right? When we finally get to the front of the line the door guy shakes his head, arms folded. I watch poor Ben pleading with him, calling in favours until he lets us in. I may as well go in too – at least he's not going to stop me this time. So I drift along, following my younger self and Ben to the bar where we sit down. Ben asks younger me if I'd like a drink and I see myself nod before I'm handed a menu which I look at in surprise. For this bar, this tragic little shithole of a place, filled with small town twits dressed in their best, specialises in fancy cocktails, the bigger and fruitier the better, and, lucky me, I get to choose one.

Seriously, why am I watching this again?

I remember what I ordered, some sort of chocolate and cream thing that arrived complete with umbrellas and cherries, and made me feel sick when I started to drink it. I remember eyeing Ben's beer with envy, wondering why I hadn't just ordered one of those, why I was sitting here in this crappy club with this guy who didn't even seem interested in me, who had nothing to say as I sipped my drink and fiddled with my hair and tried not to slide off my barstool in utter boredom and despair as I watched the heaving couples on the dance floor, women all in heels, men dancing it out and thought to myself, I cannot *wait* to get the fuck out of this town.

I lean against the bar and watch it all as it happens again. The dissatisfaction on my younger face, the flashing lights, the big cocktail and poor Ben, sitting there in silence. It's just as awful the second time around – perhaps worse. Thanks so much, death, for sharing this with me again for whatever the fuck reason I don't know.

For making me the proverbial fly on the wall when I don't want to be. I need to get out of here. I don't care if this is Hell, I don't care if there's something I'm supposed to be doing – all I know is that I need to find someone and get some answers.

Fuming, I'm about to head for the door when the room starts to spin, swirling around me as though I'm at the centre of a carousel. All I need is some hurdy gurdy music to make the image complete. There's no falling this time, just the sickening spinning and I scream again, because I don't know what the fuck is happening to me. Then the colours and lights swing to a stop and...

I'm somewhere else.

This time I'm outside. The sunshine is blinding and I shade my eyes, blinking until my vision adjusts and I can see where I am. Well, this is a surprise.

It's Bondi Beach, the great curve of golden sand packed with holidaymakers and locals, the car park filled with preening jackasses leaning on muscle cars while harried families search for somewhere to park, the promenade of shops and apartments behind looking out at one of the greatest views in the world.

I used to come here when I was younger with my friends. Sure, we had great beaches where we lived but Bondi was a scene, a place to see and be seen, and so we would get up early and catch a ride with someone who had a car, settling in for the day in a prime people-watching spot, ogling the lifeguards and muscle boys, the surfers and swimmers and pale skinned backpacker boys, giggling at their accents when they tried to talk to us. It was fun, something different, infinitely more cosmopolitan than our Central Coast lives.

I scan the beach, still shading my eyes, noticing again how the heat and breeze are barely affecting me. Like I'm not really here. Ugh. My mind shies away from that idea and then I spot... me. Younger me, teenage dream, sitting with three other girls. Sarah is there, of course, curves barely restrained by her hot pink bikini. Sophie and Cara are lying back on their towels, sunglasses in place. Sophie had an older brother with a car - that must have been how we got there today. And there I am, loading on the sunscreen, wearing my new striped bikini and trying to hide behind my arms, tugging a sarong out of my bag on the pretence of not wanting to get burnt, my golden brown hair long down my back. Sarah flaps her hands at me, making a face and I know what she's saying.

But I felt fat. I remember those bathers and I remember being talked into buying them, how the girl in the shop had said they suited me, how Sarah had nodded her approval. But fat was how I felt when I put them on and fat was how I felt on the beach. I frown, watching this memory play out. Seriously, was there nothing else I could look at in my life?

The world spins around me again, a whirl of sun and sand and deep blue sea. It's not such a shock this time and I manage not to scream. Instead I hang on, waiting until it stops, dreading what I'll see next.

This time I land in an inner city bar, one of those cool places with glass and views and boys in sharp suits. Sarah and I are standing at a high table, drinks in hand, Sarah talking animatedly to me. I see myself putting a hand to my head, taking a sip of my drink. Sarah and I look pretty good, work clothes with a twist, my sparkly cardigan getting an outing. I remember this night. I'd just had a major disaster at work, an ad going out with the wrong copy, the client going ballistic on the phone and me having to take it, meanwhile vowing revenge on the junior account manager who'd let it go to press like that. My head hurt and I'd only agreed to meet Sarah for drinks instead of going home because she said she had something major to tell me.

 I don't understand. Sarah and I did so much together, like our trip to Byron, or the winery tour where we giggled our way drunkenly around the vineyards; we'd had so many shopping days out, let alone the backpacking around Europe – why was I being shown this memory of her?

 Leaning against a pillar I watch as other me rubs her forehead with her fingers, frowning as she tries to hear what Sarah has to say over the music and chatter, obviously wanting to be somewhere else. Sarah did have something major to tell me, I remember that as well. She'd just met a guy and was convinced he was the one, that this was it. I remember having to ask her to repeat what she was saying, my mind fighting with the noise and headache and stress of the day, just wishing I could go home and sit on my balcony with a cool drink. But, wanting to be a supportive friend I'd smiled and told her how awesome it was, how happy I was for her, pushing down the sharp thread of jealousy in my mind, knowing it to be unworthy. But it was there, nonetheless. Watching myself I cringe, seeing how obvious it is that I'm not really there and that Sarah knows it too, the hurt obvious in her eyes as she sips her drink, her excitement at her news ebbing away. She'd been concerned for me, seeing that something wasn't quite right and I could never take it back, that I hadn't really been there for her in that moment. We made up, as we always did, and it turned out she was right – he was the one. He proposed to her about a year later, a romantic walk in the Botanic Gardens taking an even more magical turn, and I'd screamed for joy with her when she called me with the news, taking on the role of maid of honour with a pleasure that almost drowned out the questions in my mind – when would it be my turn, when would it be *me*?

Shit. And now she would be getting married without me. Her wedding was still six months away, though planning was well underway. Double shit. Who was going to take over now as maid of honour? My mouth twists as I watch the two of us at our table. I don't like seeing this at all, for reasons I can't even admit to myself.

The room starts to spin again and drops away. This time I welcome it, wanting to get away from the memory of that night. But when I land this time I groan. The Hell theory is starting to look more and more likely.

I'm in a café in Milson's Point. My mother and sister are there, sitting with me at a table near the window, both looking at me with concerned expressions while I, and I remember this well, am fighting the urge to get up and walk out. We had met up at my flat; we were supposed to be going into the city to do some Christmas shopping, but they had insisted on going for coffee first. So I'd agreed, never one to turn down a hit of caffeine but the whole thing had turned into some sort of attack. At least that was how I'd seen it.

I'd just broken up with a guy - Matt, I think his name was. We'd only been seeing each other for a few months but I'd taken the plunge and brought him up the coast to meet my family. He'd broken up with me a week later, saying I 'was a great girl' but that 'things were getting too serious and he couldn't handle it.' Asshole. I'd thought myself well shot of him, to be honest, but Mum and Ellie had shown up full of worry and tears, wanting to make sure I was OK and honestly, it was the last thing I wanted to talk about. Whatever. So I hadn't met anyone yet. Sorry I couldn't be like Ellie, provide another grandchild. Big fucking deal.

I stand against the wall, invisible and out of time, watching as the three of us sit and talk, Mum with that little frown line between her brows, Ellie pale and tired looking, her golden brown hair, same as mine, pulled back from her face, and me with my arms folded, looking away, wishing the place would blow up or I could drop into the ground, just so I didn't have to hear about it any more. Mum is going on and on about how I'm a great catch, having my own place and a good job and all that, how she doesn't understand it. Then Ellie chimes in, saying it's his loss, that he's obviously an idiot and I just bridle against their pity, throwing it back at them, feeling defensive. Yeah, fun times.

Huh. Well, this is great, I think, looking up at the ceiling as though someone up there can hear what I am thinking. Maybe they can. I don't fucking know. So hey, if you are listening, any more gems to show me? Any more segments of my life to depress me? I mean, so far I'm a crappy date, fat, a shit friend and a failure as a daughter. Thanks so much, Universe or Hell or whatever, for reminding me of these things. As if being dead isn't enough of a blow. Thank you very fucking much. Things start to spin again and I just go with it, hoping wherever I end up this time isn't too awful.

I open my eyes to find I'm on a beach again, but this time it isn't Bondi. It's the beach near my old home, another curve of golden sand, hot and squeaky underfoot, crackly bits of seaweed and round smooth shells lying in a fringe along the water's edge. And there I am. About seven years old and wearing my favourite pink bathers, the ones with frills on the bum and a hibiscus pattern. I loved those bathers. And, all at once, things change and it's as though I'm back in my seven year old self again. Turning my head I see Mum, sitting on a blanket with two-year-old Ellie who is toddling around, chubby legs coated with sand as she looks for 'treasure'. I'm with Dad, holding his hand as we walk carefully along the rocks at one end of the beach, me with a bucket in my free hand. Dad is wearing his board shorts, his face grinning down at me as we wobble precariously on the sharp stones, making our way to a pool carved out of the rock by years of relentless waves. When we get there I crouch down, smiling as I dip my hand in the water, warmer than the ocean, clear as crystal. I'd always thought this pool must belong to a mermaid; that she would sit there at night, tail curled around her as she combed her long hair. I'd wanted to be a mermaid too, I remember, riding the waves and swimming the green depths, wearing a crown of pearl.

The edge of the little pool is fringed with sea anemones, purple and green tendrils like soft feathers waving in the water. Dad reaches in and gently tickles the middle of one with his finger and I squeal with delight as the tendrils close around his finger. I love that trick, no matter how many times I see it. As I crouch there, sun warm on my back, my bucket full of sandy shells and bits of pebble, my big strong dad next to me, my world feels as secure as the rock on which we're standing. Looking back along the beach I see Mum. She waves her arm and I wave back.

Oh, that's lovely, I think, and as I do it's as though I step back out of myself to a vantage point further along the rocks. I watch small me and Dad a moment longer, tears in my eyes, holding onto the warmth of the moment. Oh, that's a nice one. I don't mind that memory. Let's have some more of those.

And then there's one more. The beach spins again, taking small me and Dad and Ellie and Mum away, and as the spinning stops I find myself in a church. I look around and there I am. Smaller still, sitting next to Mum in the wooden pew, leaning on the mound of her stomach, little Ellie inside turning circles. I remember a tiny fist poking me in the face and, there it is, small me sitting up and frowning. I look at small me with sympathy, remembering the feel of the uncomfortable clothes I had to wear, a stiff new dress, shiny shoes, and how I'd felt to see my mum crying. I hadn't liked seeing her like that, and I hadn't liked how quiet and sad the church was.

I stand at the end of the pew, watching little me leaning on my pregnant mother, her hand twined with Dad's, who is wiping his eyes. It's the only funeral I've ever been to. Unusual, I know, but I've been very lucky in that respect. Being there again brings it back to me, the waxy smell of the candles, the flowers wilting in the heat on my grandfather's coffin, my confusion about how he could be in the box when I'd just seen him the other day. My grandmother sitting in the pew next to dad, her face crumpled with grief. I don't think she ever got over losing him. It had been a sudden heart attack, his life over before he even realised what was happening. She had found him in the garage, slumped over the boat he'd been working on as a gift for the family. And now she had to go home alone, to the home they'd built together close to the ocean they loved.

A few years later she opened up to me one day, telling me that the pain never got any less, it was just that she had learnt how to deal with it. That she had never wanted to leave their house, filled as it was with memories of them both when they were young and the world lay before them. Even through the self centred-ness of my teen existence I had felt her loss, wondering if I would ever love like that. And here I was, dead, no chance of it now.

The scene spins away from me once more, slipping

like glitter through my fingers, fading out of time. And I find myself back on my bed in my apartment, tears running down my face. The light has changed, the day outside grey and drizzly and there seems to be more dust on everything. I lie there for a moment, but other than momentary relief that the strange trip through my memories seems to be over, I feel curiously empty. All I seem to be is emotion, raw and threading like wire, feeling as though I might fall apart and drift away. I think about the last memory, my Pop's funeral. Where is my Pop? Surely he would be here to help me if he could. I remember how he used to play music and we would dance, him laughing and laughing, lifting me up to swing around. 'That's the way, Katie,' he would say in his gravelly voice, kissing me on the cheek, the scent of his tobacco warm like sunshine. 'Like a little fairy, you are.' I wonder if I'll ever find him in this existence and hope that, when I do, he's somewhere great. It's too horrible to think that he could be like me, wandering around in some sort of limbo for the past twenty-seven years. Surely someone like him, someone with all the love and goodness that he had in his heart, would have gone straight to Heaven with an escort of angels. I'd always thought of it like that, the idea giving me comfort as a child, that he was sitting up there in the clouds, happy and well. I rub my face with my hands, unable to make any sense of it.

I hear my front door open. There are voices in the hall, the squeak of sneakers and the tap of heels. I sit up, swinging my legs over the side of my bed, still feeling strangely apart from everything. Out of mild curiosity I go to look and bam! I am back in myself once more. Because it's Mum, Sarah and Ellie, each of them carrying bags and some of those clear plastic tubs. Seeing them is like a punch to the chest, and this horrible veil between us feels like a prison as I move around them, unable to touch or speak to them, desperately wanting to.

'Okay, shall we start in the living room?' This is Mum, her voice sounding clear, her tone decisive. She is immaculate as usual, short sleeved linen shirt over chinos, her feet in shiny pewter coloured slides. Ellie has her hair tied up and is wearing a loose plaid shirt over her jeans, while Sarah is also in jeans, her t-shirt straining over her bosom. I can't help but grin when I see that shirt – it's her old Porn Star one. God, they were so cool for about a minute and then everyone had one. Her parents had flipped out when she and I had gone out one night with her wearing it, but we thought we were shit-hot. It's all faded now, the writing barely legible and I wonder at her wearing it, whether it's to remind her of me. Then I can't bear to think about it. She and Mum and Ellie are in the living room now and I stand near them, wanting to be close to them. I can't tell you how shit this is. I wish I could talk to them more than anything. They are looking at my bookcase, which is pretty huge.

'Um, Mum, I think we really need boxes for these.'

'Maybe we could call the charity shop, get them to come and pick them up? It'd be easier than lugging them downstairs ourselves.'

Oh *what*? Are they here to clear out my flat? Oh no,

that is the limit, the absolute fucking limit! They can't, they can't! I need to be able to come here, to see my stuff and feel normal and, I don't know, what the fuck! Cold horror descends on me as I see the three of them heading towards my bedroom.

'Let's start with her bedroom instead, then. We can clear out her closet, strip the bed. She's got so much stuff, we have to start somewhere.' That's Mum again, her golden brown hair, the same as mine and Ellie's, gleaming with silver as she passes through a ray of sunlight. I follow her, fists clenched, spitting with rage. For chrissakes, Mum, give it a rest! I *like* my stuff, okay?

We all go into my bedroom and I stand there shaking in impotent fury as the three of them take stock. Then reason kicks in and I take in deep breaths through my nose as I see what I hadn't before. That the three of them have red eyes, that Mum's hands are shaking as she holds them together, twisting the fingers round and round as she surveys my room. My anger fades to be replaced with resignation. Yeah, why the hell not. Just clear it all out, give it away, my life reduced to a pile of bags and boxes, my carefully chosen wardrobe hanging on a rack in the op shop, little paper tags on everything. Yeah, fuck it, whatever. Tears prickle at my eyes as I fold my arms and turn away, staring out the window, watching the leaves dance in the sunlight, feeling the coils inside me winding tighter and tighter as the three of them start work.

'I'll go with the closet, I guess,' says Ellie. I turn around to see her opening one of my closet doors revealing shelves stacked with jumpers and folded tops.

She shakes out one of the large plastic bags and starts taking them off the shelves, placing them carefully in the bag. I frown. Take some of them, El, I think, but then I realise that's probably kind of morbid of me. But seriously, there's stuff there I've hardly worn. In fact, I can see a couple of pieces with the tags still on. Mum has started on the other side and is on her second plastic bag already, hangers clattering at her feet as she packs my clothes away. There goes the beaded dress I'd bought on a whim but never worn, clothing for the life I thought I had, rather than the one I actually did. Oh well, I think with a pang as it goes in the bag with everything else. I get it, I suppose. They have to do this.

Then Mum stops. She's holding a dress and seems unable to let it go until Sarah, who is emptying the drawers of my dressing table, comes over and gently takes it from her hands.

'Do you want to keep this one, Wendy?' Her voice is quiet and I see Ellie look up, the realisation on her face as she sees what Sarah is holding. It's my old grad dress. Mum and I had gone shopping for it together and it was pretty cool, stretchy turquoise fabric with a silver sparkle running through it, halter neck with an A-line skirt and a drapey bit around the hips. It sounds awful but believe me, it was cutting edge at the time and I'd felt fab in it. I'd never been able to bear to part with it, and now it seems like Mum feels the same way. She nods, slowly, her lips pressed tightly together and Sarah takes my dress and folds it up, then puts it in a fabric tote bag that's sitting on my bed. My mum's face crumples for a moment and

Sarah goes back to her, putting her hands on Mum's arms.
'Do you want me to do all this? I can do it, you know. You don't have to-'

Ellie, who has finished bagging up the rest of my clothes, glances up again, waiting, but Mum takes a deep breath and shakes her head.

'No, no. Thank you, Sarah, but this is too big a job -'

'But you have the funeral tomorrow. Why don't we leave it for now, go and get a cuppa somewhere.'

Wait, my funeral's tomorrow? Just how long did I spend taking the tragic trip through my memories? I shake my head, frowning again. Mum has gone to sit on my bed and Ellie comes to sit next to her. Sarah has gone back to my dressing table and pulled out one of the top drawers, the one where I keep letters and photos, keepsakes from my past. She starts to go through it, seeming to want to keep busy, sorting things into piles as Ellie puts her hand on mum's shoulder, her face creased with concern.

'Are you sure, Mum? Sarah and I can do it-'

'No.' Mum's voice is louder than usual and I raise my eyebrows, surprised. Ellie and Sarah are both looking at Mum but not in an angry way, more in a way where they don't want to move, where anything could happen and they don't want to be the one who sets things off. When Mum speaks again, she sounds apologetic. 'I just need to keep busy, you know?' She takes in a big huffing breath and then there's a silence in the room. Ellie hands Mum a box from the pile next to my bed.

'Here, Mum. You do this one, I'll start on these.'

I'm watching Sarah going through my letters and

photos, arranging them carefully into piles, reading each one as though it's as precious to her as it was to me. Then I realise which box Ellie has just handed Mum and I turn, and even though I'm moving quickly it's like one of those slow motion movie scenes where you can't do anything except watch the disaster unfold. I even feel as though I'm doing one of those long drawn out 'nooooooooooo's'.

The box on Mum's lap is innocuous enough. It's very pretty, actually. It's one of those storage boxes, a bit bigger than a shoebox with a flip top lid that fastens with a bit of Velcro. It's covered with black satin fabric which has a vintage looking pattern of pink flowers all over it, bushy and voluptuous. But no. I cannot watch. And, as I can't do anything else I turn away, my hands to my face, which feels as though it should be redder than the hottest red chilli. I am dying. Well, at least I would be, if I weren't already dead.

I hear the rip of the little Velcro catch, and I know she's opened it. There's a silence in the room then, one of those silences that is full, somehow, of meaning, more powerful than a scream. And I feel defensive all of a sudden. I mean, I'm a modern woman, all grown up, mistress of myself and of my own desires. And it's not often I have a man in my life to, um, take care of things, if you know what I'm saying. So I take care of them myself. And even when I do have a guy around, it's fun to play, you know what I mean? But this is not a part of my life that I need my mother to know about. I hear her speak. Her voice is higher than usual.

'Well, they're very, um, clean.'

I hear Ellie swallowing, the bed creaking as her weight shifts. I hear Sarah making a choking sound and I turn around to see her with her head bent forward over the little piles of paper, her shoulders shaking. Jesus, Sarah! I mean, you were *with* me when I bought some of those. Remember that party we went to, the one with the guy in the G-string and those tasselly-.

Ahem. Anyway. This should not be a surprise to you. I frown at her, wondering what she's doing. And then she snorts. My eyes widen. I hear a choked sort of huffing sound at the other side of me and turn to see Ellie biting her lip, red in the face. My mother's mouth is tight, pursed as she puts the box on the floor and pushes it carefully away from her with her foot.

'Put those for rubbish, I think. Not really what the op shop wants.'

At this Sarah snorts some more and I realise that she's giggling, her shoulders shaking from hilarity rather than some other emotion. And Ellie just bursts out laughing like she can't help it, clapping her hand over her mouth and looking at my mum and Sarah with surprised eyes. They both stare at her, and I can see how hard Sarah is trying to hold it in and then all three of them burst out laughing, cackling like crazed hens as they fall about, all of them holding their sides. And I'm a bit defensive again. Are they laughing at me?

But it's Sarah who changes first, her giggles becoming sobs and she puts her hands over her face. And my mum, her own laughter ebbing away, goes to her, taking her arms to gently help her up off the dressing table chair, bringing her to sit on the bed with her and Ellie, the three of them leaning in together and hugging as they cry, the feel of release, of love and sorrow and pain filling the room with the sounds of their tears. I can see their energy again, grey and gold and sparkling like their tears and all I can do is stand there and watch them, tears running down my own face, cursing my inability to comfort them, for being the one who made them feel like this. Unable to take any more, I leave.

Death Is A Bitch And So Am I

It's the day of my funeral.
    I know where it's going to be. At St Thomas's, in North Sydney. It's where I would have been married, I guess, if I'd ever met anyone. Mum and Dad had been married there, then Ellie and Pete. I'd have preferred a park, somewhere near the harbour with a nice view. But I knew it meant a lot to Mum so I suppose I would have gone along with it.
    It's a nice looking church, anyway. Built of stone with spires and a square tower with arched doors and stained glass windows, it looks as if it was lifted from some English town and dropped here among the sunshine and palms. Going up to the door I see a sign on a stand with my name on it, so I know I'm in the right place.
    Stepping into the little vestibule I stop to look at a notice board on the wall with flyers pinned to it, some old

and curling, others new and colourful, signs for things like bake sales and Sunday school classes and faith meetings. Then I wonder at myself, that this is what I'm looking at. I really do need to go inside. But I can't bring myself to do it. Maybe I should just think myself somewhere else and not go through this.

But where else would I go?

Steeling myself, I pass through the wooden door leading into the church itself, still thinking a little bit about the wedding I'm never going to have, imagining I'm in a gorgeous white dress and veil instead of, well, you know. Sigh. Then I stop, blinking a little at the change in light. Oh. I take a step back, amazed. The church is gorgeous inside, cool and dusky, carved stone arches and lots of wood, light coming through the big stained glass window above the altar. But it's not the architecture that surprises me so, it's the people. There are loads of them. Lots more than I ever imagined would come to see me off. I drift back to the doorway again and check the sign there. 'Kate Patricia Watson.' Yep. That's me. Huh. I walk back in and look around again, trying to take it all in, wondering if perhaps there's something else going on at the same time. I mean, they can't all be here for me.

Then I see it. Front and centre. The box. The big box made of wood with silver trim and handles, resting on a stand at the end of the aisle, just where I would have been standing on my never-to-be-now wedding day. The wood is dark and highly polished and the lid is covered with flowers, pale pink and white and lilac and green, trailing down the front and sides of the thing. It's very bridal, actually, but this is a coffin.

My coffin.

Ugh. It makes me feel sick, that I'm in there. But I'm not, really. It's just the bits of me I left behind when I went to, well, wherever the hell I am now. I try to look at it objectively. I mean, it's very stylish. It's what I would have chosen, if I'd been consulted. Yes. I nod my head, obscurely pleased for a moment. But I find I can't look at it any more so I turn to the aisles instead, wondering who all these people are who cared enough to come to my funeral.

The first person I see is Jack from the newsagent on the coast – I'd had my first job there as a teenager, selling lotto tickets and gum, stocking shelves, keeping an eye out for cute guys, reading magazines when I should have been working. It's really nice of him to come along – I suppose he's still friendly with Mum and Dad, so it's nice he's here to support them. Next to him sit Sophie and Cara, both with their husbands. I'd heard Cara was on her second, but that didn't surprise me – she was always one with an eye for the boys. Nice of them to come too, though I hadn't seen them in ages, vague promises to catch up for coffee or have a drink whenever I came to visit never really materialising. Huh. Yeah, that's really sweet, actually. I pause for a second, remembering golden beach days long ago. Then the moment passes and I move on, blinking against the blurriness in my vision. There are quite a few more people from the coast - I recognise a couple of the lifeguards from the surf club and quite a few of Mum and Dad's friends, people they played golf and bridge and went on walks with and it makes me smile, to know that they have so many friends, that their lives are so full. A couple more girls I vaguely remember from school, plus... is that... Ben? Wow. He has filled out nicely, gangly lean limbs now strong with muscle, hair sun streaked and skin tan. I'd heard he'd opened a surf shop and that things were going well for him. Good on him, I think, eying him appreciatively. Perhaps I shouldn't have been so keen to brush him off after our one and only date. I mean, we'd stayed friendly, but apart from an awkward goodnight kiss that was as far as it went. A slender brunette sits next to him, skin tan like his, her fingers twined tightly around his arm. I don't know her, but she seems very keen on Ben. So, good on him again, I guess.

And there in the next pew are our neighbours, the Milnes from one side, the Johnsons from the other. I lift my hand to wave at them, thrilled to see them, then I remember where we are and why they're here and my hand drops to my side again. This isn't some *party*, I tell myself crossly. It's your fucking funeral, pull yourself together! Ahem.

Moving on, more people from the coast. Wow, Mum and Dad sure do know a lot of people. Some of Ellie's friends are here as well, which is nice for her. Then I see another familiar face. It's Annie, the girl I get my coffee from every morning at the kiosk near work. I'm confused. How does she know my parents? Her face is sad, dark hair falling forward and I'm sure, if I could still smell anything, that the delicious aroma of roasting coffee would cling to her, like some rich fabulous perfume. Well, that's nice, I think, frowning a little. I mean, it's strange, but nice that she's here.

I turn my attention to the other side of the church. Unbelievably, it looks as though my whole work department is here, taking up several rows of pews. I can't believe Darryl gave them the time off. And then I see him as well, silver fox in a dark suit, his handsome face sombre as he sits next to Carolyn, the buxom junior account manager, her blonde hair pulled back from her face, eyes lowered behind her dark rimmed cat eye glasses. Interesting. I think of who I can gossip to about this and I realise the answer is no-one. I swallow, blinking again and look at the next few rows to see who else is here from the office. There's the entire account department, everyone from the project managers and creatives to senior management, plus our PA, all of them looking suitably upset. So that's good of them, to come and make an appearance. I nod, obscurely pleased. I mean, I'm sure they've replaced me by now, but it's nice of them to be here.

There are a few other faces from work too. Interesting again. I spot Janice from Accounting. She's one of those people who paper their cubicles with photos of themselves on a big night out, you know, in case you think they're just all about numbers and boring accounts and snooooore. Huh. Still, it's sweet of her to come, and she's wiping her eyes, which is sweet as well. I mean, I used to see her a bit at the office, and a couple of times we'd had a drink after, as part of a group. She'd always seemed so excited to be included with the creative crowd, looking wide-eyed at the wild boys with their floppy haircuts, the cool girls with long lined eyes and stylish clothing. Sitting close to me she would hug her drink, asking me about my job and my day. I knew she was young, that this was her first job out of college. And now I feel bad that I never took the time to know her better, to help her out. And now I never would.

I move along the aisle and that's when I see him. Jeremy. He's still beautiful, though he seems paler than usual, his blue eyes downcast. Next to him is his latest girlfriend, sleek blonde hair, full lips pursed and looking down her nose as though someone just farted, you know the type. God, I'm bitchy. But I'm dead, as well. It's my funeral and I'll bitch if I want to. I shake myself, moving along the row, not wanting to look at him any more.

The only place I haven't visited is the pews near the front. I've been trying not to look at those ones. But now I have to and there they are. My family. And Sarah. Oh God.

My grandma looks so old and frail now in her smart black dress, a little brooch on her collar. Her face is set in folds and lines as though made from crumpled paper, squished into shape until it set. She seems resigned, more than anything, though I see her hanky in her hand. I know she's been to a few funerals lately, but I guess that's what happens as you get older. You go to more and more funerals, loved ones slipping away into the past until one day, it's you in the box and the cycle starts for someone else. Except this time it's me in the box and I'm not old. Which all seems totally unfair.

Next to her is Sarah with Bill, her fiancé. She's leaning on his shoulder, her hair bright gold against the dark of his suit and I'm happy for her, that she has him to lean on for support. She's crying and I find I can't look at her for too long, so I fold my lips and move on. But it's even worse. Ellie and Pete are next. Pete has his arm around Ellie, who is red-eyed and pale. Pete keeps wiping his eyes as well with his free hand and there's a lump in my throat that I'll never get to spend time with them again in their house on the coast, garden wild with eucalypts and palms, the ocean roaring nearby. Little David is wriggling in Ellie's arms, valiantly trying to spit his dummy out and I giggle a little to see him, his gorgeous little face and fluff of golden hair. Then I sob, completely unexpectedly. I realise that I'll never get to cuddle him again, smell his clean warm baby smell, that he'll never get to know me as his aunty. It's a choking huff of a sob, and I wipe at my face, trying to hold it all in, feeling those wires wind tight around my heart.

And then I get to Mum.

Ugh, this is the worst. She's so broken up, all hunched over. My dad has his arm around her, white hanky to his face and it's so so awful, like a thousand times worse than the worst thing I could imagine and I want so much to comfort them, to speak to them one last time, to let them know I didn't suffer, that it was quick, and that I miss them. And then it's as though space bends a little and I am between them both, even though they are still clinging to each other and I turn my face to each of them, leaning on my Dad's shoulder, then my Mum's, kissing them both, tears running down my face as I wish with all my heart I hadn't checked my damn phone and brought them to this place. The veil is still there and it feels strange and horrible to be so close to them yet not be able to smell Mum's familiar perfume, or the mingled odour of wool and clean skin and warmth that is just Dad, and my heart clenches with pain and sorrow that I will never get to do this again and I kiss them over and over.

Something happens. My Mum gets this strange look on her face. She lifts her head. 'Graham,' she whispers through her tears - her voice is all choked and it breaks me again. But then her hand comes up to her temple where I am leaning my head against hers, kissing her. Her eyes widen. My Dad looks at her and oh, his poor face, so tired and pained, so much sorrow welling in his eyes and it's more than I can stand so I kiss him as well. His eyes widen like Mum's.

'Did you…?' he whispers, and Mum nods at him.

'It's like I can almost feel her.' But then the priest calls everyone to stand and, well, what can they do but stand with the rest of the group, singing a last song, sending me on my way with their voices to accompany me. Except I'm still here, still sitting in the pew, my father's good trousers next to my cheek, my mother's soft wool skirt against me and I bow my head and weep, that I can't touch them any more, that their voices, their love, can't guide me home.

It's over now. I sit on the steps of the church, off to the side, watching as they bring ~~me~~ my coffin out of the church, my brother-in-law, my dad and several other family members sweating in their suits against the unseasonal heat. The ~~thing~~ coffin is on a wheeled apparatus but it won't go down the steps so they have no option but to carry ~~me~~ it, the wreaths on top trembling and slipping a little as they try to hold it steady. My mum is following, her hand on ~~me~~ the coffin as though she can't bear to let me go, my sister holding little David, who is crying, while trying to keep a hand on Mum at the same time and I can't watch any more. I close my eyes and turn away until I hear the muffled sound of a car door closing. The big black hearse starts driving away slowly, cars falling into line behind it like some strange coloured caterpillar moving through the suburban streets, people stopping on the pavement in a moment of respect.

    I can't go with them. I won't go with them. I refuse, I absolutely refuse to go to my own burial. This has been hard enough. I don't need to see myself being placed in the ground for all eternity. No thanks. I hook my arms around my knees, looking down at my shoes again, admiring them, wanting to look anywhere else than where my earthly remains are going, not wishing to be sucked along with them in some sort of horrific forced ride. So I focus on the red leather, the little strap and then boom! I'm back in the goddamn shoe shop again.

    50% off. Are they fucking kidding me?

The shop is pretty busy, but I'm so furious I just stand there for a moment, fists clenched as I glare at the sale rack. Then someone brushes against me, their arm passing through mine and it's just hideous, like being trapped briefly in a sticky vise. The force of it spins me around and I find myself facing another rack. Ooh, new season styles! Come to think of it, I'm kind of getting sick of my red shoes. I step forwards, drawn in by the shiny new styles and colours, reaching for a gorgeous pair of flats in burgundy leather with a pointed toe. Someone else walks through my outstretched arm and I squeal, pulling it back. I wrap both arms around myself, looking around and stepping back just in time to avoid another shopper. I close my eyes, tears starting to squeeze out and I think of my Mum, I don't know why.

Everything goes quiet. Then I hear a low murmur of voices and open my eyes to find I'm back in the church again. Everyone's gone. At least, all my people are. There's another funeral now, another shiny box, though with gold handles this time, flowers dripping petals on the stone floor, sad people in dark clothing filing in to take their seats. I blow out a deep breath. What now?

Not knowing what else to do I decide to take a seat as well, near the back. The priest starts speaking and I listen for a while, slightly impressed by how he manages to make it sound fresh, even though he's saying almost the same things he said for me a couple of hours ago. At least I think it's a couple of hours. Time seems to flash in and out, in this strange existence. I know it must be about a week since I died, but it feels like it could be a year, or maybe just a few hours.

I look around at the walls, the painted saints and angels gleaming in the stained glass windows. It all feels very peaceful, though as I've mentioned before, I'm not really the religious type. Still, it's very pretty, I think, relaxing a little. My focus comes to rest on an image of a staircase going up, a single figure on it moving towards a golden light. It's a wall hanging, a fairly modern one made of scraps of coloured cloth, with the words 'The Kingdom of Heaven,' stitched along the bottom edge.

Of course! I feel like smacking myself on the forehead for not thinking about it before, for spending my own funeral bitching about my co-workers and then crying, instead of actually listening to what was being said. Although the crying bit was understandable, really. Anyway, I need to focus now. If anywhere is going to show me how to get to Heaven, this is the place. I pay attention to the priest again, looking at him anxiously. Maybe he has some answers for me. After all, isn't he supposed to have a direct line to Heaven?

It's the bit of the service where the priest sermonises a bit, which is exactly what I need. He does some quotes from the Bible and I listen attentively. Then he says something that makes me feel as though someone has just tipped a big bucket of water over my head.

'…but after death they undergo purification, so as to achieve the holiness necessary to enter the joy of heaven.'

His voice is like a large echoing drone in my head. I know what he's talking about, vague memories of Sunday School classes coming back to me. Purgatory. The place you go when you're not ready for Heaven. When you need the dents in your soul smoothed out. Oh my God, am I in Purgatory? I mean, I've heard it being described as God's waiting room but then people also say that about nursing homes and oh my God, am I being watched?! My breath starts gasping in and out and I look around as though expecting to see vengeful angels lurking behind the stone pillars, but there's nothing. Just the sad people and the wooden box at the front of the church, the priest still talking. But, isn't Purgatory for um, people who aren't nice? God, I wish I'd paid more attention when I was younger. The only Purgatory I'm familiar with is a terrible campaign I worked on for a nightclub of that name – it was an over the top place hung with velvet and all about 'sinning', the owner throwing money around and shouting when he didn't get what he wanted. The wire coils inside me tighten, making me gasp, and I sit back against the pew, hugging myself as I watch people going up to the coffin, some of them bending to kiss the wood, wiping their eyes.

Huh. Bet whoever is in that box is in Heaven or wherever right now. Bet they're all happy, having a nice old afterlife, hanging out with lost friends and dead relatives, one big happy party time. Because they're not here. There's only me, alone, still with no idea what to do. I huff out a big sigh, the coils even tighter inside me, as though I'm being squeezed by an iron corset, some sort of twisted Scarlett O'Hara. Fuck this, I think, my mouth turning down, anger rising.

I stop short. If I am being watched, if this is some sort

of judgement thing, a very long wait at the pearly gates, then I am not doing so well here. I think back to what I've done since the accident. Wandered around, made several visits to the shoe store, sat in my apartment, taken some strange carousel ride down memory lane, attended my own funeral and bitched about the people attending. Apart from the moment hugging my parents, I really haven't done much to recommend myself to any sort of overseeing angel waiting to take me to a well-deserved afterlife.

A deep sorrow descends on me at the thought of all the missed opportunities, the chances to make change, to be a better person. All those stupid advertising parties, bars in the city, working all hours. I'd always meant to do something with my free time – volunteer somewhere, go and work on some sort of project overseas for a few weeks, but it just sort of never happened. I used to watch those disaster relief things on TV, people giving up their time and space and money to help others and I'd feel all teary about it, the world not such a bad place after all. But I never considered what I could give, what I could do, other than that it would happen 'some day.' It all seemed so far away, things happening to people I'd never met and probably never would, making it easy to turn off and turn away, I guess. And it also seemed like I had time to do it, years ahead of me where I'd have more money, more time to give. I was only thirty-two years old, for God's sake! I should have had loads of time, loads more opportunities to become a better person. But I didn't. And now my chance has gone.

I look around the church, long stained glass windows dripping colour over the aisles, and sort of laugh to myself. Well, if I'm going to have some sort of spiritual revelation, I guess a church is as good a place as any. But it doesn't seem to be doing me any good. I'm still sitting here, still alone. I stare up at the colourful windows, good old Sydney sunshine beaming through and my eyes blur at the beauty of it all. It seems as though the colours are all becoming one, glorious and shining, like a glowing pathway. And I realise, from somewhere deep inside, that all I have to do is stand up and get on it and then I, too, can be part of the light. Wow.

I stand up, almost without thinking about it. I look along the pathway and it's almost as though there's a figure standing at the end of it, arms open in welcome. I squint a bit, trying to focus on the figure as I take a step forward. But, dazzled by the brightness, I stumble. As I look down, one hand going out to get my balance, my red shoes catch my eye. The thought comes back into my mind about how they're now 50% off and how dare they and what sort of store is it and bam! The light is gone. I clench, scrunching my eyes closed, not wanting to be whisked back to the goddamn shoe store again. I almost scream with the effort of staying in place. Opening my eyes, I see I'm still in the church. Oh, this is just too heartbreaking. I step back, collapsing onto the pew where I bend forward and start to cry, wanting my mother, my father, my friends, my desk, even my goddamn crazy boss who spent his time writing shopping lists in meetings then expected me to catch him up and be on top of everything, even though he got paid three times what I did. Ugh, and there it is again, wire coils tightening inside me. None of that stuff matters any more, but I just can't seem to let go of it. I close my eyes and grit my teeth once more, not wanting to be sucked back to the office, not wanting to see everyone getting on with their lives, someone else sitting at my desk and doing my work while I'm just stuck here. I shake, my hands cramping as I try to hold onto the wooden seat of the pew and the impulse passes. The people around me start to sing, the sound echoing off the high ceilings and taking my mind away from my problems. I close my eyes to listen, tears leaking out from under my eyelids to run down my face.

If You Go, Can I Come Too?

The funeral is over and so is the day, the sky darkening to rose and gold and blue. I'm sitting on the front steps of the church, not knowing where to go or what to do. I feel like crying. In fact, I've been doing a lot of that, thinking about my family and the missed chance to go into the Light. The weird thing is that the tears seem to evaporate quickly, my hands wet for only a moment, and I don't have that snuffly stuffed up feeling I normally get when I cry. Another death thing, I guess. I suppose I should feel positive about it – another super power, yay. But I can't summon up any sort of enthusiasm at all. I just feel empty again, as though what makes me who I am is draining away with my tears.

Across the road from the church is a large three storey building, looking something like a hospital crossed with an office block, cement sheet and stone cladding giving it a vaguely modernist air. The sign on the wall at the front is lit up, a subtle glow behind each of the steel cut letters spelling out 'Star of The Sea Aged Care Facility'. Huh. A nursing home. It looks expensive, one of those places families in leafy suburbs put their elderly relatives when they can no longer care for them, their old red brick federation homes going on the market for a thousand times more than they were bought for, so long ago. I stare at it for a while, chin in my hand, a part of my mind considering that at least it's not far to go when they pass on. Good positioning, that. But it's only a vague thought and I sink back into despair.

Another glow catches my eye. It's in a window on the third floor, like a light coming on then gradually fading to off again. It's golden and sparkling and intriguing and something in me is drawn to it, shaking me out of my fugue state. I wonder what it is, feeling a little tug under my breastbone. And, just like that, I'm inside.

I am in someone's bedroom. I rub at the ache in my chest as I look around. The pale pink walls can't completely disguise the fact that this is a sickroom, the ceiling hoists and metal trolley hinting at infirmity, the wheelchair folded and leaning against the wall proof of it. Yet there are touches of home. An old cushioned rocking chair next to a low table holding photographs that span decades, laughing babies grown to tall adults, young lovers to wrinkled companions. Two small paintings of ocean scenes hang on the walls, a quilted dressing gown draped across the chair. Despite the medical apparatus, it is a peaceful place. And I am not alone.

A frail old woman with soft silver hair is lying on the

bed, wearing a dark pink dress and lighter pink knitted wool jacket. Her legs are bone slender in tan stockings that wrinkle around her ankles, her hands crossed on her stomach. A small group of people are gathered around the bed. Two men and a woman, all of them teary, while a teenager leans against the wall, wiping her eyes, black mascara smeared. A nurse is pulling a blanket up over the old woman, her voice gentle as she speaks to the bereaved family. The energy in the room is one of sorrow but also love and acceptance, joy of a long life lived, of life given to others. As the blanket covers the old lady the woman turns to one of the men and he holds her close, his hand on her hair as she sobs on his shoulder, his own eyes red rimmed. The other man also wipes at his eyes, his shoulders hunching. There is so much love here you can feel it, as though the air is thick and golden and warm with it, weaving soft tendrils around the little group. My own eyes tear up in response and I feel an easing inside me, as though the tense knot of wires is starting to relax, coils loosening.

But where is the old woman's spirit? You know, the bit of her that's like me? I can't see her anywhere, but there seems to be a sort of glow near the door, like a faint trail of sparkles that dissipates as I watch. I stare at it for a moment and an idea hits me.

I need to be there when someone dies.

God, that sounds awful and macabre but hey, I'm already dead. I'm not some snuff film fan, someone who gets their kicks from watching others leave this world. I just want to see what happens to everyone else. To see if perhaps I can meet someone who can help me, or at least not be alone anymore. After all, it shouldn't be too hard to find – this is a big city, people being born and dying every day. Pushing aside the idea that I'm in some sort of Purgatory to be judged, I figure this could, just maybe, work. I start to feel excited, considering the possibilities. Perhaps I could even tag along with them, if they know where they're going, like some sort of buddy system to get you to Heaven. I giggle a bit at this, thinking of the ad campaign you could run. Something in nursing homes, you know – *'Heaven – it's harder to get to than you think.'* *'Don't die alone, take a friend.'* I imagine Darryl in the boardroom showing mock-ups to clients and I laugh even more then clap my hand over my mouth, shocked at myself. But seriously, I need to try this. I need to do something. I can't be like this forever.

Decision made, I walk out of the room. I know, I can drift and go through walls and all that, but sometimes I just want to feel normal, you know? And walking through open doorways is a normal thing to do. I find myself in a long hallway carpeted in tasteful dark grey, the walls a restful shade of pale green. It's deserted, thank goodness. There are doors along both sides of the hall, each with a number on them except for the occasional sign saying 'Nurse' or 'Staff Only – Private.' Paintings hang at intervals in between, peaceful scenes of landscapes and mountains and leaves. I start to wander along, knowing what I'm looking for but not sure how to find it, wondering what the odds are of two people dying on the same night in the same place. But I can't think too much about that so I keep going, turning a corner into another hallway, the same as the one I just left. Rubbing at my chest where I felt the little tug before, I wonder if that's what I need to follow. Concentrating, I look at each door when I pass, but there's nothing.

When I reach the end of the hall there's a set of swinging doors that open onto a stairwell. I go down one level, emerging through a similar set of doors into a large dining room, a small vase of flowers on each table. One end of the room is set up with rows of chairs, many of which are filled with elderly people who are all watching a film, projected onto the large screen set into the wall. I stop for a moment to watch the flickering black and white images, a love story, by all the kissing that's going on. The ancient faces watching range in expression from teary to dreamy to unaware, eyes in wrinkled sockets gleaming like marbles in the reflected glow from the screen on the wall.

Then I feel something, a sort of tingle in the centre of my chest and my head turns. Something is happening, nearby. Following the feeling, I'm led out of the dining room into another grey-carpeted hallway, once again lined with doors. But I know exactly which one I need. I can see the glow, golden and unmistakable as it comes around the edge of the closed door. I think myself inside, and then I am.

Another peaceful room, pale lemon walls and another padded armchair. There are paintings on the walls here too, but these ones are religious in tone, Jesus with his heart exposed, a sad faced Madonna clutching a plump baby. A small statue of the Virgin Mary is on a small table in the corner, a lit candle in front of it. There is a pool of melted wax around the base, colourful flowers scattered on the table, their bright petals mingling with the wax.

And the glow is all around us, as though the air is full of gold sparkles, floating gently like dust motes. An old man with wisps of grey hair is lying in the bed, looking small and wizened, his eyes closed, his skin slack. His covers are pulled up to his chest, his head supported by several soft pillows. A young woman sits in a chair next to him, holding his hand, tears gleaming soft on her cheeks. A young man stands behind her, his hands on her shoulders as if to support her. She is speaking softly, almost under her breath. I can only just hear her.

'I am here, Tio, dear Tio, we are here. And if you need to go, you go, just know that we love you, so much, we will see you again one day, we know it.' Her voice is softly accented and it gives the words a beautiful cadence, like a prayer, as she keeps talking and rubbing the old man's hand so very gently, as though he is unutterably fragile and precious.

Then he dies.

Just like that, his last breath going in and then, slowly, out. It's so peaceful, especially when compared to the crash bang of my own demise. It's as though everything stops moving for a moment, even the gold sparkles hanging still in the air. They glow brightly and disappear, winking out like fireflies at dusk. Then, and this is really weird and kind of creepy, the old man sits up. Except it's not his body. That's still lying there, his hand still being held by the young woman who is sobbing now, her head bent. The dead man's spirit turns to look at her, sorrow on his face. He reaches out as if to touch her cheek and I swear she feels it, lifting her head to look around and then up at the man behind her. Once again there's a feeling of love, pure energy throughout the room.

A young woman comes in through the door and she is gorgeous. Caramel skin and dark eyes, curling dark hair pinned up with colourful flowers like the ones on her dress. She is smiling as she goes straight over to the dead man whose face lights up when he sees her.

'Maria!' he cries, taking her outstretched hands and it's as though she pulls him completely from his body and away from the bed. He pulls her into a hug, kissing her smooth skin, burying his face in her hair. And, again, this is weird but he is starting to look *younger* – his back straighter, hair going from grey to black again, wrinkles smoothing away from his face until he looks the same age as the young woman.

I make a face. This has not happened to me, I'm sure. If I could find a mirror that reflected me I'm sure I would have the same crow's feet and dark circles as always. I'd been thinking about having them 'done,' you know, some sort of injections but couldn't stand the thought of filling my face with stuff. Still, doesn't matter now. Whoops! Looks like they are getting ready to go, holding hands as they move towards the door, smiling lovingly at each other. The air is starting to glow again, but just around them. As it gets brighter I lunge forward, managing to step into the glow with them just in time. We start to ascend, surrounded by whirling lights and colours, painted Mexican sugar skulls interspersed with the Virgin Mary, fairy lights twinkling and it all spins around confusingly in a mad mix of imagery, lifting us as though we're in the centre of a tornado but it's not frightening at all. In fact, it's amazing. Whee! I'm finally on my way to Heaven! I guess the fact that I know I'm dead helps – after all, what else can happen to me? We land, and I look around in wonder.

We are in a beautiful walled garden filled with trees, the sky above bright with stars. Coloured fairy lights are strung from the trees and music is playing, a lively beat and everywhere people are dancing, women twirling in colourful full skirts embroidered with flowers, dark skinned men in shirts white like their teeth, everyone laughing and having a wonderful time. This is great. Heaven is awesome. The new arrival, the guy I followed, is being hugged by everyone as though he is a long awaited friend, and I look around, wondering if someone will come and hug me too. But there's no-one here I recognise. I start to wander through the crowd, smiling at everyone, but it gradually becomes apparent that something isn't quite right. I mean, it's not like they're nasty or anything, in fact most of them smile back at me, but I can see in their eyes that they don't know who I am and are wondering why I'm here. I end up near a long table groaning with all kinds of delicious looking dishes, but I feel strange about eating, like a party crasher with a case of the guilts. This isn't what I thought Heaven would be like at all. There's no-one here that I know, at least not that I can see and, while I love a party, it just feels not quite right. I try dancing for a bit, twirling around like the other ladies but I'm not dressed like they are and don't have a partner and so it seems weird again. I leave the dance and stand under a tree, not sure what to do with myself. My hands are sweaty and I wipe them on my skirt, looking up at the stars twinkling through the leaves, feeling like I want to cry again. I mean, I'm somewhere, this is progress, but something is wrong.

There's a tug under my breastbone and I yelp, rubbing at it. As I do I spot a man in the centre of the crowd and, I swear to God (or whoever) that his face lights up when he sees me. He is gorgeous, with unusual silver grey eyes and, ooh, will he dance with me? But then a hand touches my arm and I turn to see the young woman who came to collect the old man from his hospital room, her pretty face full of concern.

'Are you lost?' she asks, her voice heavily accented so I have to think about what she's asking.

'Yes, I am,' I nod in relief. Finally someone I can talk to about this. But all she does is smile, and reach up to touch my face gently, in between my eyebrows.

'Let me help,' I hear her say. 'I can send you on your way.' And everything fades to white. I feel as though I'm falling and I scream, though it's more of a wail. For when I land I find myself back on the street where it all started.

I could cry with frustration. In fact, I do. I stand there next to where the car smashed the life from me and I sob and sob. I was so close! And now I have to start again. I look up at the sky as if it might hold the answer but there's nothing there but cold stars and a sliver of moon, silvery clouds like feathers across it. Fuck. Where to now? I run along the pavement with my hands in the air, like I'm reaching up to the Heaven that just cast me out. I leap and jump and then I'm floating and I remember how it was just after the accident, when I started to go up before I fell and I panic. But as I think about going down to earth I start to sink and I realise that maybe, I might have some control over this thing. So I focus on my descent and I land softly, my feet flat on the ground. I stand there for a second, distracted from my problems as I contemplate this new power. Tentatively, I push off again, feeling my toes leave the ground and stretching my arms out as I rise up, turning slowly as I do it. It's a completely weird and awesome sensation and I gradually move until I'm horizontal in the air, and I think about moving forward. It's like I'm learning to drive again, in a way – figuring out which gears to use, which action will take me where I want to go. I move one way, then the other, swooping a little as I go. A tree looms up suddenly and as I swerve, trying to miss it, I lose focus and drop down, landing in someone's back garden.

    It's a small space, hibiscus and frangipani trees along one edge, a timber patio edged with pebbles and spiky plants. There's a little toy car on a wooden table, a ball against the wooden fence and I smile a little, thinking of David and the trail of toys and destruction he leaves wherever he goes. Sitting on the bench next to the table, I try to push the little car with my finger, but nothing happens. There's a light on in the house, warm and golden in the dark blue night, and it's so fucking tempting to just go in there and join whoever's inside. But my finger going through the car instead of moving reminds me of how I can never do that again. It crashes down on me that the human world is closed to me now. All I have is in between.

And I break again. Sobbing and wailing in the quiet little space, all the pain and loss and loneliness coming out, the fear that this is it, this is all that is left for me, forever to be an outsider looking in. It's an awful feeling. And I need to somehow let go of the idea that, despite all that's happened, this situation can be reversed. Because it can't.

After a while I stop crying. It just feels pointless, anyway. I briefly consider thinking myself to Paris or Bhutan or somewhere I've never been. But it just seems like a waste of time if I can't talk to anyone or share the experience. What I need to do is figure this out, because I can't sit here and wallow in self-pity forever. Or maybe I can. I mean, I just don't fucking *know*. I guess the key thing is that I don't *want* to do that. If no-one can be bothered to show up and help me, I'll find another person and tag along with them and this time there will be questions. There will be demands for assistance, and no-one is touching me and sending me away until I get some answers.

I blow out a breath and wipe my face clean of tears. It feels better to have a plan, even if it's just to find more dead people. I know, morbid and horrible, you're a terrible person Katie, blah blah but you know what, *you* try being like this.

I consider where I am, in the leafy suburbs fringing the harbour on the North Shore. I know there's a hospital near here. And I know that death will be there.

Standing up, I push off again, concentrating on controlling my flight path as I rise up out of the little garden into the night sky. It's already getting easier, and I start to enjoy the sensation as I turn myself in the direction of the hospital. I float over the night city, scattered points of light below, water gleaming lighter blue against the dark fingers of land as I turn away from the city centre, moving along the North Shore. And, wow, I can see the hospital already. It's lit up, pulsing with energy, rays of light streaming incandescent coming from the windows. One wing is enveloped in a bright silver glow and, as I draw closer, I can hear the faint sounds of babies crying and the muffled shrieks of a woman in pain. I wince, remembering Ellie going through it. No thanks. I steer clear of that area, not wanting anything to do with the maternity ward.

I turn myself towards another wing where the windows pulse softly with gold and grey light. Intensive care. Full of people hovering on the border of life and death, their families waiting in grief and hope. I choose a window and hover outside, peering in. It looks like a waiting area, so I drift inside, waiting for that tug in my chest that tells me where to go. There are a few people sitting in the leather and chrome chairs, faces dark with strain, clutching coffee cups to keep them going in the middle of the night and all at once I haven't the heart for this. I can't trade on their loss, no matter how desperate my need. I look at the signs on the wall, black lettering against a yellow background and see an arrow pointing towards a long hallway. 'Emergency Department.'

Okay. Maybe that I could do.

I focus on the hallway and zoom along, my feet just above the ground, dodging around the odd person I see. It's kind of fun, actually. But as I near the Emergency Department I start to slow. The energy here is red, gold and black, misting out from behind the double swinging doors towards me, occasional shooting rays of gold like fireworks. I grit my teeth and push myself forward again, passing through the double doors into a world of noise and light and pulsing energy. The plastic chairs are full of people sitting and waiting, some nursing wounds, some abusive, others resigned. It's busy, but this is a big city and so there's the usual assortment of overwhelmed drunks and strung out teenagers, an older woman and man sitting together, her face pale, hand to her chest. I scan the room but don't feel anything, which pleases me. At least no-one in here is going to die tonight.

I drift towards another set of double doors, following where the energy seems strongest and the scene changes again. I'm in the place where they work on people who come in, doctors moving quickly between curtained cubicles. Someone is groaning, horrible rasping creaking sounds and I move towards it, pushing down the bit of me that's saying 'no, this is gross, you can't do this.' I *can* fucking do this. I *have* to do this. But I stop at the curtained cubicle, unsure what to do. I don't want to drift through because I can't see what's on the other side and I don't want to risk going through anybody. The groaning has died down to moans and there's a lot of muttered conversation going on, the sound of plastic ripping and metal rattling. The curtain whips open and a nurse comes out, her front spattered with dark blood, her face creased with concern. I lean back as she whooshes past me then take my chance and step inside before the curtain closes again.

Oh, this is a bad one.

A woman is on the bed. She looks a bit older than me, what I can see of her, anyway. Blood is on her chest and spattered down her arms and legs, one arm is bent just wrong and her whole body is flopping and twitching unnaturally. I'm mesmerised for a moment by the mesh of energy, the silver-blue calm of the doctors as they move around her, trying to heal her wounds, and the jagged mass of darkness on her body that shows me it's an impossible task. I wonder what happened, looking around for clues. And then I see her.

It's the woman on the bed, or else it's her twin. But she's wearing the same clothes, jeans and a white singlet, her grey streaked dark hair brushed back from her face. Which is angry and dissatisfied, deep lines around her mouth, dark eyes glinting like onyx as she watches the doctors working on the remains of her body. A line of golden light still links her with it but, as she takes a step back, folding her arms and sighing as though completely inconvenienced, I see the line stretch and start to fade, the body on the bed falling still. The golden line is gone, just like that. She's dead. I go to move towards her but something stops me. It's like a voice inside warning me away from her, that she's the last person I should ask for help. Screw that, I think. I need help, and she's the only one I see dying around here. I start towards her again but stop as blackness opens up around her, like a piece torn from the night sky. From it, ugh, this is too horrible, come *arms*. Arms that shine like dull metal as they grab at her. The angry expression leaves her face to be replaced by one of screaming horror as the metal arms wrap around her and it's as though she folds in half and is pulled into the darkness and then, just like that, the rift closes and she's gone.

Holy shit.

I realise I'm trembling all over. Thank God and Heaven and all the angels and everyone else that I didn't try to join her. I mean, I know no one's shown up to help me so far but that's still better than what just happened to her. I back away, my legs feeling oh so wobbly, hearing the nearby doctors pronouncing her death as I turn and leave the cubicle, not caring about who or what might be on the other side of the curtain, just wanting to get away from that place, in case those metal arms come looking for another soul to take.

Fucking hell.

My eyes are full of tears but they are of terror, not sorrow and I just want to get out of here. All at once the energy around me is too much, throbbing with life and death and everything in between. I run down the corridor, not caring if I run into any one. Then I see a window. I'm a storey up but I don't care. Already dead, remember? So I throw myself out of it and soar up into the night sky, taking deep breaths as though I can somehow expel the image of what I've just seen, send it out into the cold stars instead.

Gradually, I calm down and focus on what I'm doing. I'm out over the Harbour again, night city lit up like a million Christmas trees in front of me and I angle myself towards it, wanting to head through and beyond. I gather my scattered thoughts enough to remember that there's another old folks home, She Oak Hills, just on the other side of the CBD, towards the golden string of beaches running from Bondi to Coogee. We did a brochure for them, a few years back, and I remember going there for the photo shoot and thinking it wasn't a bad place to end your days, not imagining I wouldn't get the chance for such a peaceful retirement. Anyway, it was a nice spot, and I'm not going back to Star of the Sea – two deaths in one night was probably unusual enough, I wasn't going to push my luck seeking a third in the same place. And forget hospitals, now and forever. So I point myself towards the skyscrapers and I think of Peter Pan, flying to Neverland, 'Second star to the right, then straight on till morning.' And I spread my arms and swoop a little and smile for the first time in what seems like ages.

After all, this flying business is very cool. I mean, haven't we all had those dreams where we're flying, soaring above the land feeling free and light as air? This is pretty similar, though I'm not so much flying as floating, like a balloon let go by a small child, taken by the wind. It's calming me down, as though I'm leaving the energy of the hospital behind, letting it stream away like smoke.

I pass over Circular Quay and then I'm among the tall buildings of the CBD, moving between the glass towers. This is really odd. I mean, I've worked in some of these buildings, so to be floating past them at night while dead and unable to see myself reflected in the windows is a level of weird I've never imagined in my wildest dreams. So I try not to think too much about that, just concentrating on my destination, enjoying the flight. There are lights on in some of the offices, a few people still at their desks, while the apartment blocks glow brightly, people at various stages of their evenings, partying, watching TV, making love, sleeping, eating. They can have no idea at all that I'm out here watching them, privy to their most private moments.

All at once below me I hear shouting, ugly and jagged, and a shock wave of hard energy knocks me to one side. Whoa! Righting myself before I slide through the wall of a nearby building I look down to see a young man running, being pursued by three more. Oh shit. He is doing his best to get away, I can see as I drop down closer to him but the other three are buzzing and fizzing with a strange energy, their bodies altered in some way that I can't figure out, until I get close enough to see their wild eyes, pupils pinpricks, the gleam of sweat on their skin. They are big men, muscles straining under tight t-shirts, their faces ugly with anger as they close on the young man who is smaller and more slender than them, and who doesn't stand a chance. I land on the pavement nearby, my heart clenching. I know it sounds morbid, to wait for his death, but I can't see any other way this is going to pan out. The drug fuelled frenzy of the attackers, the fact that there's no-one else around – I mean, you hear about this stuff every weekend, young men getting in fights, being attacked unprovoked, someone's life shattered across the front page of the newspaper, grieving families begging for people to change, to think before they act. But they never do, and the same story plays out again the very next weekend. And now it seems to be this young man's turn, his family the ones to get the knock on the door later tonight.

It's sickening to watch the three guys closing in on him but I refuse to look away, wanting to bear witness at least, so he doesn't have to go through this alone. After all, his death will be violent and sudden, and I know a bit about how that feels. He holds his hands up, trying to back away but his attackers just circle like sharks, jabbing and kicking at him, pushing him so he stumbles, playing with him. I can see their anger, the air around them thick with spikes, harsh and aggressive and I can't do anything but listen to them as they grunt and attack, relentless in the dark night.

'What the fuck are you lookin' at?'
'Think you can fuckin' look at me?'
'Faggot, dickhead, can't even punch.'

And they laugh and hit and shove, the young man's soft skin breaking under their fists, bruises darkening on his bare arms as he tries to defend himself. There's a shout and I turn to see another guy running towards the group. He's young as well, with short dark hair, white short sleeved t-shirt over jeans and he is furious.

'Bunch of cowards!' He runs without pausing right into the centre of the little group, putting himself between the other guy and his attackers, his hands up. His arms are lovely and muscly as he turns, facing each one in turn, trying to get them to back off.

'Pick on someone your own size, assholes.'

The three attackers just laugh and start swinging at him as well. But this guy is no small prey to be toyed with. He ducks under one wild swing then punches back, catching one of the attackers in the mouth so he recoils, hand to his lip, blood coming from under his fingers and the air just crackles with hate and anger as the three attackers arc up, converging on the good Samaritan, kicking and punching him so he has no recourse except to curl his body against them, trying to avoid the worst of it. The original victim is leaning against a nearby wall, eyes wide, panting with panicked breaths as he fumbles in his pocket. It's one of those ones on the side of his trouser leg and he tears the button off as he scrabbles to open it, pulling out his phone. He dials fast, not taking his eyes off the scene in front of him. His voice is distorted from the swelling on his lip, blood starting to trickle from a cut above his eye.

'I need police here, now! I've been attacked, just fucking attacked!'

His voice catches and his breath sobs in and out as he gives them the address, then he puts his phone back in his pocket and I see him looking at the ongoing fight, his rescuer covered in blood and being pushed from side to side. I see him take a deep breath and my heart breaks for him, that he is so scared yet unwilling to give up, to leave his rescuer to his fate. I put my hands to my mouth as he moves forward, wishing there was some way I could help. But it's too late. One of the attackers hauls back and kicks the rescuer in the face. He falls to the ground, out cold before he lands, hitting his head hard on the curb and just like that, it's over for him. It's so sad. All he wanted to do was help and now he's lying in the street, his attackers running off like the cowards they are, swearing and shouting, the sounds echoing off the high buildings as the scream of sirens move closer. The original victim is kneeling next to him, hands on the man's chest, his voice raw as he realises what has happened, tears and blood and snot mingling on his face.

'C'mon, man. Fuck. Oh, man, c'mon.'

I move closer and the light picks out something shining on the dead man's chest, against the no longer white t-shirt. It's a set of army dogtags, bright silver and inscribed with letters and numbers, plus another silver medallion inscribed with a strange letter, like an E with the centre bit missing, the top and bottom lines bent in. Oh, he was a soldier? Somehow that makes it even worse, that someone who would put his life on the line for his country should meet his end like this. I look around, wondering who's going to come for him. A fallen comrade? His grandma?

Door People Are The Worst

But the figure that appears with a whomp! sound is a surprise, to say the least. He is huge, blond and muscular, clad in bright golden armour and a winged helmet, a blue cape flowing behind. Oh, and he's totally hot. Blue eyes and chiselled Nordic features – it's like the guy from those Thor movies has just shown up, though he doesn't seem to have a hammer, thank goodness. My whole face stretches in surprise as I wonder what the hell is happening. The young man sits up out of his body and I can see that he is just as gobsmacked as I am. His mouth drops open, then a huge delighted grin spreads across his face. He doesn't even notice me there as he takes the hand of the huge warrior and is pulled to his feet. Fake Thor uses his free hand to draw his sword and holds it above his head, the blade shining as though it's on fire, the light growing brighter to envelop them.

'To the Hall of Heroes!' I hear him shout, and I leap quickly into the light as they ascend suddenly, air streaming around us as I try not to squeal, focusing on the bright light of fake Thor's sword. It's a fast journey, through glittering rays of light like ice crystals and all of a sudden we land with a thump.

We are, um, somewhere.

It's dusk, wherever we are, the last golden stripes of sunset reflecting from a building in front of me, a vast barn shaped structure with a roof that appears to be made of large gold tiles. A large meadow stretches off to one side and, in the distance, under a group of trees silhouetted dark against the growing twilight, I can see what looks like banquet tables, glowing spots of light along them. More golden orbs move around the table, carried by dark figures who gleam strangely where the light catches them. I blink, rubbing my eyes as I try to figure out where I am.

Fake Thor and the dead soldier start walking and I follow along, trying to take it all in. A large tree stretches up and over the huge building, leafy branches trailing across the peak of the roof where there stands a statue of a stag, fully antlered. But then the stag turns his head to reach for leaves from the tree and I realise it is no statue and that things are really starting to get weird. The stag's hooves ring with a faint chiming sound on the strange golden tiles which, as I get closer, appear to be shields. I can also see carvings on the wooden walls, twisting tangled lines and curling animal images. Fake Thor and the young man have reached the door of the building now, still without noticing me tagging along behind. Two more huge warriors stand there, armoured and muscled, both in winged helmets. Seems to be the fashion here. I am getting an inkling of where I might be when one of them speaks to the young man. He answers and I can't quite hear what he says, but it seems to be the right thing for they both smile and reach to open the big doors, lifting the carved wooden bars and pulling them back.

A wall of noise and heat hits me and I get a glimpse of long tables filled with laughing shouting men, all drinking and eating and having what looks like a really fantastic time. It kind of reminds me of a bar I used to frequent in my uni days – the University Tavern, I think it was called. And it was just like this. Long tables, lots of beer and shouting, plenty of men. The bathrooms were unspeakable but that wouldn't be an issue here. The big doors close behind the young man and fake Thor flies off again, his sword gleaming as he goes, leaving a trail like an arc of light.

The two guards have resumed their stations at the door to Valhalla. For this is where I am – I mean, there's nowhere else this could possibly be. My mind flashes back, briefly, to an ad campaign I worked on a couple of years ago, something to do with a cleaning company, the idea being they could clean up anything, even after a feast at Valhalla. Crap concept, I know, but the client loved it. Hands on hips I look up at the gleaming hall, the stag watching me with his dark eyes, and the vast spreading trees. Yeah, we probably didn't get it quite right. Anyway,

I'm here now, and I want a drink, I realise, more than anything. I'm not thirsty, I just want to sit at a table with other people and shout and laugh and get my drink on. Even if this isn't my Heaven, perhaps they'll let me stay a little while. Confidently, I step up to the two guards at the door, smoothing down my skirt and smiling my best smile.

'Hello, I'm-'

The nearest guard to me turns his head and, holy crap he is handsome. Another Nordic masterpiece, grey eyes and flowing dark hair, a head and a half taller than I am and wearing glittering silver armour from head to toe. When he speaks to me his voice is deep and strong.

'Are you a Valkyrie?'

What? What did he say? Um, I'm dead. That means I get to go in here, right? So I frown a little and move forward and his big muscled arm comes up, blocking my way, so close to my face I could have kissed it, if I'd wanted to. And I won't say I wasn't rather tempted.

'Are you a Valkyrie?' he asks again, his voice louder, speaking more slowly as if he thinks I might be deficient in some way and all at once I get it. Visions of women with braids in horned helmets singing loudly come into my head. Yeah, I'm not one of those. So I smile at him again. Honestly, this is harder than getting into the best nightclubs on a Saturday night.

'No, I'm d-'

'Then you cannot enter.'

The muscly arm stays up, the grey eyes are stern and I feel myself drooping under his glare. It's like all the times

I've been turned away at the door times a million. Tears prickle at my eyes and I feel desperate. I grab the muscly arm and whine like a little child.

'But I'm lo-o-ost!'

Surprisingly, this gets a response. The grey eyes soften slightly, the glacial features become less so.

'Perhaps you are looking for the Folkvangr?'

His voice is softer too, and the arm under my hands is feeling very nice. What did he say? The Volkswagen? I look around, wondering if some sort of celestial vehicle is going to appear and take me away, a heavenly Love Bug. But there's nothing except the endless dusk and the faint sound of carousing from behind the big wooden doors. I look at him again and he seems exasperated, pulling his arm from my increasingly over familiar grasp.

'The Folkvangr,' he says again, his voice getting louder and I stare at him in confusion. He sighs. 'Freya's Meadow. Over there. Women are permitted.'

Oh. *Ohhh!* Right. I can't go into Valhalla because I'm *female*. My mouth drops open in outrage and I'm about to make a feminist protest on behalf of all women ever but the look in his eyes stops me in my tracks. Instead I close my mouth and step away, carefully, and nod my head. 'Thanks. Um, so, over there?' I point to the distant gathering in the meadow and his hand goes to his sword. 'Never mind!'

I turn and run as fast as I can, leaving the hall behind as I head out over lush green grass, heavy with dew. I notice as I'm running that I'm not out of breath, that I seem to be almost gliding over the grass. It's actually a really nice feeling and I'm enjoying it so much I almost run into a group of women at the edge of the gathering under the trees. I stop sharply, skidding on the soft grass and they all turn to look at me with identical surprised expressions. But that's where the similarities end. Honestly, it's quite amazing. There's a teenager wearing a skirt and jumper, brown hair pulled back from her face, and an elderly lady in leopard print leggings and a spangly gold top, lipstick creeping across her wrinkled mouth. Another woman is wearing a sari, bright colours and sequins muted in the candle light, while another, her skin so dark it seems almost to absorb light, is wearing skinny jeans and a cropped t-shirt, the sparkle of a belly ring just visible. The two women closest to me are a contrast in colouring, one with white blonde hair and pale skin, her eyes dark lined, the other with dark olive skin and lush red lips, her hair dark and curling. It's just, really cool, I guess, seeing all these women together. The surprised expressions change to confusion as I don't say anything and finally the woman in skinny jeans, hair curling and cropped close to her beautifully shaped head, comes towards me.

'Hello.'

She makes it sound like a question, like there's something specific I need to say back to her, a puzzle requiring the correct response. I have no clue what that would be so I say 'Hello,' back to her, adding a smile. This doesn't seem to be quite right, their faces all looking even more confused and so I introduce myself. 'Um, I'm Katie.'

No-one says anything and I look around, not knowing what to do next. I decide to be honest. I need help, after all, and they've been dead longer than I have. 'Um, I'm lost.'

Ah. This seems to be the right thing. Understanding dawns on the women's faces and skinny jean woman nods.

'Okay,' she says. 'Perhaps we can help you. Come, sit with us.' She gestures to the end of the nearby table and I turn to see there are seats free on the long benches. I nod my thanks and look along the tables to see that everyone seated on the long benches is female, again an amazing mix of diversity. I can't imagine what these women all have in common, what would have brought them all here after death. However, if they can help me it really doesn't matter, I guess.

'Thank you,' I say, sliding in and along the bench, skinny jean woman next to me, the blonde girl and the sari lady next to her, while the elderly lady slides in opposite me, the teenager and the olive skinned woman finishing the row. I smile brightly at them all, still feeling as though I'm walking on very thin ice. Just like the fiesta Heaven, something about this doesn't seem right at all and I'm about to stand up and make my excuses when the woman on the other side of me nudges me, whether on purpose or by accident I'm not sure. I turn. She has brown frizzy hair around a careworn face, and is wearing one of those zip-up fleece tops. Her hands are clasped around a large goblet made of some pale shiny material like horn, ringed with bands that gleam golden in the candlelight. Seeing it reminds me of how much I'd love a drink and I look around, wondering if I can get one too. But all I see are the other women's eyes on me. Not mean or scary, just... waiting. I turn back to the woman next to me and see she has bowed her head to look into the cup and I frown a little, wondering if she's all right. I can still feel everyone's eyes on me and I glance across the table to see the elderly lady, lipsticked mouth pursed as she regards us both. Right, tread carefully here, Katie and remember, you're already dead. I gently nudge the woman back.

'What are you drinking?' I ask, smiling at her as she lifts her head.

'He was going to kill her,' she says in a low voice, and I can see tears starting in her eyes, bright in the light from the candles. 'He was hurting her, and I had to stop him, no matter what.'

I stare at her, not knowing what to say, feeling sorrow and love so strong coming from this woman it's like a cloud around her, a net of sparkling darkness, like the mourning jet women used to wear in Victorian times. There's a hush around us, as though all the other women are waiting to see what I'll do, like it's a test of some sort. I lick my lips, which feel dry.

'Who, um, who was hurting her?'

'He was!' She spat the words and I jumped back a little. 'He's not even her dad, and he was hurting her and I couldn't bear it, couldn't take it any more so I stopped him, even though he hurt me too. At least she's all right.' And her expression changes from fierce to loving as she turns to gaze into the goblet once more. Then she glances

A Thousand Rooms

at me. 'D'you want to see?'

I pause, unsure, but there's that whole feeling of being observed again and so I smile, nodding my head. 'Of course I do. Please,' I add at the end, wanting to be polite to this woman for some reason. She pushes the goblet towards me and I look into it. It's filled with liquid that gleams like pearl and then images start to flicker across it, like at the start of an old film on a projector. Taken aback, I look at the woman, not sure what I'm going to see, worried in case it might be some sort of death scene, World's Most Horrible Home Videos or something. But she just smiles, motioning me to look again so I do. And there's a little girl running happily in a playground, small pink shoes kicking up tan bark as she runs towards the slide, squealing with laughter. An older woman is chasing her, laughing as well and when she catches the little girl she picks her up into a big squeezy hug, kissing her rosy cheeks over and over, the little girl's hand coming up to touch the woman's face as she giggles, kissing her back. It's beautiful, and I feel my eyes welling up. I look at the woman again and her face is soft with love.

'Is that her?' I whisper.

She nods. 'It is. She's with my mum, safe now. He can't hurt her any more. And I can still see her, though she can't see me. I visit her sometimes, at night when she's sleeping.'

Ah. I nod, my lips twisting as all at once I realise what this woman has given up for her daughter, for the love that is deeper than anything. Tears drip down my cheek and I wipe at them, gently pushing the goblet towards the woman with my free hand.

'Thank you,' I manage to say. 'For sharing. That's beautiful, she's beautiful.'

There's a sort of sigh from the assembled group and it looks as though skinny jeans woman is about to say something to me when there is a shout and a bang and another woman is standing on the table, glaring down at me. She is small and skinny, wearing a breastplate and winged helmet, just like the guards at the Hall. However, she has wings on her back as well, big white sweeping ones almost as tall as she is. Straggly blonde hair comes out from under her helmet and her lined face is definitely disapproving. Her sword is drawn and pointed at me, the engraved silver blade glittering in the candlelight as the point moves to and fro. I sit back, trying to look innocent. Or something. I really don't know what I'm supposed to be but I get the feeling that my welcome has just worn out.

'Did you die a noble death?' The woman's voice is loud and along the table there are gasps, the chatter falling silent as heads turn to me. I open my mouth as the woman leans forward, her brows drawing together as she jabs her sword in my direction. 'Well, did you?'

'Um, probably not,' I say slowly, realising as I look around what is going on here. If Valhalla is for heroes, then Folkvangr probably is as well. Light dawns on me as I look at the woman with her goblet who died to save her child, at all the other women at these tables who no doubt have stories just as sad and brave as she does. Except for me. I got killed checking for a text from some guy who didn't even have the courtesy to ring me after a date. I mean, I don't know the rules here but I'm pretty sure that, as deaths go, there wasn't too much that was noble about it.

'Then you must go.'

The tiny Valkyrie is holding a spear in her other hand and she starts to bang the long haft on the table, the booming sound of wood hitting wood getting louder and louder. She throws her head back and makes this high pitched ululating cry and all at once there are winged women in battle dress all along the table, and at the very end a golden shining figure of a woman, her gleam that of sunlight on frost. All the winged women are banging now and the noise is deafening. I put my hands over my ears, closing my eyes just to get away from it and I feel myself being gently pushed and all at once I'm falling. I land with a thud and open my eyes, taking my hands off my ears. I groan.

For I'm back where it all started again.

Chandrani's Heaven

It's night-time and the shops are all closed, the pavement pretty much deserted. I walk over to the low stone wall and sit down, trying to process what I've just been through. I don't get it at all. Two deaths leading me to two entirely different places, neither of which I belonged in. I lean forward, elbows on my knees with my chin in my hands as I think. Have I really been to Heaven? I mean, I've heard of Valhalla (as you know) but it was just some concept on an Art Director's board, not a real place where people could actually go. It's kind of cool, when I think about it, and I wish I had someone to tell. But I'm still no clearer on everything. And then there was the fiesta Heaven. What was that all about? I didn't get that either. It was as though the old man had gone to his own personal Heaven when he died, instead of the whole clouds and angels and pearly gates thing we've been sold for the past however many years. Which again, is kind of cool.

I turn the thought over in my mind, considering the idea and the more I think about it the more it starts to make sense. I mean, if you were to ask a group of people to describe their idea of Heaven, like in one of those marketing focus groups I used to run, they'd probably all come up with something different, something that had meaning to them personally. Is that the key, that when you die you get to choose where you go? The revelation is mind blowing and I purse my lips and blow out a breath, staring but not seeing anything as my mind works it all out. So if that is the case, then what's my idea of Heaven? My mind goes blank and I can't think of anything. I mean, if an angel appeared right now and said, have whatever you want, I will make it happen, I would ask to go back to my life again. To see my family, to dance at Sarah's wedding, even sit happily in one of Darryl's interminable Work In Progress meetings. That would be Heaven for me, for things to go back to how they used to be, before I stepped off a curb without looking and shattered everything.

I look around, hopeful perhaps that my big revelation about Heaven and what I want will make something happen, but nothing happens. It's still dark, the cars driving past all streak and flash of light and noise, shops closed and offices locked. Nothing changes at all.

Huffing out a sigh I get up. May as well go for a walk. It's not like I need to sleep anyway, and I'm not in the mood to go back to my place yet, not wanting to see it stripped of whatever else Mum and Ellie and Sarah have managed to take away. So I drift across the road and take the first turning I come to, heading down another residential street. This one has a mix of homes, small apartment blocks like mine and larger houses set back from the road, old palm trees and iron railings hinting at the glory days of Federation, when gold made more than one Australian family's fortune. I trail my hand along the fences, peering into the big houses as I always used to do when I walked this way, wanting a glimpse inside, golden squares of lit windows like secret gates into other people's lives.

Then it occurs to me that there's nothing stopping me from going inside now, that no one could see me or throw me out, that I can wander through the rooms as much as I like. This fills me with delight, welcome after the emotional rigours of the last few hours and I grin, then laugh out loud, thrilled to have found a small silver lining to the endless cloud of my existence. I could even head down to Kirribilli and wander through the Prime Minister's house if I wanted, or into Vaucluse where the millionaires and movie stars sleep, drifting through their dressing rooms and spas, poking them in the ear and sitting on their fancy furniture. Ooh, I've always been such a real estate sticky beak, I'd even thought of becoming an estate agent, just so I could see inside other people's houses. Oh, the possibilities of this are endless!

As I try to decide which house to invade first I feel another tug under my breastbone, similar to what I'd felt in the Star of The Sea, but harder. I frown, rubbing at my chest and looking around affrontedly as though someone might have just poked me. But the street is deserted. The

A Thousand Rooms

tugging doesn't stop though, and it seems as though it wants me to swing around to the left. Still rubbing at my chest, I turn. And then I see it. A glow is coming from one of the apartments in the block opposite me. Oh, another person dying. I sigh, wondering whether I can be bothered to tag along again. But there's something different about this glow. It's intensifying, rather than petering out like the others. Huh. The glow starts to pulse and with it so does the sensation in my chest, as though I've an extra heart beating in there. I grimace, and it's as though my feet start moving without me even thinking, taking me across the road until I'm standing under the small balcony, watching sparkles drip down the edge and burst out into the night like fairy dust, beckoning me inside.

Before I know it I'm rising up, floating through the sliding doors and then I'm inside and whoa! I turn away, covering my eyes because yikes! I'm in somebody's bedroom. A young couple's bedroom, and they happen to be naked, on their bed and going for it. This is private stuff.

But there's that tug under my breastbone again, forcing me to turn around so I do, reluctantly, covering my eyes with my fingers and peeking through. I've never been much of a voyeur, preferring to participate rather than watch, if you know what I mean. But I find that I'm fascinated by their beauty, by the glow coming from them as they make love. You can tell they love each other, the way they touch each other, looking into each other's eyes and smiling, each one wanting to please the other. I mean, I enjoy sex but I don't know that I've ever felt so connected with someone like that.

I realise I'm staring and that feels rude, so I turn away, trying to catch my breath, the tight tugging pain in my chest getting worse. Then I notice the other guy in the room. He's sitting on the long low dresser against the wall, a smile on his face as he watches the young couple. Not a pervy smile, just a nice one, as though he is really really happy for them. I frown. What's his deal?

Then I get a shock.

He looks up as though he can feel me watching him, his face brightening with a smile and he waves. Oh my God, he can see me. Slowly I lift my hand and wave back at him, feeling completely weirded out. This is not a social situation I've encountered before. He grins before turning his attention back to the bed. And I stand there, not sure where to look or what to do, feeling like I've been caught peeping when I shouldn't have been, hot with shame. But wait. *He can see me.* And if he can see me, maybe he can help me. Pushing down my embarrassment I casually wander over and perch myself on the edge of the dresser next to him, trying hard not to notice what is going on in the bed in front of us. But things are really starting to heat up. It's kind of hard to ignore.

'Hey,' says the guy, turning to look at me. He is still smiling, still looks so very happy and I'm not sure at all. But I have to try.

'Hey,' I say, trying to be casual. 'Um, so, you can see me?'

'Well, yeah.' He frowns at me a little, like I'm confusing him. 'They didn't tell me I was getting a twin.'

'Wait, what?' It's my turn to frown at him.

'Well, I'm waiting, right?' He tilts his head in the direction of the couple on the bed, who are really going for it now. 'You know, to join.'

I make a face. I can't help it. 'What, like, you're waiting to join in?!' I shake my head, trying to understand what he is on about. Perhaps I don't need to understand. 'Maybe I should just-'

'No, not join in,' he says, looking at me like I'm insane. 'These are my parents, right? So I'm waiting for my moment. Didn't they tell you, when you chose your life?'

'Wait, what? No, I mean...' I stop, trying to pull myself together. I *need* to speak to this guy but I'm so gobsmacked I can't get the right questions out. He's still looking at me as though he's really worried about my state of mind. I try again. 'OK, you said they, who are they?'

'You know, the Guardians? The ones who reassign us? I'm really excited about this life I'm getting. I've been told it's got the potential to be great. So, er, you're not my twin?'

'No.'

'So, what are you doing here?' He looks at me as though he's getting angry, and I totally get it. The embarrassment comes flooding back as I realise that I'm in totally the wrong place at the wrong time. I'm not here to perve, honest, but what other reason can I have for coming to sit with him while his parents are, well, you know. Other than the fact I'm hopelessly lost, of course. I open my mouth, wanting to apologise but he turns away, his face lighting up. The couple on the bed are reaching a crescendo, all systems go if you know what I mean.

'That's my cue,' he says, looking at me with such a joyful expression all I can do is smile. Then he, sort of, dives at them both and at the same time shrinks down to a tiny point of light. I watch then, I can't help it. Because it's amazing. As his little spark reaches the couple they light up, glowing golden in the room, little twinkles of light all around them. It only lasts a few seconds, but enough time for him to merge with their glow. Then it fades, though the woman holds on to a small amount of it, a faint gleam all around her.

Ah, so that's the pregnant glow people are always going on about, I think randomly as I back away out of the room, leaving them all in their private moment of joy.

I stand alone in the dark street, shaking. I mean, wow. I can't believe what I've just seen. It was beautiful, once I got past the embarrassment of it. I kind of feel privileged, in a way. But I'm still no closer to getting anywhere, other than the mention of the mysterious Guardians. But while I'm stuck here I have no more chance of finding one than I do of finding a date. After all, it doesn't look as though they're coming to find me.

A pale shimmer in the distant sky lets me know dawn is on its way, another night over. All at once I feel tired. I wander down the street a little way further, my feet dragging, without even the energy to drift. The houses open up to a small park and I sit down on one of the benches there.

It's a peaceful place with grass and trees and a corner with a slide and swing set, tan bark piled around the base. It reminds me of the little girl and her grandmother, her mother watching her from Freya's Meadow and my eyes tear up, the dark silhouetted shapes of eucalypts blurring and shaking against the dawn. I know it sounds weird to say I'm tired – I mean, I'm dead, after all – but that's how I feel, as though my tiredness is something that's in my soul, rather than physical. I wipe my eyes and stare up at the brightening sky, thinking about my life, about the couple in their small bedroom, the obvious love between them shining so brightly.

I would have liked to have kids one day, I suppose. I'd considered the single mother route, but still felt like I might meet someone, plus I was only thirty two. I was supposed to have had time! And I'd liked my life the way it was, having my own place, being able to do what I want when I felt like it and I knew kids would change all that. But I'd still known I'd do it one day. I adored my little nephew, the chubby deliciousness of his little legs and arms and cheeks, the way he giggled and clapped when he saw me, how he clung to his mother as though she was his whole world. I used to watch them together, thinking about how that would be me on some indeterminate date yet to come, the shadowy figure of the man I'd yet to meet standing with me as we cuddled our child, a full circle of happiness. But I'd never really met anyone I'd even have considered having kids with – I suppose Jeremy might have been the closest, but we know how that worked out.

Still, it had always felt like it was going to happen, that I would meet that special someone, that it was just a matter of when, rather than if. But all my whens and ifs are gone and now it never will.

The trees around me are starting to rustle, lorikeets flying in colourful clouds of red and green and blue feathers, shrieking and chirping loudly as they greet the morning. It's almost light now, the sky streaked with lavender and blue and gold and red, lights coming on in the little houses around me. But still I sit here. I just can't think of where else to go. Valhalla has shaken me up, to be honest. I half smile to myself, thinking it probably does that to most people. But it's made me realise how little I've done of any worth. I think back to that strange carousel ride through my memories, all those places I'd visited, the scenes from my life and I nod.

Of course.

That's what I had been shown, the fact that nothing really important had ever happened. Maybe that's why I'm stuck here, because I just don't matter enough to get to go to Heaven. I start to feel very sorry for myself, sitting there alone in the golden morning light, birds swooping around me as the park comes to life. The first few early commuters start arriving, heels clicking on the small paved path as they walk through the park to the next street, obviously on their way to work. Men and women, most of them wearing dark suits and carrying shoulder bags, their hair fresh from the shower. I hate all of them. I know it's unreasonable, I know that more than a few of them probably have crippling mortgages and aren't that happy at work but still I hate them because they have what I don't. They're alive. They still have a chance to change, to become something more than what they are and be accepted when they get to the other side.

As the flow of smartly dressed workers starts to slow, they're succeeded by strollers and prams. Oh God, this is all I need. One small group of women arrive together, each pushing a pram, their bodies still holding the soft roundness of being recently pregnant. One of them spreads a colourful blanket on the ground under a nearby gum tree, while the others park their prams around the edge. Then the babies are brought out, waving chubby fists and squawking like the birds above them, wide-eyed little faces looking around as their mothers sit together, smiling and talking despite the tiredness in their eyes, the swollen breasts. A few have coffees in hand, sipping away as they cuddle their babies, setting them down in the centre of the rug to watch the leaves dance above. It's gorgeous and it breaks my heart, that it will never be me, that I can never be a part of it.

Ugh, I've had enough of this.

I get up and walk away. I haven't the heart to float or drift so I take the path through the park instead. It leads to another residential street, a long one that heads downhill towards a gleam of water and something about the distant silver ripples calls to me so I head towards it. The houses on this street are larger, some old and red brick, others with timber cladding, a few modern homes obviously built after knocking the original house down. I just want to get to the water – perhaps I can hitch a ride on a boat or something, take a little harbour tour. I don't want to go home and spend another day sitting on my couch, but when I think of leaving Sydney something deep inside curls and coils. It feels like fear.

As I walk I start to hear the faint sound of chanting. It gets louder, the sound twining tendrils around me. I'm captivated by the rising and falling sound, almost like a song, though with an unmistakeable thread of sorrow running through it. On impulse, I decide to follow it and, as it gets louder, I start to feel that tug under my breastbone again. Something is happening.

The chanting leads me to a modern brick house almost at the end of the street, rippling water just metres away. The house is huge. Like, five or six bedrooms at least. Big money, especially in the harbourside suburbs. The windows are white framed and a white tiled portico shades the front door, which is open. As I stand there a car pulls up and a man and a woman get out, both dressed in white, the woman's hair long and dark and loose around her shoulders. When they reach the front door I see them both nod, putting their hands together in front of them, before stepping inside. The tugging feeling is getting stronger, though there's no glow I can see, so I follow along behind them.

Inside the front door is a wide hallway with a large staircase heading to the second floor. A man is standing in the hallway. He's also dressed in white, his hair, dark as his eyes, cut very short. He looks tired and sad and I feel sorry for him, though I don't know why. The chanting is very loud now and seems to be coming from the room to my left, so I go through the door, still feeling like some sort of will-o-the-wisp, just floating on the wind and going wherever because nothing matters any more and what's the point anyway.

I stop short when I get inside. The room is filled with more people dressed in white, all of them sitting on the floor in the middle of the room, the furniture pushed up against the walls. To one side a man sits, slightly separate from the group – it's he who is chanting, his eyes closed, a deep furrow between his brows as he sings, moving from side to side. In the very centre of the room is a simple wooden coffin with the lid open and I pause, realising I'm at a wake. The strange swirls of energy blink into view again, soft wisps of golden sparkles around the room, twining around the mourners and linking them together. I blink once more and the energy's gone, though I can still feel it. Moving closer I get a better look, though I'm careful not to walk through any of the mourners. Inside the coffin is an old woman dressed in orange and red robes, her long grey hair braided carefully, a design in orange powder on the wrinkled skin of her forehead. Her eyes are closed and her hands rest on her chest, a garland of flowers around her neck.

'Pretty nice, hey?'

Shocked, I turn to see a young woman standing next to me. Her eyes are bright and long lashed, her hair a dark shimmering rope braided down her back. Her robes are orange and red, just like the woman in the coffin. And she is talking to me.

'Er, I'm sorry, did you just, um...?' The words jumble

and tumble in my eagerness to get them out, wanting to talk to her before she decides to get born again or send me away. But the young woman simply smiles at me, her teeth pearl white against her smooth golden skin. She is gorgeous, and I smile back, laughing a little in relief that she doesn't seem to be going anywhere yet.

'Talk to you?' Her eyes twinkle and she seems amused. 'Of course I did. It seemed only polite, as you are in my house.'

Oh. My mouth comes open and I feel like an idiot. What was I thinking, wandering in here like this, interrupting a family in their private moment of grief? I am the worst, the absolute worst. I'm about to apologise when I stop, shaking my head. I'm still dead, right?

'Um, I'm sorry, how is it you can see me?' is what comes out instead of the apology I'd meant to make. 'Are you a medium, or something?'

The girl laughs, shaking her head. 'No no, silly. I'm dead, just like you are. That's me, in the coffin.'

'Ohhhh!' The light dawns. 'Oh, right.' I turn and look at the old woman, then at the young beauty next to me. 'So, that's you?'

Of course it's her, she just told me it is, but I just can't get it straight in my head. And what is with everyone becoming young and gorgeous when they die? Everyone except for me, that is. I'm surprised I'm not walking around with a giant head wound that gradually festers, like the dead friend in that old movie my dad loves, An American Werewolf In London. I mean really, with the luck I've been having, what difference would it make?

Still, the young woman is talking to me and so I try to look polite, putting my sour face away as I listen to her.

'It is. I died a few hours ago, so now they are making the preparations.'

'The preparations?'

'For my burial. Well, cremation really.' She looks fondly on the group of people sitting around the coffin and I see a resemblance in some of them to the woman next to me, the same long lashed dark eyes, shimmering black hair.

'So that's your family?'

'It is, and they are doing me proud. It is all as I wished.'

'But, wait, don't you feel sad, that you're leaving them?' I remember how devastated I'd felt in the church with my family, the sadness of the irrevocability of death, that we can never go back to our lives or anyone we knew. But none of this seems to be affecting the young woman next to me. Instead, she seems perfectly excited about the whole thing. 'And, where are you going to go? Is someone coming to meet you?'

The young woman is frowning a bit, a faint wrinkle in her perfect satin skin. 'Sad? Why should I be sad? I have lived my life as best I could, done the best I can. I will see them again, one day. And now I can go on to Samsara, to find my place on the wheel.'

'The wheel? And, did you say Samsara, like the perfume?' This all sounds confusing and I can feel myself frowning as well. I've heard of Samsara – I think I've even worked on a campaign for it once, through one of the big department stores. But I haven't the faintest idea what the connection is between the perfume and the afterlife. The young woman is looking at me with her lips pressed together, her eyes kind, exuding patience as she starts explaining it to me as though I'm a child.

'The great wheel of life. We move through, each life teaching us something, and our place in Heaven, or Samsara, is decided by our actions on this earth.' She smiles, looking so beatific and peaceful I can hardly bear it. Here is someone who knows exactly who she is and where she's going. I am about to beg shamelessly for her to help me when she says, 'Of course, I don't know where I'll end up, but I hope it will be lovely.'

Oh, right. Well, that's what I'd hoped too. I must look upset because she puts her hand on my arm, looking concerned. 'Are you all right?'

I shake my head, my mouth all twisted up because I can't speak, the disappointment so strong inside me. Tears prickle at my eyes and one escapes to run down my cheek. I can feel the coils tightening inside me and I don't know what to do.

The young woman looks even more worried now. 'Oh dear,' she says. 'Come, let us talk.' Taking me by the arm she draws me out of the room into one next door. There are low benches against one wall and she leads me over to them. We sit down and she pats me gently on the leg, looking at me with those beautiful dark eyes, lustrous with concern. 'Tell me what is wrong.'

My mouth untwists enough to answer and it all comes tumbling out of me. 'I'm lost. I died two weeks ago and I don't know where to go or what to do or anything! And I heard the chanting and I came in here because...' I am deeply ashamed by what I'm about to admit. 'I've been following dead people.'

I think of that little kid in the movie as I say this and a completely inappropriate giggle comes bursting up from my chest. Then it becomes sobs as it hits me again how awful this all is. The young woman is great, though, patting my arm, not running off and leaving me to my fate, though she would be completely entitled to do so, a complete stranger coming into her home and interrupting her funeral. She simply sits patiently, waiting for me to stop crying. I do, after a few minutes and she smiles a gentle smile.

'Well,' she says. 'There is a simple solution to all of this.'

'There is?' I look at her, starting to feel hopeful in the face of her calm self-sufficiency.

'Yes, of course. You must come with me when I go. It won't be long now – they will come to take my body away soon and I won't go with them. So then we can go together.'

I frown at her, though I try not to, not wanting to seem ungrateful. 'Um, thank you, I mean, that's lovely but, that's what I've been doing, you see. Tagging along with other people. And it hasn't worked out so well this far.'

'But this time it will be different,' she says, patting me on the arm again, her face shining with her faith, her certainty that this will be so. 'For I know you are coming with me, so I can ask on your behalf when we get there.'

'Oh!' Okay, that actually does sound reasonable. 'Um, so, your Heaven...'

'Is all Heavens. It's all connected, right? Just don't tell anyone.' And she winks at me. I gape, then giggle a little. There's movement nearby and we both turn to see the coffin being carried from the house, the man with very short hair leaving a small white ball of something on the threshold as they go. The young woman beside me waves at him, her eyes bright, then she turns to me and takes my hand.

'Right,' she says. 'Let's go.'

We stand up and a wonderful swirling energy is all around us, the faint scent of sandalwood in the air. Still holding hands we start to ascend through the golden air, big white and red balls of chrysanthemum flowers tumbling like huge snowflakes as we rise up and out of this world. It's beautiful and I feel tears in my eyes at the thought that finally, I might get to where I need to be. As though she knows what I'm thinking I feel the young woman squeezes my hand, her dark hair and eyes tinted gold as she smiles at me.

We approach the edge of what looks like a long platform, white polished marble inlaid with curling patterns of coloured stone. We land, light as a feather and I look around. Well, this is kind of what I'd thought Heaven would look like, sort of clouds and pillars and stone. It's very serene, the golden mist still swirling around us and I smooth my hands down my skirt, waiting to see what will happen next. The young woman is standing close to me, her delicate profile silhouetted against the glowing air, her posture straight. A figure emerges from the mist. He bows to us, his hands held together in prayer position in front of his chest, naked except for a swathe of fabric around his hips. He is beautiful, dark hair and skin, his bare chest muscular and garlanded with flowers and I take a breath as he comes closer, smiling at us both.

'Chandrani,' he says, looking at the woman next to me and she bows to him, smiling, a blush in her cheek. 'Your Heaven is waiting for you. Your life has been blessed.' He holds out his hand to her. She glances at me, then places her hand in his. Before he can lead her away she says,

'Wait, if you please. I have one more request before I leave this life.' The man waits, his face gentle. 'My friend here is lost. Can you help her? Do you know where her Heaven lies?'

The dark eyes turn to me and he gets a confused look on his finely drawn face, his head tilting slightly as he regards me.

'Your name does not lie with me,' he says eventually, still so gentle. 'But I can tell you three things. One, that your life has also been blessed. Two, that Heaven contains many rooms, that what you seek may lie sideways, rather than down. And three, that the way to Heaven-' he reaches out to touch me, one long golden finger coming to rest on my breastbone, '-can be found in here.'

I look into his beautiful eyes and all my frantic questions go silent in the face of his calm certainty, the otherworldly energy moving around him. The tight coil inside me releases slightly and I smile.

'Thank you,' I say. Then I look at the young woman who brought me there. She has done more for me than anyone else and all of a sudden I'm so grateful I could hug her. But I restrain myself, as it doesn't seem quite like the right thing to do. She seems to get it, though, reaching out to squeeze my hand with hers before letting go. I smile at her. 'Thank you so much, for everything.'

'It was my pleasure.' She smiles at me. 'And good luck with your search. Who knows, we may meet again.' Then, just like that, she and the young man dissolve into the golden swirling mist and I'm alone once more. The mist keeps on moving, coiling around me and it picks me up, lifting me away from the platform. I try to remember that I'm already dead, that I can't die again and whatever it is that's happening to me it is as least *something*, which is an improvement on my previous situation. So no screaming, don't panic, everything is going to be fine, right? At least this is better than being pushed out of Heaven by an angry Valkyrie, I think as I tumble through the air, trying to hold on to some of the calm I had felt from the young man.

But then the mist dissipates and I am in a sort of blue space, floating. I start to fall and, as I do, the words of the young man echo in my head. 'Sideways, not down.' Okay, I'm going down, so that's not going to work. I need to go sideways. And as I think it I change direction, sliding along faster and faster as though I'm on some sort of slippery slide and then...

I land.

A Thousand Rooms

I'm in a pure white room with no windows, lit with its own light. In the middle sits a man, eyes closed, on a perfect white fluffy rug. His hair is grey and cropped close to his head, his skin smooth. He looks, I don't know any other way to say this, expensive. Like the boss at my old agency, the big boss, Tony. He wasn't a terribly attractive man, you understand, but everything about him was groomed to perfection, as sleek as could be. And that's how this guy looks as well.

'Um, excuse me,' I say, stepping forward. 'Is this… your Heaven?'

His eyes snap open and look at me, annoyed. 'Well, it was,' he says, 'until you came along.'

My mouth drops open and I step back.

'My whole life,' he goes on, his voice growing louder, 'I had to deal with people. And when I started working it was all phones and noise and emails and taxis and planes and people, people everywhere! All I ever wanted was to make enough money to be alone and I finally did it and

then I fell and hit my head and now I'm here.'
'Er, right,' I say. 'So, you're, um, not happy here?'
'I'm very happy!' he says, glaring fiercely at me. 'This is *my* Heaven. And I want to be alone in it. So go away!' He holds his hand out, palm up and it's as though he pushes me and I fly out of the room. But I remember the instructions. Sideways, not down. I push back and feel myself slide sideways and I end up in…

… a dark room. It is calm, the darkness warm and welcoming, almost embracing, like a soft blanket of night. The walls are darker shadows, indistinct, and in the centre of the room is a long table around which a group of men and women are seated. Candles lit along the length of the table cast gold onto their faces, which look as pale and peaceful as an old painting. The man seated at the head of the table has his eyes closed, his hands laid flat on the table with the palms facing up, fingers curling slightly as he speaks in a deep musical voice, the language unfamiliar to me. As I glide into the room heads turn, dark eyes on me and I stand still, not wanting to disturb them. The man speaking seems to sense a change in the atmosphere and he opens his eyes and looks at me too. His eyes are large and dark, filled with kindness. He smiles at me, beckoning me to join them, to partake of the delicious food on the table, wine dark in glass goblets, the smells and soft light and serenity of this place making it very appealing. The other faces turned to me smile as well and I feel welcomed, which is a nice thing. I am considering whether or not to sit when there is a little tug under my breastbone, just where the young man had touched me in Chandrani's Heaven. It's as though it's saying to me, 'not here, not this place.' A-ha! Is this what I need to listen for? This is starting to make more sense.

So instead of joining the little group I nod and smile apologetically, then I close my eyes and push against the ground, as though I'm going to jump into the air. I feel myself start to slide and remember to go sideways, not down and...

...I open my eyes...

... to see I'm in a grove of trees. This is nice. I've always liked the woods, the leaf patterns and quiet and majesty of tall trees reaching to the sky, hidden worlds lurking under their branches. This is a particularly lovely grove, an almost perfectly circular arrangement of trees around a soft smooth lawn, small flowers dotted around the edge. It has a gentle energy, one that pulses quietly with happiness and I think to myself that this feels more like Heaven to me than any of the other places I've been. I turn around, looking up at the shapes the leaves make against the sky. Beyond the grove I see a field, green with long grass and, running through it is a group of women, all in long dresses in different colours, their hair unbound and flowing behind them. They are all smiling and laughing, seeming excited and I wonder what the big deal is. Then I realise they are coming toward the grove and me and I panic a little, thinking maybe I should go. But it's too late as they all step between the tree trunks to form a ring around me, still smiling.

'Welcome,' they call, voices like bells chiming. 'Welcome to our sacred grove.' They start to dance around me, a dipping weaving type of dance and I turn with them, feeling confused, their soft voices calling to me, singing a welcome but, you know what, this really doesn't feel like my thing. As I think that, the dance seems to get faster and faster, the coloured dresses whirling around me, petals flying through the air, sweet scented dots of colour and I hear the song change to one of farewell as I spin away from that place and think…

… sideways not down…

I slide sideways again and I'm in a bar, one of those old wood panelled places with glass and chrome gleaming, bottles and glasses lined up against the mirrored backdrop. A guy is standing there, polishing a glass with a checked cloth, and there are several people sitting on barstools, all with their backs to me. As I arrive the bartender looks up, his smile welcoming.

'What can I get you?' he calls, and the people sitting at the bar all turn around and wave their glasses at me in a sort of salute but I shake my head, smiling, not wanting to offend but, as mentioned, I'm not much of a drinker so I know this Heaven isn't for me. I push off again, seeing the gleaming glass turn to sparkles like stars as I move further away from the bar, still going sideways…

… not down…

This time I land in a crazy colourful place, big platforms and cartoonlike palm trees, everything blue and red and green and yellow, bright primary colours against a dark blue backdrop, music playing in the background. It reminds me of an indoor play centre I went to once with Ellie and David, the same loud colours and music playing, although it's not full of screaming children, which is kind of a relief. The music is fun and bouncy, but the colours are a bit bright and glary. I'm about to push off when a small figure bounces down from one of the platforms, followed by another shooting what looks like red lasers from his wrists. The figure takes a shield out of mid air, blocking and deflecting the lasers so they bounce harmlessly off the platforms and trees. I can hear both of them giggling, high pitched and I realise they're both children. The one with the lasers spots me and turns around, waving.

'Hey!' he calls. 'You wanna play too? We're having the best time!'

'Yeah!' pipes up the other one, with the shield.

'Um, no thanks,' I call out. 'Not really dressed for it.'

I spread my hands, feeling a bit sheepish and the two little boys shrug, then the one with the lasers runs at the platforms, bouncing up the side of them and laughing his head off as the other one takes off in hot pursuit, the two of them leaping into the distance. I watch them go, feeling a bit sad. I mean, everyone I've met so far has been dead, but they've all been adults, you know? They all got to live a little. These children had such short lives. Still, this video game Heaven seems very cool, I suppose. But, I think I need to move on, and, as I think this, I feel a little nudge under my breastbone again. I look around and see that a hole has opened up in the ground next to me, but it's like the entrance to a tunnel or a waterslide, striped in bright colours to match the rest of this place. As I look into it I get nudged again and I think, what the hell, why not and then I don't think about it any more. I just jump.

And I'm sliding, the stripes whirling around me and it's fun and scary at the same time though I have to remind myself that I need to go sideways, not...

... down...

And as I think it the tunnel bends and opens up like a giant funnel, spitting me out onto a pile of soft velvety pillows where I lie for a moment, trying to catch my breath. I hear laughter and sit up, looking around. When I see where I am I laugh too, because it's amazing.

I'm outside, the sun is shining and there are palm trees waving next to an enormous blue swimming pool, a pillared arcade running along one side of it. A white platform in front of me has steps leading up to it and on the platform are four pillars and a chaise longue, upholstered in what looks like hot pink velvet. But what's made me laugh is the lady reclining on the chaise longue. She is fabulous. Her hair is dark and curling around her face, her figure voluptuous and barely clothed in a bikini and several spangled scarves. She looks to be in her mid fifties and is smiling widely as she tosses her head and leans back.

And no wonder.

For around her are half a dozen well built young men (and when I say well built I mean it, if you know what I'm saying). They are oiled and muscular and wearing little tiny shorts that cling beautifully, and their sole purpose seems to be to meet this woman's every demand. I enjoy this immensely, grinning so hard my cheeks hurt as I watch the young men fan her and bring her iced drinks and feed her fruit and kiss her brown shoulders and rosy lips. Ha ha. This is Heaven, all right. I laugh again and the woman hears me. She turns, opening her cat-like kohl lined eyes to look down at where I'm sitting on her cushions. Her face lights up like I'm an old friend.

'Care to join me?' As she calls out she waves her hand and a second chaise longue appears next to hers. One of the young men pats the upholstered seat, winking at me, all white teeth and cheekbones, muscles rippling and I'm tempted, I must say, though it's the sort of thing I think would only suit me for a short while, not forever. Then I feel the nudge under my breastbone again so I shake my head and smile back at her.

'Thanks, but I have to keep going.'

'That's fine, darling, but come back and see me anytime. I can highly recommend this sort of thing. Oooooh.' Her head goes back and she reaches a languid hand to touch the smooth skinned chest of the man behind her, who has started massaging her shoulders and arms. Hmmm, tempted again, but the nudge comes once more, harder this time and I wave goodbye as I push off, sideways and not down...

…

And then there is screaming and fire and I see dragons, figures running through smoke and flame, arrows flying from a dark stone castle looming in the background and I don't even need to feel the heat of the flames to know this one isn't for me so I push off again…

… speeding through blue streaked with stars, sideways not down…

… and I arrive in a sort of grey neutral place, mist wreathing around me as I come to a stop. My mood changes, responding to the strange calm in the air, though there is an undercurrent of sorrow, drifting like the smoky tendrils around me. A young man is kneeling a few feet away from me. He is bent over, his arms wrapped around himself. His lips are pulled back and his eyes closed, as though he's refusing to look at the group of people standing in a semi-circle in front of him. The young man is groaning and hugging himself and I can see tears, crystal on his cheeks. The other people are a mixed group, men and women, old and young. There are babies there and a few children peeping around the adults, clinging to their mother's skirts. All of them are looking at the young man with such serious and sorrowful expressions that I wonder what is going on. I notice a gleaming figure standing behind the young man, almost hidden by the mists. It bends to rest a silvery hand on his shoulder.

'You must face this. You must see what you've done, look on the faces of those you killed. Then and only then will you be permitted to move on.'

He killed all these people? My eyes widen as I look again at the sombre group, feeling them waiting for the young man to lift his head and face his victims. He screams instead, twisting and turning his body.

'I didn't think it would be like this!'

The figure still has a hand on him and I can see it is wearing a long robe, drapes rippling in the silvery fabric. Its face is like an ancient statue, calm carved stone. But the features move as it talks, gentle yet firm.

'You can do this. You can learn from this, then move on. But you must face them.'

The young man screams again, his voice agonised and cracked and I don't want to see any more of this so I push off again, needing no nudge under my breastbone to tell me this is not the place for me. I fly through the clouds, feeling the pull become stronger as I move sideways once more...

.... not down...

And all at once I am on a beach.

It's lovely, and just what I need after the last two places I visited. The air is fresh and clean, feeling like it does at the end of summer when the nights grow cooler but the days are still warm, the water retaining the last of the summer's heat so it's like silk on your skin. I stand on the shore looking along the rugged coastline stretching in both directions, cliffs eroded by water and wind edging long golden beaches. Moonah and sea shrubs and bushy grasses cling to the dunes, the sand white gold. It looks like the south coast to me, where only Tasmania sits between you and Antarctica, ferocious winter storms and treacherous currents claiming ships for centuries, their wrecks now a diver's paradise of fish and corals. This beach is wild and gorgeous, blue water striped with straight lines of perfect waves running parallel with the shore. I sit down, wanting to catch my breath after the mad slide through all the different Heavens. I know where I need to go now.

I need to find my own Heaven.

Somewhere, in all those layers, all those different rooms, there's a place for me. I wrap my arms around my legs as I think about what that place would be like. I wonder if this is it. The tug under my breastbone seems to have stopped for the moment so I take in a deep breath, enjoying the warmth of the sun on my skin, the blue whispering sea in front of me. I notice a surfer out there, dipping and curling in and out of the waves, his body black against the water, board white as it kicks up spray. If this is my Heaven I like that they've included a surfer. Makes sense, really. I've always had a soft spot for them, their salty sun kissed skin and tousled hair, the way their wetsuits cling so nicely. I grin, breathing in the spicy scents of salt and vegetation, the freshness of the deep sea, sand warm beneath me. I watch the surfer as he comes closer, taking one last wave before diving in, legs long against the blue sky before he disappears. He pops up a moment later to grab his board, lying on it as he coasts in to shore, standing when the water gets too shallow. He stops at the water's edge, undoing his leg rope before tucking his board under his arm and heading towards me. Towards *me*.

Shit. I tense, thinking of the Heaven with the angry loner in his empty room. Maybe this rolling beach isn't my Heaven after all. Maybe this guy will be grumpy too, sending me away before I have a chance to speak. There is a pang in me at this, rejection welling in my chest as I watch the surfer come closer.

He's tall, maybe a bit over six foot, nicely built with broad shoulders, dark blond hair sleek against his head. And there's something so familiar about him, but I can't put my finger on it. He comes to a stop a few feet from me and pushes his board end first into the sand so it stands upright, like some sort of sandy monolithic tribute to the God of Surf. I get to my feet, brushing sand off my skirt, feeling nervous. I smile, because that's what I do when I'm nervous. Or mad. Or whatever, really. Default expression, I guess.

He smiles back.

And he is rather gorgeous. His eyes are silvery grey, his smile wide, skin tan from the sun and water, droplets gleaming in his hair, on his black wetsuit.

'Hi,' he says. There is something *so* familiar about him.

"Hi,' I say back to him, still smiling. He looks at me, then at my feet.

'Nice shoes.' He winks at me and, flustered, I look

down at my feet, realising I'm still wearing my red shoes. And bam! Just like that, I'm back in the goddamn freaking shoe store again.

A Meeting Of Souls

I cannot believe it. I cannot fucking believe it. I feel like bursting into tears as I stand there next to the table where my shoes used to be. It's full of boots now, a new season taking over. But I am too upset to care. This is for several reasons.

    a) I am dead, so I don't need new shoes.
    b) I was *so* close!
    c) Now I have to find another dead person to take me back to Heaven, or whatever the fuck it's called, again.

Wire coils twist tight inside me as I leave the store, not pausing to trail my hand across the shiny new leather boots, not even a little. I'm in the middle of the city and I don't want to be here. There are way too many people, for starters, and you know how I feel about people walking through me. So I close my eyes and think of home, trying not to dwell on the fact that I'm wearing red shoes as I do so, and all at once it's quiet. I sigh in relief as I open my eyes. I'm home. At least I can take a moment and figure out what I need to-

Wait. This is not my home.

It's my flat. Or it was. Sydney's fast moving property market means that it wouldn't have stayed mine for long after I died.

Someone else is living here.

I wander around the living room, feeling sick as I see someone else's things, someone else's furniture, where all my stuff used to be. I wonder where my stuff is now. I wonder how long it's been since I died. I wonder if I'll ever find a way out of this mess. And all the time the wires are twisting tighter inside me, making me catch my breath and gasp, my arms tight around my middle as I realise that there is no home for me here now.

I leave. But I do it how I used to. Through the front door and turn left down the stairs, letting my hand slide along the curving metal rail, taking in the plain painted walls for what I know now is the very last time. I can't come back here any more. And I feel sick to my core.

I walk out into the grey day, Sydney sky gloomy like my mood. I start walking, because I don't know where else to go. My mind no longer seems to work. I can't focus on anything, and I don't want to go anywhere, I just want this to be over, whatever it is. Tears fall endlessly, then evaporate. I don't care enough to wipe them dry. I wander through the streets for hours, sticking to the back roads where I know there won't be many people, past old brick homes and small wooden cottages, each one renovated and shiny and beautiful, born again for a new generation. But who cares any more. I'll never own one. My life is over and now I'm stuck here, nowhere to go, haunting the Sydney streets forever. The clouds burn off, the sun comes out, trees shady as I continue to roam. Sobs well up, then go as I trail along. Nothing changes. I don't get tired or hungry or thirsty. I just walk, because there's nothing else to do. In this dark state of mind I continue on until finally, as the sun starts to set, I end up by the water.

I'm in one of my favourite spots, or at least it used to be when I was alive. A small grassy patch at the harbour's edge, almost directly under the great bridge, a brick support tower rising like a small castle behind me. A road curves around the base of the bridge support, leading towards the Art Deco swimming pool. A restaurant I used to like is tucked against its side, looking straight out at the magnificent view. At this time of night it's filled with people, the small patio noisy and lit with lanterns and glowing heaters, everyone laughing and drinking and eating and it hurts to see them glowing with the life I'll never have again.

Turning away, I wander over to a bench and sit down, staring out over the water. Colours change in the sky as the sun sets over the city, lights glittering in the buildings and along the sails of the Opera House, their reflection broken into a million more smaller lights on the swirling water, competing with the stars coming out above. It's beautiful, but I may as well be sitting in a large black hole, for there is a melancholy inside me that beauty cannot touch, binding me tight.

    I sit and I stare. The cars going over the bridge become fewer, the lights starting to go out as the city finally goes to sleep. This is the best time, I think, trying to summon some positivity, to use it as a ladder to climb out of my pit of despair. This is the time when the city belongs to me. When I was alive it was rare that I was out alone at this time. Safety and all that. But now no one can hurt me and I can sit here and look at the view all I want. So that's something good to cling to, I tell myself as I look at the rippling city reflected in the ancient waters of the harbour. At this time of night you can almost imagine the place as it was long ago, the tall ships arriving, the gentle people who used to live on these shores before they were forced away. Moonlight lends magic to the scene, shifting shapes so that buildings become trees, lights become campfires, a distant hum of traffic the roar of the sea.

    I drift off into reverie, feeling the darkness inside me melting away, wondering if perhaps I can just dissolve along with it and make an end to all this. I don't want to move any more, sort of how I'd felt that day in my flat when I sat and watched the jacaranda leaves, waiting for something to happen.

    Then someone sits down next to me.

    Not super close. About a foot away from me at the other end of the bench and so I don't bother looking at them at first. I mean, they can't see me, right? But something, I don't know what, makes me turn my head

and look. And I'm jolted out of my stupor.
Because he's looking at me.
It's the guy from the beach Heaven, the surfer. He's not wearing his wetsuit anymore – instead he's dressed in jeans and a sweater, one of those cream ones with a woven pattern through the wool, chunky and masculine. His hair is dry and brushed back from his face, long legs stretched out in front of him. He's smiling at me and wow, he's gorgeous.

'I'm so glad I found you,' he says, his voice deep. My eyes widen. 'I've been looking for you. Ever since I heard about the accident. And today. I didn't mean to send you away.'

My mouth opens and shuts. I frown at him. 'You've been looking for me? Are you my, um, guardian angel?'

He grins, shaking his head. I realise what else he said. Anger comes like a hot flare in my stomach and I glare at him.

'You knew about the accident? Where the hell have you been! Ooh!' I'm so mad I stand up, fists clenched at my side. His mouth drops open a little as I keep going. 'I've been wandering around, it's been the worst time ever. I'm all alone! I mean, what the hell!' I choke on the words, unable to say anymore, so I march down the little slope to stand at the very edge of the water, my arms folded, the harbour lights bobbing and blurring. I cannot fucking believe this! I feel him come up behind me and I'm about to turn around and let him have it when he speaks.

'I'm sorry.'

That's all he says but honestly, he may as well have set me on fire. I am *raging*. All that I've gone through, all the loneliness and sorrow and fear come up in this unstoppable surge of fury and I turn around and just shove him, my hands hard on his chest. But he doesn't move and my hands just stay there. He reaches up and gathers them into his own and, all at once, I'm warm. And I realise I haven't really felt much, you know, since the accident. Temperature doesn't bother you when you're dead. But there is a warmth coming from him that feels so good I can't believe it. He's looking at me with the strangest expression, I don't recognise it at first.

'Katie, I'm not your guardian angel,' he says. 'I'm Jason. Your soul mate.'

Oh. It's love. That's how he's looking at me. As though I'm everything he's ever wanted. And my anger slips away, quick as it came, as I realise that every word he's saying is true. I know it like I know my name, or how my skin feels, or how to breathe. It just... is. My mouth has come open and I don't know what to say, but I feel as if a giant wave of relief is washing over me. I'm no longer alone.

'I know,' he says, looking at me with such love, his eyes silver grey in the light from the city behind me. 'I get it. And I'm here now.'

He does. I'm amazed. He gets it.

'And I've been trying to catch up with you. It wasn't expected, you see, when you died. It wasn't supposed to happen like that. I would have been there, otherwise.'

'You would?' His hands are still holding mine and it's

very very nice. I try to concentrate on what he's saying.
'Well, yes. You're not supposed to come through by yourself. It's all planned out, you see. But you had to step off the curb at the wrong time...' His tone is teasing but I can see his mouth twist, see worry in his eyes and it makes me feel warm all the way through, that he worries for me, that he cares.
'I know. I shouldn't have been-'
'Checking your phone?'
My mouth drops open. 'Wait, how do you know about that?'
'Well, we found out afterwards, once I realised I couldn't see you anymore. I asked the Guardians and they told me-'
'Who are the Guardians?' I can't help interrupting him, but he doesn't seem to mind. He just smiles at me and I feel warmth from him again, rippling through me. It's the most wonderful feeling, almost distracting me from his answer as I move a little closer. All at once all I want to do is talk to him and hear what he has to say.
'The Guardians are the ones who run this show, I guess. They look out for us, help us with our transitions between life and death.' His fingers are gently massaging mine and, oh, it feels so good. I inch a little closer.
'Right. The, um, transitions. So, who came for you, you know, when you...?' Then I stop, shaking my head. 'I'm sorry, that's personal. I don't need to know.'
'It's fine, Katie.'
Love is there again, shining in his eyes and he is just so damn familiar! I blurt out, 'Did we ever, I mean, have we

met, you know-'

He shakes his head. 'Well, we have, but not for a while.' I frown at him, not sure what he means and see pain flicker across his face. 'We were supposed to, but I just never got born into this life.'

'What?' I shake my head. 'I-I don't understand. How can you be my soul mate if you were never born?'

He shakes his head, mouth quirking up in a half smile. 'Sometimes it just happens like that. Either the baby doesn't make it, or people choose not to have a kid.'

This is all too much. I mean, just my luck. I have this gorgeous soul mate waiting for me and he doesn't even get born. Mentally I shake my fist at the Universe. Then I get a grip.

'But that's awful-' He is shaking his head and I stop, mesmerised by how the light shines on his cheekbones, the flash of white teeth as he smiles.

'It's fine, it's not just about me, you know. The choice isn't mine to make. '

'So, I still don't get how you're my soul mate. Although…' My brows come together as I concentrate, flickers of memory coming to me from somewhere deep inside. He squeezes my hands gently.

'I wasn't born into this life, but we've been together before, many times.'

Oh. Wow. This is all getting a bit deep and I don't know if I'm ready to go there yet. He's looking at me with those familiar silver grey eyes as he moves closer and now the warmth is everywhere, pulsing in me as he puts his arms around my waist and gently pulls me against him. 'And we're here now,' he goes on, his voice lower, a rumble against me as I wind my arms around his neck.

Wow.

Even though I'm dead, I can feel everything, everywhere he touches me thrilling and fizzing with energy. My heart is beating so hard it feels as though it's going seventy miles a minute, like I might explode. This is a literal meeting of souls and it is *electric*.

He bends his head and I reach up to him and as I do so I realise I can smell him. He smells delicious, and it's the first thing I've been able to smell since this whole death thing came along to change everything. And then the thought is gone as he kisses me.

Wow again.

My eyes close and behind my lids it's as though stars are exploding, bursts of light and colour as I swing out into space, taken on a wave of feeling stronger than anything I've ever felt before. It's extraordinary. I kiss him back, feeling the soft/hard of his lips on mine, the heat of him so close and it's as if I'm dissolving into him, his arms tight around me, my hands in his hair and it is the most sublime thing ever. Finally the kiss ends and I open my eyes to stare at him in wonder, feeling as though the world has been tilted on its axis, as if fireworks are about to come shooting from the metal arch of the bridge above, a New Year's Eve display just for us. He is staring at me too, then a slow smile appears on those kissable lips.

'I'd forgotten,' he says, looking at me like I'm everything again.

'What?' I manage to say.

'How it is, when we kiss. I mean, I knew it was good, but the reality of it is so much more -'

And I'm watching his mouth as he's saying this, nodding slightly in agreement and I think, I want more and reach up to kiss him again, cutting him off mid sentence. Well, I have some catching up to do, right? *I can't remember what it's like to kiss him, so I need to do more research.*

Hmmm.

Research is proving that it is, in fact, amazing kissing him and he doesn't seem to mind at all, kissing me just as enthusiastically, his hands moving on me as we press together and my mind starts to go to hotter, less clothing required places. Then he lifts his head and smiles at me again.

'Shall we?'

'Shall we what?' I mean, not like I care. Whatever he wants to do, I'm in. He grins at me and I know he gets it. Again.

'Shall we go?' He looks up and I realise what he means. He's going to take me away from all this, like a Calgon bath or a prince in a fairy tale, coming to lift me out of my existence. I can't believe my luck. But I realise that there's one last thing I need to do so, despite the heat in me, the desire surging like a wave, I step back slightly. He waits.

'Can we, I mean, I'd like to see them. My parents. One more time.'

His face is so gentle, so loving I can't speak any more, and he gathers me close. I can feel the wool of his jumper against my cheek, soft and warm and I hear him murmur. 'Of course.' And then there is a moment of falling. When I open my eyes, we're standing in Mum and Dad's living room.

It's still night-time, the moon shining through the big window to paint everything with silver and grey. I look at Jason for a long moment and he kisses me on the forehead before letting go of me. I feel bereft, cold, but I know what he's doing. He walks over to the big cabinet and starts looking at the photos, pointing to one of me in high school, taken around the time I'd had an unfortunate experiment with bleached hair. He doesn't say anything but quirks his eyebrow and I huff out a laugh, unable to help it. I know he's just trying to cheer me up but it's pretty funny, just the same.

'What can I say? I thought blonde was my thing.' I spread my hands and try to look innocent. He laughs.

'I'd have still thought you were beautiful.' Something passes between us, warm and deep, giving me the strength I need to do this. He comes to me and takes my hand, his silver grey eyes creasing a little and I know it's time. 'Let's go and see them,' he says and I nod. 'I'm here with you,' he goes on. 'I always will be.'

Okay. Holding onto that thought, I close my eyes and think about Mum and Dad's room. And we are there.

And it's so, so very hard to be standing next to their bed. To see the familiar carved wooden headboard, frilly pillows against it where I used to sit and bounce and giggle when younger, Ellie and I playing on lazy Sunday mornings. Dad used to complain about the frills from time to time, saying it wasn't a very masculine room but we knew he didn't mean it, that he adored Mum and would be happy to be with her anywhere, no matter how frilly.

But Dad isn't here. Mum is, sleeping, her hair spread across the pillows looking more grey than when I last saw her. Dad's side of the bed is empty, the book and reading glasses missing from his bedside table and I feel a stab of fear that makes me sag and gasp, Jason's hand the only thing holding me up.

'What is it?' He lets go of my hand to put his arm around me and I turn into his embrace, trying to take comfort from his warmth.

'It's Dad. He's not, he isn't-'

I can't say it. I can't bear the thought that he might have died and I've missed it, but Jason is shaking his head, his hand coming up to my face and wiping the tears running down my cheeks.

'He's here. Next door. It's okay, you're okay.'

He folds me into a hug but my mind is reeling. Dad is sleeping next door? In the guest room? What the hell is happening? I break free of the hug and move closer to Mum, laying my hand on her shoulder. She stirs, turning and sighing in her sleep and I snatch my hand back. Her face looks more lined than before, sorrow etched in her features and then I notice the pills on her bedside table. I can't pick them up so I bend down to read them.

Take one with water nightly. To alleviate symptoms of insomnia.

What?

Jason's grey eyes are full of sympathy. 'Grief takes time, Katie. You can't put a number on how long it will take, or what form. Losing you was hard for her.'

And she can't sleep. It starts to make more sense now, why Dad isn't here. He's a light sleeper anyway and having Mum up all night wouldn't help. Oh, but my heart breaks to see her lying there alone, like a broken vase or misaligned picture, something not right in the room. I touch her again, my hand on her hair and I can just feel the softness of it, imagine her perfume and I bend to kiss her on the cheek, tears dropping and dissolving before they touch her skin. And as I do so she sighs and smiles a little and my eyes widen. I straighten up and turn to Jason and I don't need to say anything.

'The living feel us most when they are sleeping. It's when they are closest to what we are, more open to our presence.' He pauses and I stare at him, waiting. 'You won't wake her, but she'll know, deep down, that you were here.'

Oh. That's awful and lovely at the same time. Oh, Mum. My hands come up to my face and it's the same as it was in my apartment, when I realised it wasn't my home anymore. Except it's a thousand times worse, because I'm not just saying goodbye to walls and floors and clothes. This is my *mother*. Memories flick through my mind of my life with her and I gasp in a trembling breath. There is so much compassion in Jason's face I can hardly bear it. I rub my face again and look at Mum one last time, wire coils sharp around my heart. Then I take Jason's hand and I look at him and nod.

'Okay.'

It's all I say but he knows what I want to do. In a moment we are next door in the guest room, familiar patterned bedspread and curtains, small chair in the corner of the room now with Dad's clothes draped across it, the humped shape of him in the bed. I don't hesitate, moving towards him and touching his shoulder, the faint feel of flannel under my hand and he too turns to me, and I bend and kiss him, wishing I could feel his warmth and smell his dad smell, teardrops dissolving again. And I see him smile, colour coming into his pale lined cheeks and it's just the worst. My heart feels like it might crack under the pressure and I curl over, hugging myself. Then Jason is there, lifting me and turning me into his embrace, and I cling to him and sob as he soothes me, his hand on my hair.

I finally calm down and lift my head. He's waiting, lips soft on my cheek as he kisses my tears away. I know he wants to go, but there's one more thing I need to do.

This time it's me who makes it happen. As I think it we are both outside on the balcony looking out over the sea, darker jagged rocks made visible by white foam around their base, phosphorescent in the moonlight. I look at my old town, a few lights on along the road heading down the hill. I can just see Ellie's house but there's no way I can go there. I need a minute to sort myself out. Jason is standing close to me, his steady warmth keeping me together.

'Nice view,' he says and I try to smile but can't hide how I feel and his face changes, sorrow washing over it.

'Oh, babe.' He wraps his arms around me and holds me close, his hand smoothing my hair as I lean against him. 'You don't have to do it all now. You can come back here, whenever you want. See them whenever you want.'

I look up at him, then over his shoulder to the faint gold light at Ellie's house, bright in the darkness. She's probably up with David and yeah, I can't face it. But I don't know if I'll ever be able to. I think I just need to go. And, once again, he gets it.

'Shall we go?

I nod again, not able to speak. His arms tighten around me and I hear him say

'Hold on.'

His lips touch my brow and we start moving upward and sideways, the beach and ocean and town disappearing as we soar to the stars, shooting lines of light around us against an indigo sky. I hang onto him, not because I don't want to fall, but because I never want to lose him, ever ever ever. It feels as though the world is falling away from us again, that we are all that is left and I don't mind at all. And then we land.

This Has Got To Be Heaven, Right?

We are back on Jason's beach.

Oh, it's glorious. It feels like early morning, cool breeze off the rapidly brightening ocean, promise of a warm day to come. But I am a wreck. The pain in my chest is like paper cuts and salt, bitter and hard, the wire around my heart so tight it takes my breath from me. I cling to Jason, glad of his support as he murmurs to me, comforting phrases that barely dent the sorrow I feel. Finally he stops talking and gently breaks my hold, waiting until I look at him.

I raise my eyes to him, all blurry in the morning light. 'Come on,' he says. His voice is so gentle and I take his outstretched hand, wanting him to lead me away, to leave my pain like shattered glass on the sand. He takes me a little way into the dunes, to a sheltered spot where a blanket waits, laid out on a gentle slope. We both sit down but all I can do is stare at him, my breath gasping and slowing until finally I take in one deep breath and let it out. Seeing I've calmed down a bit he lies down, pulling me to lie next to him.

'Just rest, Katie,' he says, strong arms coming around me and I bury my face in his shoulder, warm wool comforting on my skin. I start to relax and I hear his voice, feel the vibration in his chest against my cheek. 'I've got you now.'

I close my eyes and start to drift, my pain easing as I listen to the waves, the breeze in the soft grasses, Jason's arms a warm anchor keeping me in this place, safe so I don't have to run anymore.

And then I sleep.

I wake slowly, feeling calmer and more rested than I can ever remember, at least since I was alive, anyway. I know it sounds weird to say I slept – I don't really need to do it, but that's what it feels like I've been doing. Jason's arms are still around me and I carefully disengage myself before sitting up. He's still sleeping, eyes closed, his mouth a relaxed curve, so beautiful and familiar that I cannot believe my luck. Waking up with him feels like the most natural thing in the world, nothing strange or awkward about it at all and once again I curse my luck that he'd never been born. If he had, then I wouldn't have had to check for stupid texts and I'd still be alive and none of this would be happening and –

Right. Get a grip, Katie. Because it *is* happening. And you know what, for the first time I'm sort of okay with being dead. Because I'm with him, I guess.

I get to my feet, needing to walk, to see more of where

I am. For this is Heaven. It must be. I know, I know, many rooms and all that, but this place feels closer to my heart than anywhere else I've been.

    I take the little path between the dunes to the beach where I stop and take a breath, the salt air fresh in my lungs. There's sand in my shoes so I sit down and unbuckle them to take off. I stop, realising that it's the first time I've taken them off since the accident. Carefully I ease each foot out, placing my shoes next to me in a neat pair, just as they were by my body as it lay at the side of the road. I stare at them for a moment, brushing a few grains of sand from the still shiny red leather. Then I get up and leave them in the sand. I walk towards the glowing ocean, stopping at the water's edge and feeling the cool silken foam of it between my toes, lapping around my feet and ankles as my eyes fill with tears, relief that I'm finally here overwhelming me. The sun is setting, a red orb sitting just above the horizon, eggshell smooth sky golden shading to blue. The first few stars are out and I look up at them and laugh, my tears turning to joy. Arms come around me and I tense, remembering the woman in the hospital but warm lips kiss my ear and I turn to see Jason, his hair sleep tousled, smiling at me. I reach up to kiss him, feeling the sweetness of it moving through me in honey tendrils. He lifts his head and we stare into each other's eyes, goofy romantic moment. There's a noise from the sea, like the faint sound of horns and we turn to look.

    'Do you see them?' Jason points, his other arm wrapped around me as I lean against him. Oh, I see them.

Wow.

There's an honest to God pod of whales out there, humped shapes dark against the bright water, spouts misting against the multi-coloured sky. I hear them calling again, distant sounds like pipes and bellows and moans, echoing in the cool soft air. Jason is warm against my back, his arms around me and it's all that I have ever wanted, right there in that moment. It's the most beautiful thing I have ever experienced and I don't want to move, ever again. I watch the pod weave through the waves, swimming off into the distance as the sky darkens to violet, the stars silver above us, and I let out a deep sigh as the last of them disappears.

'That was amazing.' Words are inadequate, really, but I feel the need to say something. I turn in Jason's arms and he bends his head to kiss me and, well, it's pretty fucking fantastic. Again I don't want to move or for it to stop ever, and the thought comes to me that it doesn't have to, that I'm dead and he was never born, so the two of us can just stay here in this blissful place and be happy together forever, like we were supposed to be. But as I think this there's a tug under my breastbone and I break off the kiss in surprise.

'Ow!' I rub at my chest, and the feeling passes. Jason is looking at me with concern.

'Are you all right?'

'I'm fine,' I say. 'It's nothing.'

'You sure?' I nod, putting my arms around his neck again and he obliges with another of those mind-blowing kisses. This time it's him that breaks it off, smiling at me.

'Come on, let's walk for a while.'

He takes my hand and we wander along the beach a little way until we find a sheltered spot against the dunes, a nook carved out of the sand, perfect for the two of us. I guess that's how it is in Heaven though, everything's just as you want it to be. I'm so pleased to finally be here I don't even stop to consider the lack of angels or my Pop, or any of the other stuff I thought I'd see. I just want to be with Jason.

We settle back onto the sand, his arm around me and I lean my head back to watch the stars wheeling above us. After all I've been through, all the pain and loss and sorrow, all the fear and not knowing, this is the most gigantic relief. To know that I've made it, that I'm here. But as I think it there's that pain again, the tug in my chest and I yelp in surprise, my hand going to rub at it again.

'What *is* that?' I sit up, humphing out a sigh. Jason frowns at me.

'Katie, are you feeling a tugging sensation, just here?' He reaches out to touch me gently, just like the young man in the golden swirling Heaven and I nod, frowning back at him, not wanting anything to spoil our time together. The pain is subsiding again but I'm feeling a bit freaked out by it, not able to speak for a moment.

His face clears, his mouth curving in a half smile as his hand presses flat against me, between my breasts. All at once I feel a surge in myself, lower down, lust rising. His silver grey eyes start to smoulder and I think he feels it too as his hand slides up to my cheek, his thumb caressing my face. It is probably the sexiest thing that has ever happened to me and I close my eyes, turning to kiss his palm.

'Katie.' I hear his voice, deep as he moves closer.

'Hmm?' I sigh.

'It's Heaven.'

'Yes, it is.' I sigh a little more, waiting for him to take me in his arms and ravish me senseless, but instead I hear him laugh softly and I open my eyes, feeling slightly affronted. Jason is grinning at me.

'No, Katie, I mean it's Heaven calling you. The pain you're feeling?'

'Wait, what? I thought this was Heaven?' I'm outraged, especially when he laughs again. But it's nice laughter, not like he's making fun of me.

'Oh, it is,' he says. 'It's my Heaven and-' he moves closer and his arms slide around me, '-now that you're here, it's perfect.'

Oh, that's better, I think as his lips come down onto mine. Much better. As we kiss I think to myself, this has to be Heaven. What is he talking about? Then rational thought becomes a bit blurry as things get more heated, his hands sliding under my cardigan, mine moving lower down his back, pulling him against me. Yep, Heaven. Definitely.

'Ow!'

That fucking tug again! I open my eyes and sit up, Jason having rolled off me as I yelped in pain. I stare at him, gasping a little, feeling my eyes wide with worry, my hand to my heart. The tugging sensation has stopped but the aftermath is still there, a sort of tingling ringing

feeling.
'What the hell?' I say. 'Why does it hurt so much?' I stop short, a horrified cold shock washing over me. 'Am I, is it... am I not supposed to be here with you?' I mean, I can't imagine why that might be, but I don't know the rules here and so what the fuck, right? If it's true it seems terribly unfair. But Jason rolls over to kiss me again, holding his weight just above me so as not to hurt me, I guess. Hmm, that's quite sexy, I think. Then I think of how much I love him. I realise what I've just thought about and there's a brief moment of panic. And then it's all okay.
I love him.
Of course I do. It's meant to be and we're soul mates so everything will be all right, just like in a story.
He's looking at me, blond hair tousled around his face, silver grey eyes bright.
'You are supposed to be here,' he says, touching my cheek with his hand and I smile, my fear smoothing out under his touch. 'With me,' he goes on. My smile gets wider and I take in a breath on a gasp, about to tell him my big revelation. 'But-'
Uh oh. There's a 'but'? Why is there *always* a 'but'? My words die unspoken as I wait for him to tell me what he means and there's that feeling like threading wire in me again, tight with pain.
'You have to leave at some point.' He softens his words with another kiss but they freak me out so much I push at him. He raises his head, looking at me quizzically and I try to hold a non-panicked facial expression.

'Don't send me away,' I begin, wanting to sound nonchalant and cool about the whole thing, to keep the terrified wobble from my voice. But I can't help adding, and it comes out as a whisper, 'Please.'

'Oh, Katie, no, that's not what I mean,' he says, tender with worry as he pulls me close, touching my hair, gentling me like I'm a horse about to bolt. All my pretence is gone, my barriers down. I am trembling all over, so scared I'll have to go back to my old dead existence, except this time it will be about a million times worse. Because he won't be there. I breathe in the smell of him, the safety I feel in his arms and I can't bear the thought of being without him. He speaks again, his voice a rumble in his chest against my cheek as he continues to caress me. 'I would never send you away, Katie. Never. All I want is you.'

And just like that my heart opens. It's a very strange thing but that's the only way I can describe the sensation, as though it's a heart shaped box with a hinged lid, or a flower unfurling in sunlight. I feel as though I'm glowing, as though a million sparkles surround me and the words come to me again and this time nothing will stop me from saying them.

'I love you.'

I feel him stop what he's doing, his hands, his lips falling still. I lift my head and see him looking at me with those silver grey eyes. They look even more silvery, like they're underwater.

'I love you too,' he says, his mouth, that oh so handsome mouth, turning up at one corner. I pull him close to kiss, wanting that mouth on mine and oh, it's wonderful again as he pushes me gently back against the sand, cool against my skin. I push at him, wriggling a little and he stops, waiting. I see a twinkle in his eye and get the feeling he's being very patient, what with me and all my questions and stopping him kissing me. I find I love him even more for that.

'So why do I have to go?' I frown at him. 'Why can't I just stay here, share your Heaven with you?'

He takes my hand, twining his long fingers with mine. His body is heavy against me, his skin warm and wonderfully rough/smooth.

'Katie, you can stay as long as you like. Forever, as far as I'm concerned. But you know...'

'I need to find my own place.' I huff a little, sounding resigned, but I know it's true, remembering my big realisation the first time I was on his beach. 'So that's what the pulling sensation is.' And as I speak I can feel it again, a little tug inside me like an itch on my soul that I can't scratch, deep under my breastbone. But at least he doesn't want me to go. That's something.

He nods. 'Yes. That's your Heaven, calling to you. It won't get any better if you ignore it. In fact, it will get worse. You might even lose it, or they'll send a Guardian to get you.'

'A Guardian?' I think about what he told me, that they run this place, so to speak, and I can see how having one come to fetch you might not be a good thing. I think of the metal arms in the hospital, the silvery figure I'd glimpsed in the mist, like a living statue and I shiver a little. Jason, however, seems amused.

'You've no need to worry. All they'll do is send you on your way, but it's always better if you can get there by yourself.'

Hmm. Righto. I know I can trust him, the same way I know that he's the one for me so I relax a little more, the pain in my chest subsiding. Night is unfurling above us, the sunset just a few pale streaks above the horizon, stars like silver glitter and I wriggle my feet in the cold sand, enjoying the rough feel on my skin. I hear the sound of the waves as they come closer, and Jason starts kissing me again. Bliss. Then I tense, pushing at Jason again so he rolls off me.

He lies to the side of me, resting his head on his bent arm, his other hand warm on my stomach, fingers brushing my skin above the waistband of my skirt. I can see the twinkle in his eye again, but I sense his patience is starting to wear slightly thin. I don't blame him, really. He's been waiting a long time for me. And I have for him, I realise, feeling heat rising in me as he touches me. But I need to do something first.

'You okay?' There's a line between his brows. 'I promise, the Guardians are nothing to worry about. You'll see-' But I hold up my hand. It's not the Guardians I'm worried about anymore. It's my shoes. I've just realised the tide has come in quite a way, waves roaring up the beach to fizz on the sand and I'm worried it's taken my shoes. After all, they're the only pair I have and they have to last me for eternity.

'It's my shoes.' I turn such a worried face to Jason that

he shouts with laughter, which isn't very flattering. But, true gentleman, he schools his expression and gets to his feet.

'Where did you leave them?' he asks, and I point to where I think, hope, pray they still are. Hardly worn, remember? And I paid full price.

He heads down the beach and I can still hear him chuckling, and I admire the cut of his jib, so to speak, as he walks away, sandy denim on his long legs, broad shoulders under the cream jumper. It seems only a moment before he returns, my shoes in hand. 'They are nice shoes,' he says, laughing a little as he hands them to me and I examine them anxiously. Other than a little sand, they seem none the worse for wear. 'But then, you've always been into fancy footwear.'

I look at him curiously as he sits down next to me again. 'What do you mean? Oh, like when you could see me, when I was alive?' I pause, a little embarrassed at the thought of him knowing about the extent of my shoe collection. I place my red shoes carefully onto the sand next to me. 'Were you watching me all the time?'

He shakes his head. 'Not all the time,' he says. 'I missed your accident, remember?' The silver grey eyes are bleak for a moment.' And I didn't like it, seeing you with those other guys, never being happy. No, I 'm talking about when we lived together before, in our other lives.'

In our other lives? I feel my mouth drop open. Reincarnation. That's what he's talking about. I mean I've heard about it, seen a couple of those shows where they hypnotise people, but I've always thought of it as being a vaguely hippy sort of thing, a nice idea, that you get to have another chance and start over again. But then I remember the guy in the apartment bedroom, watching his parents making love until his moment came to join with them. I remember him talking about being 're-assigned'. And I remember Jason telling me down by the harbour that we'd been together before. Shit.

I stare at Jason in astonishment and he gives me a look that combines tenderness and amusement in a way that's entirely captivating. In fact, I'm becoming more and more captivated by our closeness, heat starting to rise in me again and I turn, wrapping my arms around him, wanting to feel him against me again. He obliges, shifting so he's half on top of me as we lie back on the sand.

'So, when have we lived before?' I ask, still not totally believing it, playing with the hair at the nape of his neck.

'Oh, loads of times,' he says, looking at me with those grey eyes. There is mischief in his gaze and I push him gently, moving my shoulder against his.

'Hey, I'm new to this, remember?'

'Okay,' he says. 'But are you sure you don't remember anything?'

I shake my head. 'I just know that I know you. That I always have.'

'Well, that's a start. 'He grins, then moves slightly, shifting his weight. Hmm. I'm starting not to care about the answers any more. But he seems to want to tell this story, his eyes intent on mine. 'So, in one of our lives you were the wealthy, privileged daughter of a fine household. And I was the gardener.' He waggles his eyebrows at me and I want to laugh, but his words are reminding me of something, fragments of memory, images coming into my mind.

'Wait, did I live in a big white house?'

'Yes, backing onto a lake, with a pine forest. It was beautiful.'

'And I loved you? The gardener? Very Lady Chatterley of me.' I wriggle against him and he laughs.

'Nonetheless, that's how it was.'

'So what happened? Did we get married? Did we run off together?'

A shadow crosses his face and he glances away for a moment.

'It didn't end well,' he says, finally. 'They wanted to marry you off. That's what they did in those days.'

'Those days? Wait, how long ago was this?'

'Oh, about two hundred and fifty years ago, give or take a few.'

My mouth drops open. 'So, what did I do?'

'You killed yourself, rather than be without me.' His grey eyes are pained, and I can see he's remembering it. I'm kind of glad I can't. Remembering one death is quite enough, thank you very much. But there is something about the story that feels very personal, and my voice is a whisper as I ask him.

'What did you do, when I died?'

'I died too,' he says, his eyes bleak. 'Oh, not straight away. I went on for a little while but I was young, and I couldn't live without you. So I ended it as well.'

'Oh.' I don't even know what else to say to this so

instead I reach up and kiss him. He kisses me back and I can taste salt on his lips. I wrap my arms around him, sorry for what I'd done, for the pain I'd caused him, even though I can't remember it. He lifts his head, finally, and there's a long moment of us just looking at each other. Then his mouth quirks up in a half smile.

'There was also the time you were the knight sent to guard me. A poor innocent maiden I was, and you came along and stole my heart.'

'What! *I* was the knight! How does that work?' The anatomy pressed against me is definitely male, and I know I'm female. He grins.

'Oh I know,' he says. 'But that's the great thing about love. It doesn't come from gender, it comes from in here.' He touches me with his fingertip between my breasts, just at the point where I can feel the tug under my breastbone, the call of Heaven. And it makes sense that love would come from the same place when I think about it. And, as he touches me, I can see it. A vision of myself standing at the water's edge, armoured and helmeted and carrying a spear, guarding the lady who swims there, trying not to look at her white skin as she moves through the water, the way her hair streams out behind her. When she turns to look at me I can see the same silver grey eyes in her face as those looking at me now.

'I remember,' I say, my voice soft as I touch his face, my fingertips moving over his skin, over the eyes that close, lashes dark on his cheeks as I touch him.

'There have been other lives as well,' he says, opening his eyes. 'There was one in India…' He trails off, smiling to himself and as he says it I get an impression of heat and colour, sun on bright fabric and painted stone, and love, hot as the air around us. I blush, and his grin gets wider. 'That was a good one,' he goes on. 'But we've had lots of lives, all over the world. And wherever we are, whenever we are on the earth at the same time we find each other.'

'Except for this time.'

He nods. 'There have been other times when we've been alone, but yes, this was one of them.'

'It doesn't seem fair. It still doesn't.'

'It doesn't?'

I shake my head as he kisses me once more and he stops.

'So, do you want to keep talking all night, or…'

He raises an eyebrow at me in a meaningful fashion and I giggle, unable to help it. Yeah. We can talk later. No more questions. I reach a hand down to his belt buckle and I don't need to say anything. He knows what I want, and he wants it too, I can see it in his eyes, the pupils dilating as he takes in a breath. He sits up, delicious weight leaving me for a moment as he pulls off his jumper to reveal a t-shirt, thin enough so I can see the smooth contours of his chest and stomach through it, his arms strong with muscle. It's my turn to take in a breath. I start to undo the buttons on my cardigan but he reaches to stop me, his hand on mine.

"Let me,' he said, his voice close to my ear as he leans in to kiss my neck, his hands already working on the buttons. "It's been so long, and I've missed you so.'

And what can I do but give in?

Wow.

Is there a word bigger than wow? I can't think of it at the moment, my mind and body ringing with pleasure, golden and glowing and sweeter than anything I've ever experienced. Jason and I are twined around each other, our legs and arms and bodies pressed so close it's as though we're trying to merge into one. My breath starts to slow and so does his, hand languorous on me, my nerve endings still tingling from our lovemaking. For that was what it was. It was sex, but so much more than that and as I lie here with him, breathing in the scent of his skin, the soft tickle of his hair on my cheek, exchanging kisses, slow and warm, I realise that Sarah was right.

She had tried to tell me what it was like; how you felt when you knew that someone was 'the one'. How it was about personality and enjoying each other's company but also how they made you feel when you were alone together, the way that no one else could. It had nothing to do with technique or equipment or longevity - rather it was about intimacy and trust and the feeling when they touched you that no-one else could ever give you, that connection between two souls. It was intangible and inexplicable, one of those things that you can't really describe to anyone; you just have to let them find out for themselves. And as I lay there with Jason, our hands moving on each other, our breath warm as we found our comfortable spaces, curved around each other, I could feel it. It was like nothing I'd experienced with any other lover, and it wasn't that he was better than the others, not at all. It was just that he was the right one, the one who matched me best.

The sand is cold and soft against my back and I shiver a little, the night breeze blowing around us. Jason untwines himself from me, reluctantly it seems, kissing me as he lets go and sits up. He reaches to one side and, somehow, a soft blanket is in his hand. He lies down with me again, pulling it over us both, tucking me back into the warm safety of his arms.

But where did he get the blanket? It wasn't there when we sat down, I would have noticed. I realise this seems a strange thing to be wondering about, considering where I am and who I'm with, but that's always been the way with me, my mind moving, always asking questions, thinking of ideas. The blanket is snuggly soft fleece, perfect against naked skin and I wonder if it's a Heaven thing again. Then I figure, stop wondering and ask.

'This is nice,' I say, as I snuggle against him and I feel him smile against me.

'It is,' he agrees, tightening his arms a little. 'Just nice?' There is a bit of doubt in his voice and I giggle, getting what he means.

'No, I mean that part was, um, amazing. I mean really it was. Like nothing I've ever, um…' I trail off, unsure whether he'd want to hear about my other experiences. Then I figure he knows about some of them anyway. This is going to take a bit of getting used to, the way he knows so much more about me than I do about him.

'Hmmm,' he says, half a sigh, his hands smoothing circles on my skin and I can tell he's pleased by my

answer, so that's cool.
'So where did the blanket come from?'
'Do you like it?'
'It's lovely. I mean, perfect. I don't really want to get dressed...' That's true, actually. Now that my clothes are gone I realise how sick I was of them, how wearing the same thing for weeks on end had been getting at me without me even realising. A bit shallow, I guess, but I do love clothes and dressing up.

'I don't want you to get dressed either,' he says, a grin in his words as he touches me in a very sensitive place and I gasp, all thoughts of clothes and blankets going out of my head. Oooh. Another nice side effect of being dead. No waiting time in between, it seems. If you know what I'm saying...

Wow again.

Time passes in a haze of heat and languor, our bodies finding their natural rhythm. And we do rhythm very well together, it seems. The night is waning, moon sinking low as we drift in and out of sleep, clinging to each other. Though the breeze has died down it's still cool and I'm glad of the blanket, pulling it around my shoulders. Jason feels me doing it and lifts his head, his hand on my face, love and tenderness shining in his eyes. Oh yeah, Heaven.

'Feels like Heaven to me,' I say, pushing a lock of blond hair back from his face and he grins, eyes crinkling at the corners.

'Oh, it is,' he says, punctuating his words with a kiss. 'It's my Heaven, but because we're so connected, it feels like home to you too.'

'So it's true? Heaven is what you want it to be?' I fall silent for a moment, thinking of my dead self sitting on a silent dark street, trying to work it all out. At the time all I'd wanted was to go back to my old life – that would have been Heaven to me. Now I'm not so sure. I feel the tug again but it's softer, more like a little nudge and I don't need to rub at my chest. Instead I consider. What would my Heaven be like? I still have no idea. I think there might be trees, but that's all I can think of.

'Yes.' Jason is looking at me, like he's waiting for something.

'So what makes this Heaven to you?' I'm very interested in this.

He smiles, kissing me. 'Other than you being here? Well, it's just where I love to be. I've always loved the water and, when I wasn't born, I imagined this life for me here instead, thinking it might be something like how my life would have been.'

'Huh.' I think about that for a moment. There is something so sad, yet beautiful about the idea. 'Were you disappointed, when you weren't born?'

He shifts his weight a little, his skin on mine. 'A little. Mostly because I knew you'd be coming along. But I knew I'd just have to wait for you instead, that we'd be together again one day.'

'Really? That sounds awful.'

He looks thoughtful. 'Well, it wasn't the best. But here, well, it's like all the strong emotions, the hurtful ones, they don't really matter. They are fleeting, at best.

The only one that matters is love. It's like the songs say, love is forever.'

I'm not sure about this. I can still feel the wires around my heart if I think of them, guilt and sorrow and loss when I look back at my old life, despite my current situation. But maybe it's just something that comes with time, the emotions getting worn away like rocks on the seashore, ground smooth.

'And anything is possible here.' Jason nudges me and I realise I haven't answered him. 'You can do anything you want, so it's really not a bad place to wait.' He seems a bit worried and I reach up to smooth out the crinkle between his brows.

'What do you mean?'

'Well, if you want something, you just ask for it.'

I raise an eyebrow at him and he huffs out a laugh. He sits up and I pout, not liking the heat of him moving away from me. I sit up as well, clutching the blanket to me, about to protest when he waves his hand and a little bonfire appears on the sand nearby, a driftwood one ringed with shells, flames hissing blue with the salt. It's warm and welcoming, the crackle and pop of the wood reminding me of the wood burning stove at my parents' house, toasting marshmallows with Ellie when we were young.

'Ooh!' My mouth drops open and I reach out my hands to the flames, enjoying the golden heat. 'Oh, that's really cool! Okay, now it's my turn,' I shoot Jason a mischievous glance. 'I would like, um, an ice cream. Chocolate, in a waffle cone. With sprinkles.' I hold out my hand but nothing happens and he grabs it, laughing a little.

'This is my Heaven, not yours. I'm the only one who can ask for things here.' He grins at me and I pout again and all at once the ice cream cone is in my hand, just as I'd asked for. I take a lick. It's delicious. It's also the first thing I've eaten since the accident and I get a little teary, realising how much I've missed feeling normal, doing normal human things. I devour the ice cream, savouring every delicious creamy mouthful and, when I've finished, Jason reaches for me and kisses me, licking the chocolate from my lips.

'Very nice,' he says, all sexy again and I'm about to leap on him when his expression changes, becoming more serious.

'I asked for something else, Katie. Something for when you arrived. Shall we see if it's here?'

I look at him wide eyed, my mood changing with his to a wild excitement, the kind you feel as a child before a holiday or on Christmas morning.

'Show me,' I say, and he gets to his feet, holding out his hand. I take it, and he pulls me to my feet and into his arms for another kiss. I could really get used to this, I think.

'C'mon,' he says, breaking the kiss, and I can see the same excitement and anticipation in him as is in me. We wrap the fleece blanket around ourselves, giggling as we try to cover up against the cool night air. Our feet sink into the soft sand as we walk along the beach, smiling at each other, the stars above silver bright, the dark blue ocean whispering beside us. We walk a little further along the water's edge until he steers me between two dunes, feathery grasses and low shrubs growing across them.

We come to a stop and I gasp.

He pulls me close, his arm around me. 'D'you like it?' Do I like it? Is he kidding me? I love it!

'It' is a small cabin, set behind the dunes and raised up so it has a view across the sand and shrubs to the ocean. It's one room, really, built of timber bleached silver grey by the elements, a rough shingle roof sloping up, the wall facing the sea made of glass. Two chairs sit on the small decked area out front and, as we walk closer, I can see the golden glow of a fire inside. Jason leads me around the side of the little cabin and I notice a shower head sticking out of the wall, a tap below, hooks on which to hang your towel, completely private as there's no one else here. I have to pinch myself, almost, reminding myself that I'm dead, that this place exists as part of Heaven, that I'm not actually on the south coast somewhere on an extra extended holiday. We stop at a door made of the same wood as the walls so it blends in, a single metal latch keeping it closed. Jason opens it, pushing the door before standing back so I can go inside first. I'm kind of glad he hasn't tried to carry me over the threshold or something like that – it's a bit too over the top for me. But I guess that's why we're perfect for each other – he gets it, and so do I. He relinquishes the blanket to me and I wrap it around myself before stepping inside. It's wonderfully warm. There's the slippery softness of polished wood under my bare feet, then the rough warmth of a rug. The fire is burning in the fireplace on the wall opposite, scenting the room with salt and herbs, making me realise how chilly I'd been feeling. I look around, taking in the glorious view through the glass, the wooden beams painted white in the ceiling, the bleached timber walls, silvery grey like the outside. And the bed.

It's the only piece of furniture in the room, and it's huge and comfortable looking. I want to jump into it immediately. The pillows are soft and fluffy and there are lots of them, all in smooth white pillowcases, while the quilt is patchwork, blues and greys and greens like the landscape outside, intricately embroidered with a pattern of threads. Another similar quilt is draped across the end of the bed and I know I could pick it up and wrap myself in it and sit outside, warm and secure. Two robes, grey and velvety, hang side by side on hooks set into the wall, and that's it. That's all there is. Jason has come up behind me and I can feel he's waiting for me to respond, that he's wondering what I think. I turn to him.

'It's beautiful. Perfect.'

His face lights up in a huge grin and I go to hug him, dropping the blanket and kissing him, happiness like I've never known coming over me. He kisses me back, then pulls back to smile at me.

'I'm so glad you like it. I made it just for us. I knew you'd be coming here one day so I planned it, wanting to be ready.'

'Wait, you built this?' I look around in amazement, taking in the craftsmanship, the shaped and polished timber, but he shakes his head.

'No. Well, not in the truest sense of the word. I designed it, and I had it in my head and then, when you arrived, I asked for it.'

Ohhhhh! Right. Of course. This is his Heaven and he can ask for whatever he wants. How cool is that? And how amazing, that he would make such a place for us. I look around again and I come back to him, one eyebrow arched.

'Just a bed?' I look at him meaningfully and he laughs.

'Well, there are a couple of chairs outside, but, yeah. Just a bed.' His eyes change then, his pupils dilating as he leans in to kiss me, the kiss becoming deeper. 'Besides,' he murmurs against my mouth, 'if we need anything else we can just ask for it.'

I cannot argue with this on any level, nor do I want to. And I was only teasing him about the bed. As far as I can see, it's all we need. We don't need the bathroom, we don't need to eat (though we can ask for food if we want it), and we don't really even need to sleep. The kiss is becoming more passionate and he is moving me towards the bed, his hands on me, my own touching the smooth skin and muscles of his back, feeling him move under my hands. My legs hit the edge of the bed and I sit, then lie back with him on top of me, still kissing. The mattress is just right, just firm enough. And that's about the last rational thought I have for a while.

Later we sit together on the small deck and watch the sun rise, me wrapped in the quilt from the bed, Jason in the soft fleece blanket. I've asked for a cup of tea and it's in my hand, the warm curve of the mug so comforting and familiar it makes me all teary again. And it's a really good cup of tea. I'm not sure why I keep crying at the drop of a hat, but it feels like reaction to me, like I might need some time to heal from what's happened. Here is a good place to do that, I think as I sip my tea and stare out at the waves. The whales are back, hooting bells in the dawn light and I listen and weep and think that there can never be anything better than this, ever. Heaven can wait, for now.

Goddamn City Boys

I don't really know how long I've been here for. Not that I'm bothered, really. I think maybe it's been a couple of weeks but, as I say, I'm not sure. Whatever the amount of time, it's been the most blissful of my entire experience, alive or dead. And it hasn't been just shagging, although, let's be honest, there's been a fair bit of that. And swimming, though we're naked for that so it often ends in shagging too. But there's also been talking, time spent sitting out under the stars, opening our hearts to each other. I'm remembering more about our other lives together, even surprising him, like the time when I remembered him as a fisherman, me as his long-waiting lover, standing on shore wishing him safely back to land. And he's told me more about Heaven, and every so often I get that tugging in my chest, just to remind us both that there's still more to do, that we have more to accomplish together. But so far he says it's not time yet, and I don't want to argue, wrapped in love and desire as I am, all of my dreams fulfilled. I tell him more about my life, my most recent one, and, while he knows some of it, he doesn't know it all. He was outraged when he heard about the Stag and Doe date - at least I think he was, but it was hard to tell with all the laughing he was doing. Huh. I have never loved anyone like I do him, never felt this close to anyone in my life (or death). And the wonder of it, the miracle of it all is that he loves me too, words whispered in the night or spoken as we drift in the currents together, limbs twined like seaweed around each other, heart to heart.

Today is much like any other day. We wake together, slowly, taking our time, no alarms to shriek us into wakefulness, just the slow drowsy feel of being together, not having anywhere to go or anything in particular to do. Jason's arm is across me and I turn into his embrace, breathing him in, kissing the soft skin on his shoulder as his arm tightens around me. It's strange, all the sleeping we do. Like I say, we don't need it – it's almost like we do it as a holdover from our lives on earth, a continued pattern of behaviour that we don't need to follow, but that we do for no other reason than it brings us pleasure. It's like the eating as well. I start the day with breakfast, just like I did when I was alive, the only difference being I don't have to cook it and I don't need to eat it. Although Jason doesn't seem to need food like I do he humours me just the same, laughing at some of the things I ask for then kissing me, telling me he likes to taste them on my lips. He just asks for whatever we want, although sometimes it's only me that eats, sitting wrapped in the quilt on the deck as I watch him ride the waves, a distant black figure against the blue and white foaming ocean.

I wriggle out from his arm and slide out of bed. There are no cold feet, no unpleasant chill as I walk to where my robe hangs and put it on. The temperature in here is perfect – cool enough to sleep by, warm enough to be comfortable. That's Heaven for you, I guess. Running a hand through my hair I walk to the window and stand there, watching the waves. I hear the rustle of covers as Jason moves and turn to see him sitting up, chest bare, golden against the white pillows. He grins at me.

'The usual?'

I smile back. 'Yes please.' And a steaming mug of tea appears in my hand, just how I like it, strong and sweet. There's a joke there about men and tea but I can't bear to make it, so I turn to the waves instead, watching the sparkles of light, the shadows changing as the sun rises behind us, turning the day to gold.

There are times, you know, when I forget that I'm dead. It all seems so normal. I mean, a pretty blissful kind of normal, but there's not much to distinguish between this and a holiday week away on the south coast, long walks on the beach, dinner under the stars, the scent of salt and sand and seagrass on our skin as we dance together, slow, by the fire. But every so often something reminds me. There's the absolute solitude, the fact that it is just the two of us here. No other walkers come along the beach or through the dunes, no dogs or children play in the waves. And the fact we have no need of a bathroom. I do use the outside shower though, mainly because I like the feel of it, the freedom of being naked outside, the warm water on me. To be honest, I think maybe I'm trying to forget. To put the pain of it out of my mind, the guilt at all I've caused my family, the shock of being dead and lost with no one to turn to. Jason is pretty great about it all. He knows I don't want to talk about it, but he's there when I need him to be, or when the tug of my Heaven pulls strong. I know I need to move on soon, but for now I'm happy to just drift here, feeling those tight coils inside me growing looser each day, choosing to forget whenever I can, just being in the moment.

And Heaven, as it turns out, is a pretty interesting place. For starters, I can eat, taste, smell and hear just like normal, except that alcohol, or what appears to be alcohol, has zero power to get me drunk. And I can eat whatever I want, whenever I want and nothing changes. I don't gain weight, I don't lose weight, there's no need to exercise or count calories or feel guilty about having a second piece of pie (not that I did, really, in my old life. I was lucky that way, I guess.)

And every day I think of new things to ask Jason about.

We talked about my accident, of course, and why no one was there to help me when it happened. Turns out it wasn't supposed to be my day to die, after all, just as he told me when we first met.

Although, me arriving on his beach during my mad slide through Heaven wasn't the first time we'd crossed paths either. (At least in *this* lifetime – I know, it's confusing, right?) Remember the first Heaven I went to? The fiesta Heaven, filled with dancing and light and music. I'd felt so out of place and gone to stand under a tree, then been sent on my way with the best of intentions. But just before the young woman pushed me back to Earth, I'd seen a man in the crowd. A man with silver grey eyes.

Of course it was Jason. He'd been searching for me, just as he said, as soon as he realised I wasn't where I was supposed to be. As we were so close it was easiest for him to find my trail, so to speak. So he'd almost caught up with me when I was sent out of Heaven, and then he lost the trail again until I showed up on his beach a few weeks later.

It saddens me that it wasn't my time to die, especially when I think about my family. And I'm furious when I think about the missed chance we had to be together, all the fruitless time spent wandering through Sydney, tagging along to strange Heavens with people I didn't know. But then I remember the wonder of Valhalla, the beauty of the woman who died for her child. The joy and peace of Chandrani's Heaven, the young man who told me my life had been blessed.

That didn't make sense either. I mean, I didn't have Jason in that life, so how was I blessed? All I had was some city boy who thought he was a superstar, without even the courtesy to call me after a date. Just treating me like another city girl to take out on a date, wine'em and dine'em and, if you're lucky, get into their knickers, then don't bother to call or text or...

Okay, I need to stop thinking about him. Because it only takes me to that place where wires coil tighten around my heart. I know it upsets Jason, too. In fact, we kind of had a little fight about it. Or a disagreement, at least. A very small one.

It was another lovely day, cooler, the bite of autumn in the wind when you stood in the shade, but the sun still summer warm. Turns out that's Jason's favourite time of year as well as mine, just another way we connect.

We were on the deck, soaking up the golden light, slow start to a languorous day. But instead of enjoying it, I was thinking about the text and how silly it was, the fact I couldn't wait to check my phone costing me so much.

I don't know what it was that made me think of it. My phone was long gone and I felt no need to have one – who was I going to call, after all? Anyway, so there I sat, wrapped in my blanket with my tea and for some reason I thought about the text and it annoyed me, that this jerk hadn't bothered to get back to me. I mean, I thought we'd had fun.

(I know, right? I'm a complete idiot. Sitting here in Heaven with my very own gorgeous soul mate and I'm thinking about a text that may or may not have been from someone else. Sometimes I think they're right when they talk about the mysteries of the female mind. God knows I don't understand myself some of the time.)

'Heaven bothering you again?'

'Hmm?' I looked up, startled out of my reverie to see Jason looking at me, his face midway between amused and concerned. I grinned at him. 'No, it's nothing.' I went back to my tea but he was still looking at me.

'It's something,' he said. 'You had that look on your face, the annoyed one you get sometimes.'

Oh really? I felt a flare of anger then I took a deep breath, not wanting a fight. 'It's fine, I'm fine.' But my mind went back to the text again and oh my God, maybe it *was* him. I never found out, did I? So I spoke before I thought, never a good option.

'You know the day of the accident, how I was checking for a text-'

'Oh, Katie, it wasn't your fault-'

'No, um, I know that, although really, it kind of was. But I never knew who it was from, who was texting me.'

'What?' Jason looked half annoyed, half amused.

'Well,' I plunged on, in for a penny, in for a pound.' I had been on a date, you see, and the guy had promised to message me and so I was just checking…' Jason was starting to look annoyed now. 'Anyway, I still don't know if it was him.'

'It wasn't.' Jason sort of snapped the words out then took a deep breath in through his nose, as though he was counting to ten or something. He flashed a silver grey glance at me. 'It wouldn't have gone anywhere anyway. He was nowhere good enough for you.'

Now I was cross. 'Well, what was I supposed to do? You weren't even born. God!' I folded my arms and twisted in my chair, wire coils tight. I hadn't felt them for a while, not like this anyway and I didn't like it. Honestly, what had gotten into me? I stared out to sea, waves blurring into silver blue sparkles and I wished I'd never brought it up. I took in deep breaths, trying to calm down, to release the coils of pain and then I heard the creak of Jason's chair as he got to his feet and came to stand in front of me, blocking out the blue shimmer.

'Hey.'

I took another breath and wiped at my eyes, blinking a little before looking up at him.

'I'm sorry,' he said, and I could see he meant it and that made me feel even worse. I shook my head.

'No. It's me who's sorry. I shouldn't have said anything.'

Which is true. But then I can't be perfect all the time and, I guess, neither can he. Sometimes stuff is just going to come out and cause arguments like this one. And I'm still annoyed, unreasonably so, that the stupid text that took my life wasn't even from this guy. As far as I know, he doesn't even know I'm dead. Asshole. I don't know why it's so important, for me to have approval from someone who so obviously wasn't into me. I mean, who did he-

Oooh. Stop right there. Back to the disagreement.

Jason's beautiful eyes were full of sympathy. 'It'll take time,' he said, his voice more gentle than I deserved it to be. 'You have to get through it all to let it go.'

What? I looked at him in confusion.

'Your life,' he went on. 'It stays with you, a little while. Especially if you go unexpectedly, like you did. It's a shock on a lot of levels. So I get it.'

He got me, all right.

I stood up, not wanting to be upset with him or myself or anything any more.

'I'm sorry,' I said again, and I really meant it. I slid my hand into his, feeling his warm fingers and he pulled me close against him, into a hug, then released me.

'It's okay,' he said, smiling at me. 'Shall we go for a walk?'

I nodded, taking his arm and leaning close to him as we stepped off the deck and started along the soft sand. We wandered along in silence as I took it all in, thinking about what he said. I remembered sitting in my apartment just after the accident, thinking to myself I might be in shock. And I nodded, as it began to make a bit more sense. We walked a little further along the golden beach that seemed to stretch forever, no one there but the two of us, leaving footprints in the sand. I thought about this a little. Then I considered how had I slid through all the heavens.

'Hey, so can other people come here? You know, if they're lost, or looking for something?'

Jason looked surprised. 'Um, yes, they can,' he said. 'But it doesn't happen very often. Maybe because I wasn't born this time, I'm not so connected to the human world.'

'But they do come?'

He nodded, sliding his arm free to put it around me as he looked at me, grey eyes amused. 'Does that worry you? No one has the power to harm you, especially not here.'

'But what about the Guardians?'

Jason's brows drew together. 'The Guardians? Why would they ever hurt you?'

'Well, I saw this woman...' I began, telling him the story of the woman in the hospital. He listened, holding me close as we strolled along, calming my shivers as I relived the cold horror of that moment in the emergency room.

'Okay.' He nodded his head. 'I see what you mean. Did you know the woman?'

I shook my head. 'Nope. Never met her. Just saw her standing there as they worked on her body, then she was just... gone.' I shuddered again.

'So you don't know anything about the kind of person she was?'

'No.' Then I stopped, thinking a little. About her unpleasant facial expression, her dissatisfied posture. The way she had seemed so annoyed about everything. Still, I didn't know her life. My mouth twisted before I spoke, as I didn't want to seem judgy. 'Well, she seemed kind of angry...' I stopped again and shook my head. 'No. I really don't know.'

Jason nodded. 'Okay. Well, it may be that the Guardian took her because there was something she needed to do. Or she needed to face something she'd already done.' Then he sort of laughed. 'I mean, I don't really know either. I've spent a bit of time here, but they're still a mystery to me.'

I shivered. 'They scare me.' Then I told him about the young man with all the other spirits, waiting for him to face them and he looked at me, his eyes wide.

'You saw that? I mean, I've heard about it- wow. That's pretty profound, Katie. That was, I guess you could call it a judgement.'

I thought about that. Judgement is a Biblical sounding word, something that always makes me think of worlds ending or intervention by a higher power. Which seemed pretty true, in this instance.

'The Guardian, it was telling him he had to face it, then he could move on.' I paused, considering. Yep, it made sense. I mean, you couldn't spend your life killing or abusing people or being generally unpleasant and just expect to go to your Heaven, everything all hunky dory. At least that's what I thought. You had to face up to what you'd done at some point, surely. Otherwise you'd never learn anything. Which seemed to be one of the most profound revelations I'd had yet.

The sea sparkled next to me, birds calling above, running light footed across the sand and leaving little pronged prints and I could feel the peace of this place just washing through me, the joy as I walked with Jason. Yep. I didn't think I would deserve anything like this if I'd not at least tried to be a decent person. And I had tried, honest. He was looking at me, half smile, waiting while I figured things out, patient as always.

'Okay,' I said, still thinking hard. 'So, Guardians are like… angels, then?' My voice went up on the last part of the question, because I still wasn't sure, even though it did seem to make sense. Jason squeezed me a little before answering, hard body against mine.

'They are what we would call angels, at least in a spiritual sense. Others have called them gods or spirits. But they are here, they've always been here and their job is to look after us, as far as I can see. To help us see who we are, and the potential of who we can be.'

'So why didn't they know when I died?' This was important to me. Was my death such a small thing that it didn't matter? This made the wires coil in me again as I thought of my family, of Sarah, the loss and sorrow in their lives.

'I know.' He hugged me to him again, and I knew he knew. 'Sometimes things happen outside of fate, and so they get missed.'

'Outside of fate? What, like my destiny?' This sounded a bit too trippy, but Jason was in earnest as he continued.

'Yes. We all have a destiny, a potential life we can live, a time to die. But within that we have a freedom of choice that can change how things happen, steering us to a different path, so to speak. And so if you make a choice such as, say, checking a text at the wrong moment,' he winked at me,' you can change your fate. You weren't supposed to die that day, and so that's why we weren't there to help you.'

And I flushed a little, not wanting to be reminded of it, or of the almost argument we'd had earlier. It's all fine now anyway, our relationship back to its usual laughing loving self, nothing awkward remaining between us. It's like our connection ran deeper than all that petty stuff.

Later we lie on the sand together, listening to the crackle and hiss of a little bonfire keeping us warm as the breeze grows cool. Stars come out overhead and I gaze up at them, thinking of how I used to wonder what it would be

A Thousand Rooms

like to fly among them, when I was a kid. Now I suppose I can, if I want to. But I'm quite content to be here for a while. I'm getting the vague impression that it's necessary for me to be here, that I need the time to get over the shock of my lonely death. And also to be with Jason, of course.

But it's still a mystery to me. How I could live such an uneventful life and yet end up here, in such a blissful place? I mean, that trip through my memories just seemed to reinforce the fact that I'd not done much of anything except complain and be a disappointment. I don't know how to share this with Jason, not wanting him to see me as less than perfect, I guess. Even though I know I'm not, and I know he knows that too.

Seems like relationships are complicated no matter where you are.

He nudges me, gently, and I turn my head. His cheekbones are gilded by the firelight, eyes gleaming in the almost dark. He is beautiful, and my heart swells again to see him.

'You hungry?' I almost laugh, coming back to reality. Then I think about it. Actually, I wouldn't mind a little something…

I don't really have to say anything – a paper parcel appears on the sand next to me and I know what's inside. Fresh fish and chips, hot as though just out of the fryer. Chips juicy, real potato, the fish white and flaking inside golden crispy batter. It's one of my favourites and he knows it.

I grin, sitting up and crossing my legs, pulling the

parcel between us and opening the paper, releasing steamy salt and vinegar scents. I pop a chip in my mouth, offering the meal to him as well, but he shakes his head and smiles, seeming happy to see me happy, I guess. And there it is again.

What have I done to deserve all this?

'So um,' I start, reaching for another chip as I think about how I want to ask this. I chew thoughtfully and he laughs.

'So, um, what?' he says, poking me in the leg.

'Well, remember that guy I told you about? The one who was waiting, you know, for his new life?' I blush, thinking of how embarrassed I'd been and Jason laughs out loud.

'Yeah, I remember him.'

'Well, how did he get his new life? I mean, he talked about being re-assigned. How does that happen? How do we get the lives we get?'

It's the only way I can think to ask about what I want to know. Jason looks at me a long moment and I raise my eyebrows. But I know I can't hide much from him.

'Well,' he starts, tracing circles in the sand with one long finger. 'I don't know too much about it, but as I understand things it's up to the Guardians, really – they send you to the best place for you, the place where you can learn.'

'Okay.' I think about this, breaking the fish and starting to eat the crispy batter, burning hot against my fingers. I swallow. 'So, what about if, you know, you aren't a nice person? Do they send you somewhere you can learn to be nicer?'

'I think they try and help you first, to see if your spirit can grow before it gets sent back to earth. But it's really complicated, Katie. I mean, they're the only ones who figure this stuff out. It's like a mystery, that perhaps we're not meant to understand.'

I stare at him, my mouth twisting a little. I get that, absolutely I do. And I know people get born into lives that are terrible from the get go, through no fault of their own. I was very lucky, really. And as I think that there's a fluttering tug under my breastbone again and I jump. It's been a while since I've felt it. I rub at my chest, breathing hard, my face screwing up. Jason sits up, reaching for me, full of concern.

'Are you okay?'

'Um, I think so,' I reply. And I am, the pain passing. I rub my face with my hands. Maybe that was a little warning, reminding me I'm just not meant to know about some things. Right. Got it. You don't need to tell me twice, I think, looking up to the spangled sky, just in case the Guardians are there, hiding amongst the stars. But all I feel coming back to me is… laughter. As though someone, somewhere, is amused.

'And what about us?' I decide to change tack. Surely they won't mind me asking about this. After all, it's important, right?

Jason raises an eyebrow. 'Us?'

God, why are men so obtuse sometimes? I resist the urge to roll my eyes. 'Yeah, us. You said we've been together, loads of times before. So, how does that work?

Do we get reassigned together?' All at once there is a great panic in me. That is how it works, right? I mean, it's got to be. I bite my lip and breathe in through my nose, staring at Jason. 'That's what's going to happen, right?'

Jason holds my gaze with his own, silvery gleam in the firelight. 'It is usually the way. I mean, I can't really remember the in between times, when we were here before. Only the lives we've lived. But, from what I know about it, it has to be. So, wherever you are, after this, if I'm alive I'll find you.'

I swallow. 'And if you're not?' My voice is a whisper. Jason looks down.

'I'll still be with you, just like I was this time.' *Except for when I died.* The thought flashes through me, then goes, leaving me feeling empty. The fire is starting to burn lower and Jason lifts his hand as though to bring it back to life. But I grab his hand, stopping him.

'Can you, can we go back to the cabin?' I say. 'I just, I want to be with you. Inside.' I shoot him a look that tells him exactly what I want and he gets it right away. But he doesn't see the other part of it. At least I don't think he does.

I just want to forget. Perhaps I'll never know why I had the life I had, or why he wasn't there to share it with me. But I'm here with him now and all at once I just want to be done with my old life. With the questions and worry and wire coils twisting, Heaven tugging at me. I just want to stay where I am, dammit. After all I've been through it seems only fair.

The Magic Pool

So, this is bliss.

I'm in bed with Jason, half sitting against the soft pillows with the covers pulled up to my chest as I gaze out at the sea, enjoying the way it's never the same, changing with the sky and the wind and the weather, a constant moving canvas. Today it looks stormy out there, the wind kicking up whitecaps, huge waves crashing into the shoreline. I'd asked Jason about it, why he makes it so the weather changes and he told me it keeps things from getting boring, that that's how it is in the real world, change making things exciting for us all. So a wintry day today but it doesn't matter, cocooned as I am within warm quilts, the fire crackling in the fireplace, Jason's heat next to me. He turns his head, smiling up at me, grey eyes full of love. His hair is all messy from sleeping, or whatever it is we do here, bits of it sticking up and for a moment he reminds me of my nephew, David, and how he looked when Ellie would pick him up from his nap, his golden hair sticking up.

I tense, a creeping feeling of guilt and horror coming

over me. Jason must have seen my face change for his does as well.

'What is it? Is it Heaven again?' He pulls himself up to sit close, his shoulder leaning against mine as he puts his hand on my chest. All I can do is shake my head and stare at him, my eyes filling with tears. 'Babe, what is it? Tell me.'

'It's my family.' As I say the words two big tears overflow from my eyes and run down my cheeks. Jason is still looking concerned, and also a bit confused. 'I haven't seen them, or thought about them or anything for, well I don't know, weeks or months or however long I've been here with you! Oooohh!' And I bring my hands up to my face, letting out a big wail. Jason has me, his arms coming around me to pull me to him and I hug him back, crying hot tears of guilt into his neck.

I cannot believe it. I've been so wrapped up in all this, in being with Jason, that I haven't even thought of them. I remember how they were at the funeral. The way Mum and Dad were so broken, poor Ellie so distraught, none of them wanting to let me go, then seeing Mum in bed alone, no Dad to comfort her as she slept her drugged slumber and I feel awful that I've just gone and left them to it. I sob some of this out incoherently against Jason's neck – I'm babbling so much I don't know how much he understands - and he just lets me cry it out, stroking my hair and making me feel safe and loved in that way only he can. Finally I calm down, pulling back and wiping my face on a corner of the quilt.

'When I was in Valhalla...' I start, and Jason looks at

me, amazed.

'Katie, of all the things you could have said, that is the last thing I expected.' He huffs out a laugh and then so do I, realising how ridiculous it sounds.

'But I was!' I say, feeling injured.' Remember I told you about it?' He nods, still grinning and I go on. 'They wouldn't let me in or anything, so I was sent to the meadow where I met some women, and one of them had a glass through which she could watch her daughter, you know, on earth.'

Understanding dawns on his face. 'You want to see them?'

I nod, feeling tears welling up again. 'I do.' And my voice is all croaky and breathy at the thought of it. 'Do you have a magic glass thing here?'

'No,' he says, 'but let's get dressed and I'll show you something just as good.'

It feels strange to be back in my clothes again. I haven't really worn anything other than my robe since I've been here, or a blanket wrapped around me, fleece soft against my skin. I bring my shoes out onto the deck and slide my feet into them, doing up the buckled strap, wriggling my toes against the enclosed feeling. Jason is already dressed, his jeans and cream sweater again. He's not much of a one for clothes either. I don't mind that at all.

He reaches out his hand and I stand up to take it, swallowing a little at what's to come. But I have to do this, I have to see how they are. Guilt is pulling the wires tight in me, tighter than they've been for a long time. But at least the tug under my breastbone is mercifully absent.

We walk between the dunes to the beach, turning to walk along the shore towards a line of rocks some distance away. I've been out on them before, standing like a figurehead against the waves, watching Jason surf, then picking my way carefully among the shells and sharp edges back to the soft sand and warm pools of trapped seawater, miniature oceans among the wind-twisted stones.

'So where are we going?' I say, wanting to say something. The weather is calming around us, the sky turning back to blue, the sea shining and calm. Jason squeezes my hand, his eyes crinkling as he smiles at me.

'Somewhere special. I think you'll like it.'

When we reach the rocks he goes first, stepping onto a large level stone, water pooled around its base. He turns, holding out his hand and I take it. He helps me climb up and get my balance before he starts across the slanted slippery surfaces, boot heels crunching on shells. It's a little harder for me with heels, but his hand is warm and strong around mine and I'm not worried about falling, knowing he would catch me.

He takes me further along the rocks than I've been before, out to where they meet the ocean, deep blue water washing against the jagged edges. There are more pools out here, some fairly deep, so I'm a little more careful now. The seaweed is green and slippery, still anchored to the rocks, shells lodged in crevices hurled there by the force of the waves.

And then I see it.

A perfect round pool in the centre of a large flat rock. And all at once I flash back to being seven again, my hand in my father's as he takes me along the rocks. This time it's Jason's hand holding me tight, keeping me safe. There is a warmth, then, love surging through me anew and the coils loosen a little.

When we reach the little pool I crouch down, trailing my hand in the clear water. I poke a finger into one of the little anemones, smiling through my tears as the soft tendrils close around my finger, feather light.

'Dad.'

I breathe the word and it's as though my breath is taken into the pool, the water misting over and becoming opaque. I take my hand out, hardly daring to breathe again as the mist coalesces and... there he is.

There they all are.

My legs give way and I sit to one side, not caring about the water soaking through my skirt, my hand outstretched as though I can reach through and touch them. My family.

Mum and Dad are sitting on the sofa in the big living room at their house. There are stripes of sun and shadow coming through the window, falling across the faded colours of the cushions and wallpaper. Mum and Dad are both smiling, looking at something spread out on the low coffee table.

David is toddling around, holding what looks like a piece of paper in his chubby hands, golden hair a fluff of light around his rosy cheeks. He is giggling, and as I watch the sound becomes clearer and I can hear it, that irresistible baby laughter. Pete appears in the frame, chasing after David whose giggles become squeals, sturdy legs moving faster as he tries to outrun his father.

'Oh!' I say, softly, my hand coming to my mouth. Jason, who is sitting beside me, puts his hand on my shoulder. I can feel the warmth of it through my cardigan.

'Oh, look at how big he is! Oh...'

Pete by now has caught up with David, scooping him up and kissing him over and over, while managing to get the piece of paper from his sticky grasp. He hands it to Mum, who has her hand outstretched and is laughing too, her mouth and eyes wide. She adds it to the pile on the table.

Ellie comes into frame and my eyes widen as I notice the obvious swelling around her abdomen, see the faint glow around her. It's too much and I start to cry. I hear her speak. 'So, Mum, are you going to art class tomorrow?'

Art class? I turn to Jason. 'She always wanted to do art,' I whisper, my voice rasping in my throat. His arm slides across my shoulder and he leans against me.

'Keep watching,' he murmurs. I turn once more to the pool, conscious of the weight of his arm on me, his warmth against my side, like anchors holding me together, stopping me from breaking into pieces and flying away.

For this is so hard.

I'd... not forgotten, exactly. But I'd let them go, not able to deal with thinking about them too often, other than with a sort of distant fondness, as though I were really on holiday and would be seeing them again in some vague future. But this brings it all back again, my pain and sorrow at having to leave them, to leave my life behind.

I look at the room, at the familiar paintings of hibiscus flowers and sailing ships, the way one edge of the rug curls up. I remember sitting on the couch, pushing at the edge with my foot, not even really realising I was doing it until Mum asked me to stop, the feel of the wool against my bare foot soothing. I huff out a sob, looking at the shelf with our old photos, the ornaments behind glass doors. I notice a new photo at the front of the shelf. Well, it's not that new. It's of me, at Ellie's wedding, a single portrait the photographer shot at the last minute. Sun is shining gold in my hair and I'm smiling against a backdrop of roses and gumtrees, so happy for my sister. But the frame it's in is new – it's silver and quite ornate, small sparkling jewels set at intervals around the edge. Very pretty. Next to it is a little silver vase with a single flower in it, a rose, pale pink like the ones in the photo. I sob again, hanging forward over the little pool, my tears dropping into the shimmering images.

Mum picks up something from the coffee table and hands it to Ellie, who has come to sit down in one of the armchairs. Pete is sitting on the carpet with David, both of them playing with little toy cars, pushing them around as David laughs, waving his chubby arms. Ah, it's beautiful.

Ellie goes to hand the piece of paper back to Mum and she drops it. It lands face up on the carpet and I see what it is. It's a photograph of Sarah, radiant in white silk and lace, smiling up at her new husband. Oh, she's married. Oh…

I can hardly bear this and turn away into Jason, putting

my face into his shoulder. He hugs me close. 'Katie, it's okay. They're okay. Keep watching. I'm here with you.'

He gently turns me to the pool once more and I see Dad going to retrieve the dropped photo for Mum, handing it to her, his smile gentle, his face lit up in the old way it always is when he looks at her. And I see that sparkling energy once more, the dense swirl of grey mist around them all, though the light in it is much brighter now as it twines through and around my family, holding them together. And the loose ends that had flapped and flickered, searching for me are still there. But they have changed, knotted together in a shape like a heart, the link to me with them forever, though I am gone.

And then I hear Ellie speak, but I can't really see her any more because my eyes are blurred so completely. 'It's a girl,' I hear her say, faint over the crashing waves. 'I thought, if it's okay, Mum, we might give her Kate as a middle name. What do you think?'

I can't take any more.

I plunge my hand into the water, swirling it around and the images break up, fading away. I feel like I might do the same, something big inside me pushing at all my edges, a mix of love and sorrow and pain that threatens to explode out of me. It's huge and I don't know what to do with myself at all, my face twisting as I curl over the water, wondering whether I'm going to scream or throw up or simply come apart, floating across the waves.

'Katie, Katie, are you okay?'

Jason is rubbing my back, his voice dark with worry. But I can't answer him. Am I okay? I am and I'm not. I'm okay because I know they're all right, that life is going on and it's awesome and terrible at the same time. I'm not okay because life is going on and I'm not part of it anymore. And it's this that seems to be tearing me asunder, choking me and taking my breath as I try to encompass it all.

'Ungh,' I manage, pushing Jason and sitting back on my heels, staring at him. He is waiting, love and pity gentle in his silver eyes, the sky turning grey, clouds moving across a sign of his turmoil at seeing me in pain. The waves are whipping up too, salt spray dashing across the rocks to where we sit, spattering into the pool. 'It's, I'm all right, I think I just need to-'

But what I think I need to do is lost as there is a tug under my breastbone so fierce I yelp in surprise, my hand going to my chest and rubbing it as though I can make it better. I manage to sit up, hunched over, my hand to my chest as I look at Jason, feeling my face twisting in agony. 'What's happening to me?'

'Don't worry,' he says, getting to his feet as I stare up at him. 'I know what this is. I think it's time for me to show you.'

'Show me what?' I manage through gritted teeth. But he says nothing, just holds out his hand and I take it, still holding my chest with my other hand as he pulls me to my feet and into his arms.

'Trust me,' I hear him say and I cling to him. Then I feel his kiss on my brow as we start to fall.

We come through the clouds together and I can see we're over the harbour once more, the familiar view still breathtaking, no matter how many times I see it. The water, the Bridge, the Opera House and glittering city move closer and closer as we fall, vapour streaming around us. As we near the ground we start to slow and we land as softly as thistledown, our feet gently back on earth once more. We come apart and I look around, wondering where we are. It's early morning, the sun just turning the sky apricot and gold, just enough light for me to recognise our surroundings. I'm still clutching my chest, feeling as though my insides are one big mass of tightly coiled wires, and then I realise where we are.
We are back at the scene of the accident.

This again! I groan in frustration and Jason puts his hands on my arms, forcing me to look at him.

'Hey, tell me what's different about all this.'

I look around. The seasons have changed and spring is flowering in the city, lilac jacaranda blossoms littering the pavement. But other than that, it's all the same. I can't believe I have to start all this shit again. But at least I'm not alone. And then it dawns on me. That's what's changed. That's what's different to all the other times I've been here. I smile at him and see relief in his eyes.

'I'm not alone,' I say, my hand moving from my chest and sliding around his waist. The tug has calmed down to a dull ache and I press against him, my eyes closing as I rest my head on his shoulder.

'That's right,' he says, his hand coming up to touch my hair, his voice a rumble in his chest under my cheek.

'You're not. And this is what was supposed to happen, when you went. This is how it works.' I open my eyes and realise our surroundings have changed. We're inside that bar in Thompson's Point once more, the one where I had my first proper date with Ben from my high school. And there I am again, sitting on a bar stool with my elbow on the bar, chin in my hand, looking at the dance floor and sipping my ridiculous cocktail as my date casts around for something to say. I frown at Jason.
'What are we doing here? I've already seen this.'
'Have you?'
He directs my attention back to the scene again. This time, it's as though a lens drops away, the Katie prism through which I viewed my world dissolving, and now I can see all the things I'd missed before. It's extraordinary.

My hair wasn't so bad, for starters – the soft curls around my face were kind of flattering, the little clip just the right amount of sparkle in the darkened room. And the nightclub wasn't so bad either, everyone in there laughing and having a good time - except for me. The boy on the stool next to me is looking at me, but I didn't notice. I didn't see the appreciation in his eyes, the warm glow he had for me. I didn't see that his silence came not from boredom, but from shyness and a desire to impress me, that he thought I was wonderful, that he had wanted to take me here because he thought it was special. That if I'd stepped outside of my own desire to be anywhere but where I was, I might have had fun as well. For I loved the little town where I grew up, the friendly faces, the simple beauty of the coastal lifestyle. I'd been so lucky to grow up somewhere like that, I just hadn't been able to appreciate it while it was happening. But I can see it now and as I do it's as though the tight coils inside me loosen a little. I turn to Jason, my eyes wide.

Then the air around us begins to whirl, just like the mad carousel of my first trip through time. I know what to expect, so I just hang on to Jason and wait for it to stop. When it does, we're in the small café on Milson's Point. There I am having coffee with my mother and sister and, once again, I can see things as they were, not how I thought they were. I can see the love in my mother's eyes and hear concern in her voice, not judgement, and I know that all she wanted was for me to be happy. That's what she'd been saying to me, that it was okay for me not to be married, that it didn't matter, but all I'd heard was an attack, that instead of me being perfect as I was, I was lacking in some way. And my sister. I can see the glow in her now, early pregnancy and I realise how sick she must have been feeling. But all she had been worried about was me, that I was okay. The love was there, all around us, all around me, the love of the women closest to me. But instead of embracing it, accepting it, I had pushed back. I feel my heart unfurl, the coils loosening a little more. Tears come to my eyes as I realise how much I miss them, how I regret not seeing more of them when I could.

The swirling takes us again, all lights and colours and I close my eyes. When I open them the café has been replaced by the chrome and glass and pulsing music of an inner city bar, and there I am with Sarah again. I'm not sure about this one. I mean, it was what it was. Sarah needed me to be present, and I couldn't be. But as I watch the scene again, the concern in her eyes as she talks to me, me trying so hard to be there for her, I see the bigger picture. That I was beyond fortunate to have had a friend like Sarah. That I was going to leave a hole in her life that couldn't be filled, and that she needed me as much as I needed her. It was almost as though she was my soul mate, but in a friendship sense and, as I think this, I catch Jason out of the corner of my eye, nodding as though he agrees with me. And I see that it doesn't matter that I wasn't able to concentrate on what she was telling me, that she understood. I see how lucky I was that, when she had something huge to share, she chose me as the first person to share it with, just as I always did for her. That our backpacking and crazy schoolies trips and shopping and dancing and talking for hours, all of it added up to something more precious than almost anything on earth. Tears roll down my face as I watch us both, seeing the bonds between us, golden and sparkling, as we laugh and lean in close, sipping our drinks, and I realise how lucky we both were to have each other. And then I think of how much I love her and as I do so the coils inside me loosen even more, so I can hardly feel them.

The world swirls again and we end up on hot sand under a bright sun. Jason lets go of me, looking around. Then he whistles.

'Nice bikini.' He grins at me appreciatively and I blush a little. I look across to where I know my teenage self is sitting and see with my new clarity of vision that he's right, that I was beautiful, my skin smooth and firm, the swimsuit accentuating my shape just so. But I can see much more than that now. How fortunate I was to have been young and free in such a beautiful place, to have had such good friends. I see the joy in our faces to be sitting on that famous beach, the giggles as teenage me forgets her self consciousness, laughing with her friends, eyes shining, spirits free in the way that only teenagers can be, before work and bills and life experiences came to shut us down, to make us forget who we were, all our dreams and ideals. I see that day on the beach for what it was, a perfect moment in time, blessed. I think of the young man in Chandrani's heaven and how he had told me my life was blessed and, I think I'm starting to get what he meant. As I think this, the coils inside me loosen a little more and I laugh out loud for sheer joy. I turn to Jason and wink at him. 'Hey, maybe I'll put it on again for you later.'

He laughs as well, throwing his head back, then the world spins and shakes once more and we grab onto each other, still giggling as we spin through time.

But when the spinning stops I realise I'm back at work. Huh. Well, that's kind of a let down after the shining beauty of Bondi. I look around at the shiny glass and wood and chrome, then at Jason, confused. This isn't one of the memories I'd visited on that carousel. I'd actually been in the office, the day after I'd died, thinking it was all a mad dream until I turned up at work just by thinking about it. So this is different. He motions with his head and I turn to see we are near to my desk. The flower is still lying on my keyboard and everything else is the same too. That's weird. I would have thought they'd have found a replacement by now. But then I hear the Velvet Boom coming faintly from Darryl's office.

'Isn't this what you do?'

And I realise I'm back here again and it's the day after my death. I'm still confused, but everything I've just been through gives me an inkling there might be something more to see here. I remember how subdued the office had seemed, but I'd put it down to the big meeting that everyone seemed to be going to. I look at Jason again and he jerks his head towards the meeting room.

'Shall we go and take a look?'

'Um, I guess so.' Not sure why, though. I can feel the coils tighten a little as I think this and I don't like how it feels. But before I can tell Jason about it we are in the boardroom.

And I am amazed.

It's a nice room, oval shaped with pale walls, a big wooden table in the middle, a matching low buffet with glasses and paperwork along one wall. The furniture is shiny and modern and really, it's not a bad space to hold a meeting. One end of the room has a glass panel looking over the city, glimpses of blue water visible between the buildings. But it's not the view or the décor that has me so gobsmacked. It's the people and what they're doing. All around the room, on the walls and spread along the table, are photographs. Photographs of me. At work functions, in the office, laughing and serious. There's one of me in my costume at last year's Christmas party, a laughing elf in a too-short skirt. Another of me running a meeting – there are several of those, part of a promotional shoot we did for a company brochure. There's the headshot they put in the annual report, and another of me standing by the copier pretending to scream at the amount of work I'm waiting for. And there are more arriving, people from all over the office coming to drop off images or sign a big sheet of paper on the table. Sally, our PA, is putting the photos together into a sort of collage, wiping her eyes as she does it, a box of tissues on the table next to her.

Then Jeremy arrives. He's walking slowly, his face tight, blue eyes dark. He comes over to the table and stands there, silent, looking at all the photos. Sally sort of glances at him, and puts her hand on his arm. He turns and looks at her, seeming a bit surprised. Then he reaches inside his suit jacket and pulls out a photograph, laying it on the table with the others.

I take in a breath. It's a photo of us. When we were younger, working together. A shot someone must have snapped at lunch, sitting outside at a city café, leaning into each other and smiling. It's a really nice photo. And I've never seen it before.

I turn to Jason and he sort of shrugs. He seems nonchalant but I frown at him. And I get it. I look at Jeremy, at the photo he had of us for all this time and I realise. He's the guy who could-have-been. That maybe, if things had been different, if the timing had been better, if we hadn't gone on that disastrous date, there might have been something for us. He's not my soulmate, but he could have been good for me.

Oh. Regret flashes through me, fleeting, as he turns to leave, one hand coming up to his face as he exits the boardroom. I watch him go, coils around my heart. Even though Jason is standing with me and I know he is all I've ever wanted, there's a deep sorrow for Jeremy and what might have been. I realise he had his own coils holding him back from what was important, and I hope he finds his way out of them. Jason comes closer, putting his arm around my shoulders, and I lean on him, taking comfort in his warmth. The door opens again and Janice hurries in holding a tissue to her face, dropping yet another photo on the table before turning around to leave.

And my vision blurs as it all rolls over me. Because it wasn't a meeting. It was for me. This was all for me. People weren't subdued because they'd had a big night or a tight deadline – it was because they were in mourning. *For me.* I turn and bury my face in Jason's chest, overcome with it all, with the love I can see around all the people here, the way they cared for me. It shimmers golden through the air, so beautiful, and I cannot take it in.

Then, just like that, we're in Darryl's office. He's still yelling into the phone, but this time I can see his face, his eyes watery, one hand rubbing over those silver fox features as he talks to HR. And this time I get to hear what he was saying about me.

'Of course. I mean, it couldn't have happened at a worse time. It's just the most awful thing. We're all devastated.'

There's a pause while he listens, rubbing his face again.

'And her poor family. I know, I know. They're doing

something now, and we'll be sending flowers of course. D'you know when the funeral-' He nods again. 'Right, right. No, we'll all be going.'

He listens again. 'The client can fucking wait! This is far more important, that we're there for her. Christ, I miss her. Don't know how we'll replace her, really.'

My eyes fill with tears as I listen to him, old Velvet Voice Darryl. To think that he'd felt that way, that he missed me. I mean, I've no doubt he'll have replaced me by now and that my successor is doing fine, but still, it's nice to know. Then I notice the flowers lying on one of the shelves next to him. A bunch of pink orchid type blooms, pointed petals spotted with brown, bright yellow stamens leaving dust on the dark wood. I realise who it was that had left the flower on my desk, and the coils loosen even more, like a sigh of tension long held and my eyes close, my body starting to feel as though it's dissolving.

'Hey, not yet.' Jason touches my chin and my eyes open to stare into his. He kisses me and it jolts me back into myself, though I feel pleasantly drowsy. I squint my eyes at him. 'One more place to go.'

Of course. The beach with my dad and the mermaid pool. How lovely. But I've already seen that as it was, a time of pure love and security in my life. Still, it will be nice to see it again, one last time. And the world starts to spin, but more slowly this time, as though the air around us is thick like honey, one of my hands coming free to trail through the kaleidoscope, wakening sparks of light and colour.

We land on the beach and I see little me with Dad, little Ellie with Mum and I just sob and sob at how beautiful it all is. I know crying sounds like a strange reaction but it feels like a release as I wipe my eyes and laugh through my tears, watching my big strong Dad holding my hand, holding me steady as he always did, making sure I don't slip. And Mum, her face glowing with love as she watches us all, little Ellie stopping to wave her shovel at us as we pick our way further out to the magical mermaid pool. And I see myself crouch down, Dad crouching next to me, and I see myself giggle and know he's done the anemone trick and oh, my heart feels as though it could burst with the beauty of it all.

'Can you see it now?' Jason's voice is soft, his breath warm on my ear as he stands behind me with his arms around me and I lean against his chest.

'Yes, I see it.' I twist in his arms to look at him. 'But my life would have been so different if only you'd been there! To show me, to help me see it!' Frustration colours my voice and I can feel the coils inside me winding tight again but all he does is shake his head, those silver grey eyes so beautiful.

'No, Katie.' He speaks so gently. 'Maybe I would have been able to show you a little, but you had to find it inside yourself. You're the only person who can help you, in the end.' I take in a deep breath, staring at him, before I turn again to little me playing in the rock pools, my Dad, his hair dark instead of silver, watching over me. And I see it. I see it so clearly.

I *was* blessed.

I was loved beyond reckoning. I lived, and I was fortunate to do so. And I see that love comes in so many different shapes and sizes, but it's all around us when we look for it. It doesn't have to be romantic to have meaning, and I'd had more love than I ever knew in my short life. The realisation washes over me like a wave and I feel the coils loosen one last time. Then they're gone, and there is only bliss.

And I finally let go.

Of everything. Of the life I had, the stuff that weighed me down. And all that's left is love. Love for my family, my friends, for the life I'd had the chance to live and for the man holding my hand, his fingers tight with mine. I see the whole universe spread out around me like a network of twinkling lights, blinking on and off as souls enter and left the world. I can feel the trees and the earth and the animals, the wild free flight of a bird across the mountains, the hot gush of blood in the mouth of a predator as it takes its prey, the love of a mother for her newborn child, the death of a tree as it falls in a great forest and I realise that I am connected to it all, that I am part of it and always have been. Through it all Jason holds my hand, his being a glow of warmth beside me as I spin through the dimensions, the world around and within me all at once and I remember my favourite book as a child, Horton showing us that the whole world can fit into a single drop of water and that's how I feel, as though I am the water and it's all inside me, though I am just a drop in a mighty river of souls. And I feel my family, my connection to them, see the lines connecting us, past and present and future possibilities, knowing I'll see them again one day, the love that binds us unbreakable. And then there is Jason. I can see the threads of all the lives we have lived, our love for each other woven through the ages and the glow of it is almost blinding. It all merges together into one great big shining light and I'm in it and it's surrounding me and....

I fall back onto earth.

But it's a green and growing earth, the sweet smell of grass and flowers all around me. I open my eyes to look up into blossom, petals drifting down from the tree above me, delicate pink and white glowing against the warm sunlight filtering through the branches. It is perfect. The temperature, the flowers, the smells, the faint sound of water, birds singing in the trees. And the fact that I'm not alone. I turn my head to see Jason next to me, smiling, his grey eyes full of more love than I could ever have imagined.

'You did it,' he says. 'You're here.'

'I am?' My voice is soft and it trails off as I turn my head to look up again, at the petals spiralling down, feeling complete. For this is my Heaven.

I sit up, looking around in wonder. There is no tug under my breastbone now, just a swelling joy that is sweeter than anything I've ever felt. I scramble to my feet in the falling petals, my hands out as they whisper feather soft between my fingers and I laugh out loud. Because everything is perfect – the glowing woodland, the ground underfoot soft and green with grass, flowers blooming everywhere. Jason is sitting against the tree, watching me with smiling eyes, and I know he feels it too, the joy inside me.

Then a figure arrives with a sizzling sort of zap, making me think me of a star falling as it comes down to earth. The figure is silver and shimmers as it lands, shining draperies shifting around it. A faint glow of light surrounds the figure, long hair flowing down its back and it has the face of a carved stone deity, beautiful and terrible to look upon. I freeze, completely petrified as it comes toward me and my Heaven shakes and shivers, leaves falling from the green trees. Jason comes to stand behind me, his hands on my arms.

'It's all right,' he murmurs as the figure stops, what looks like confusion on its perfect silvery face. This makes it seem more human and I relax, slightly, as Jason gently rubs my arms. 'It's a Guardian,' he goes on, but that doesn't really help my fear at all.

'Yes,' says the figure, still frowning a little. 'I am your Guardian, Katie, and I'd like to welcome you to Heaven.'

The stone features stretch into a smile and I smile back uncertainly, casting around for an appropriate greeting. Then something it (they? him? her?) said to me registers.

'Wait, you're my Guardian?' The words slip from my mouth and I clap my hand over it, not wanting to offend. The figure's smile slips a little and, this is very strange, it looks slightly embarrassed.

'Yes.' I am definitely not imagining the slight note of apology I can hear. 'Er, I should have known when you-'

Oh. This is about the whole dying alone thing. I wait

for the flare of anger to come but there's nothing except a faint twinge of regret, as though I'm thinking about something that was briefly painful a long time ago. Guess my time with Jason helped in lots of ways. I pause to consider that for a moment. Then I realise the Guardian is waiting for me to say something. And it looks upset. I consider how I feel for a moment longer, but all I get is compassion for the beautiful being waiting for me to speak. I don't want them to feel bad.

So instead of getting angry I just smile. My Heaven is back to normal, the birds singing again, blossom smelling candy sweet and it's fine, everything is just fine. I hold out my hand. 'It's fine,' I say. 'Really it is. I got here.'

The being reaches out and takes my hand gently in theirs, but instead of the cold hiss of metal all I feel is warmth, comforting like the sun on my back. It smiles again, the beautiful silver stone face mobile, eyes gleaming in the sunshine. 'Then, it is a pleasure to see you here.' The being's voice is strangely accented and has a melodic sound, like bells chiming and I find myself relaxing more in its presence. Jason is still behind me, close enough to feel his strong presence and I'm glad of it, as I'm still not one hundred per cent confident about the whole thing.

'So, um, what now?' I venture, not knowing what I need to do but wanting to fill the gap in the conversation.

'Well.' The being looks at the palm of its hand as though it's a book and they're consulting it. Then it turns its silver gaze on me once more. 'It seems as though all the requirements have been met, all the challenges passed.' It sounds a bit officious and I bite back a nervous giggle. But honestly, if it had produced a clipboard from inside its robes and started ticking things off I wouldn't have been surprised. It goes back to perusing its hand.

'Yes, that's all for now,' it goes on, sounding satisfied.

'Wait, for now?' Again. Words just slipping from me, like it's all cool, like I know what's going on. But it seems a reasonable question. The being looks at me, eyebrows slightly raised as it tilts its head.

'Well, yes. There are things still to come, Katie. But for now you are free to rest and enjoy.' Another of those slightly unnerving smiles. 'My name is Dezariel. If you need me, call for me.'

Before I can ask anything else the being looks up, hair rippling long behind it, silver feet lifting so it's balancing on its toes. Then with another zap it's gone, streaking like a comet into the sky. I just stand there and watch, my mouth hanging open, feeling myself start to shake. I turn to Jason.

'What the he-. I mean, what was *that*?'

He is laughing, but in that nice way he does and he pulls me into a hug. I hold onto him, still shaking. I start to laugh too, but in relief, that I've made it, that we're here. Gradually I calm down, and I consider where I am. I lift up my head and look into Jason's eyes.

'Give me a minute,' I say. He raises an eyebrow but says nothing, letting me go. And once again I love him for it.

I walk away from him, into the woods, to a space I know will be waiting for me. I don't linger to look at the flowers, or trail my hand along the mossy trunks of the tall trees – there will be plenty of time for that. Instead I concentrate on one thing only, shaping it in my mind, focusing and sending the idea ahead of me so that it will be ready when I get there.

And it is.

What Comes After All

I built us a house.

As I stand here looking at my creation, warm pride welling in me, I hear someone coming through the trees behind me. I turn and see Jason, pushing the leafy branches aside. I run to him, taking his hand, my smile wide as I pull him towards the cabin, his mouth stretching in an answering grin.

'It's for us,' I say, somewhat unnecessarily.

'I know,' he says, putting his arms around me. 'And it's perfect.'

It is pretty good, if I say so myself. I think I'd had it in my mind for a while, to be honest. Certainly it's quite similar to Jason's beach house, which makes sense when you consider how happy I was there. Made of wood and stone and glass, my house is built to blend in with its surroundings, a part of the whispering woods. Instead of a deck there's a front verandah with two chairs, where we can sit and watch the woods as they change and shimmer. I grab Jason's hand and pull him along, both of us laughing, our feet banging on the wood porch before we go inside.

It's a single room, really – large enough for a big luxurious bed, a fireplace burning bright in the stone chimney breast. There are a couple of differences from Jason's place, though. I've added a very small kitchen in one corner, just a couple of cupboards, a counter top, a sink and a kettle. I couldn't resist. It just feels weird to ask for everything, and I enjoy the ritual of it, the ceremony of making tea or coffee. I go over to the cupboard and open it to find four cups – well, you never know, someone might come to visit. I take two and put them on the counter, fill the kettle and set it to boil, and it all feels so real and normal and wonderful.

I hear Jason laughing his head off and I smile, knowing what he's found. You see, I couldn't resist adding one other thing. A closet. Tucked away behind the wall against which the bed sits. Ooh, it's lovely. Ha ha. I mean, I haven't been to see it yet but I know what it looks like in my mind. Lots of hanging space and shelves and drawers, all in smoky grey wood. The kind of closet I'd dreamed of having once, a long time ago in a different place. After all, this is Heaven, right?

Jason emerges from behind the wall and comes over to me, his arms sliding around my waist, his lips on my neck.

'Tea can wait, don't you think?'

Hmm. Maybe he's right.

We wake, later, wrapped in each other, warm under the soft quilts. My clothes are on the floor, as are his and I realise I really don't want to put them on again. But I don't want to be naked all the time, either. It was okay at Jason's beach Heaven, where we were in the water and there was no one around. But here feels different. I never lounged around in my undies at home in my old life, and there's still a part of me that doesn't want to be like that here, either. What I really want to wear, when I think about it, is something soft and comfortable, like those really expensive lovely lounge pyjamas, all in soft colours with matching cashmere wraps. So I have a little think and I know that when I go into my closet there they'll be.

But for now I'm comfortable as I am, Jason warm against me. He lifts his head, one silver grey eye closed as he squints at me.

'So, now what?'

As the days pass I become more accustomed to the way things are. It helps that where I am is just perfect, my ideal place. My woodland isn't large, but it's big enough for me. There's a stream, clear water tumbling over grey stones, where Jason and I sit on warm days, watching the dragonflies dance over the water, silver fish slipping through our fingers.

I haven't forgotten about my life, of course I haven't. But the pain of leaving it so suddenly is now a distant memory, my travels through the afterlife something to wonder at, rather than a source of frustration. Because I understand my place in it. That I'm on a wheel, that I have to let it take me where I'm meant to go, not fight it or force it to be what I think it must be. And I'm in Heaven, literally and figuratively. I have Jason, and he has me, and we're beyond happy together.

And I still get to see my family. I have my own magic pool, a deep bowl carved into the riverbed, a large flat stone next to it perfect for sitting on as I watch their lives drift on the surface of the water. I go back there, sometimes, as well – Jason has shown me how to fall to earth, and, now that I know where it is, my Heaven is easy to find.

I was there with Ellie when she gave birth, urging her on as she screamed and pushed, weeping with her as Charlotte Kate emerged into the world, her little face red and screwed up like a rosebud. I've been to see Mum and Dad as well, pleased to see them back in the same bedroom once more, Dad's familiar grey hair among all the frills, holding on to Mum in the night. They're getting older, but they're still busy, their lives and friends and family sustaining them, even though I know my loss will always be with them.

I've come to terms with that as well. I can't change it, so I have to accept it for what it was, a chance mis-step. The regret is always there but I've learned to manage it with Jason's help. It took me a little while to get there but the time I spent at Jason's beach helped, healing my battered soul.

I've seen my Pop, too. I didn't go back to his funeral, didn't need to. Instead he came to find me, showing up just after Jason had helped me to find Heaven, walking with that gangly long legged stride he had, still in his pale shirt and dusty jeans, baggy around his legs, his thinning white hair combed back like it always was, his face lined and lit up with joy to see me again. I ran straight into his arms and he picked me up and swung me around just as though I was a little girl again, and I wept as I smelt his tobacco-y sunshiny smell, realising he had always been there, that he had never left me.

'So, shall we go to the beach later? I think I might need to go surfing again.'

Jason and I are sitting under our favourite tree, just talking, as we like to do. He has his back against the trunk and I'm leaning against him, his arms around me, my hand twined with his, playing with his fingers.

'Sounds nice,' I say, half drowsing in the warmth. 'I might pick up some more shells to bring back–'

Then there is a sizzling zap sound and my eyes snap open. A figure is falling to earth, like a silver gold statue. But it isn't Dezariel. Alarmed, I twist around to Jason. Who is staring at the figure, a look of apprehension on his face.

'What? Wh-what is it?' My voice is shaking, I'm not even sure why. But he has tensed, his muscles hard, his arms squeezing me. He mutters something under his breath. It sounds like 'Oh no.'

I really start to panic now. The figure is coming closer, perfect chiselled face regarding us both with a vaguely sympathetic expression.

'Jason.'

It's just one word, but it cuts through me like ice.

'Oh no, oh–' He lets go of me and I get to my feet so he can as well, standing with his arm around me. My stomach is falling, dread all through me. The Guardian surveys me for a moment and makes a noise like a soft sigh, before returning focus to Jason.

'You have been reassigned.'

What? Oh no! I grab at him and he pulls me to him, those beautiful eyes of his looking into mine, one hand coming up to my hair. Then he kisses me.

'We knew this would happen.' He sounds calm, but I can hear a slight roughness to his voice and I hug him, burying my head in his warm chest, breathing him in while I feel as though I'm being ripped apart.

'C'mon, Katie. C'mon.' His voice breaks and I lift my head, tears running down my face. 'You have to let me go,' he goes on, as though it's so easy to do, even though there are tears in his eyes as well.

I nod, but I am panicking and as I do it sets my world, my little piece of Heaven, shaking, clouds moving across the sun, a wind whipping up the leaves, sending confetti showers of petals from the ever-blooming trees.

'Hey, hey, it's going to be okay,' he says, holding me tight. But it isn't going to be okay. How can it be? I cling onto him, thinking in some disordered part of my mind that if I don't let go of him he can't be taken from me and everything will be–

A warm hand is laid on my arm and I turn to see the Guardian standing close to me. The beautiful face shimmers in the light, leaves and petals still raining down from above.

'I am sorry,' it says. There is compassion and infinite love in its eyes, which, up close, are like glass, stars falling through them.

'Please don't take him,' I whisper. 'I don't want to be without him again.'

'Katie, remember what I told you,' says Jason. I look at him, uncomprehending. I remember every word he's ever said to me but at the moment I can't pick just what he means. I frown. 'That it's not just about us. It's time for me to go.'

I'm so hurt I can barely breathe. 'So,' I whisper, 'you're just going to go, just like that? Because you've been told to?' My voice squeaks on the last word.

The Guardian has let go of my arm and steps back, waiting.

Jason shakes his head, and now I see tears in his eyes. 'I don't want to leave you,' he says. 'Of course I don't. But we will meet again. We always do.'

'But when?' I wail.

Jason opens his mouth but it is the Guardian who answers, surprising us both. 'You will not be apart for long, my child. There is one more thing for you to do here, then you will be sent to him. Both of you will have a good life, full of joy.'

'Together?' I say, looking at the creature. It nods, a faint smile curving the silvery gold lips.

'Together,' it says. 'As it should be. But if I do not take him now, he will not be born.'

'So we'll find each other.' I turn to Jason, looking into his eyes, trying to imprint the moment in my memory so that I'll recognise him when I see him again.

'We will. I promise.'

We stare at each other a moment longer, then he bends his head to kiss me, his lips so warm, soft on mine.

'I love you,' I say, against his mouth.

'I love you too,' he says. He lifts his head. 'Always.'

He lets go of me and I swear I can feel tearing, as though the ties that attach him to me are being broken, as though they are physical things anchored into the heart of me. I sob, because I can't help it. I don't want to be sad for him, not when he's the one that has to go. So I straighten up and wipe my face, trying to smile as best I can against the tearing of my soul. And I nod.

'See you soon.'

He nods as well, and his face twists for a moment. Then the Guardian takes him by the hand.

'It's time to let go, Jason,' it says. He is still looking at me, smiling, and it's the last thing I see as he starts to fall, the Guardian letting go.

Then he's gone.

I want to break, to sink to the ground, but I don't want to do it while the Guardian is watching me. It comes closer.

'You are not alone here, Katie,' it says. 'And you will be joining him, soon. Do not lose heart,' it says, so gentle, one silver gold hand coming to rest briefly on my arm. 'Enjoy your time here, for it will pass before you know it.'

It looks up, hair rippling like gilt around its perfect

form. And with a zap, it leaves, ascending like a bright comet against the blue grey sky, fading to a last spark before it's gone.

Just like Jason.

I stand there for a moment, leaves falling all around me. Then I turn and go back into my cabin. I get into the bed, so large and empty without him, and I hug the pillow to myself as I curl up into as tight a ball as I can manage.

And I sleep.

Waiting...

'Mornin', Katie.'

The call from outside wakes me, and I blink against the soft morning light, uncurling from the pillow and stretching myself out. I brace myself, waiting for the pain to hit me, the realisation that he's gone. But instead of raw hurt, there is calm acceptance, as though my sleep has smoothed out all the broken edges. I miss him, so much, but from somewhere deep inside comes the knowledge that I'll see him again.

There's a knocking on the window glass and I see my Pop looking in at me, smiling, his white hair fluffed up around his head. I smile back.

'Tea?' I call, and he nods as he takes a seat in one of the chairs, the wood creaking faintly. I get up, pushing the covers back, and I sit and take a deep breath in and out. Then I go and put the kettle on.

Jason was right, you know.

About the whole emotions thing. I mean I miss him, so very much, but it's not the kind of missing that hurts and burns and colours everything I do. Those emotions don't seem to work here, in my happy Heaven. No, instead it's missing laced with acceptance and gratitude, acceptance for how things are, gratitude for the way things were.

So I sit on the verandah hugging my mug of tea close, looking out at the whispering green forest. Pop glances over, his eyes serious.

'He gone, Katie?'

I nod, my mouth twisting a little. 'Yes.' I clear my throat. 'Um, yesterday. He was reassigned.'

'Ah,' says Pop, taking another sip of his tea. He stares out at the trees too, rocking slightly in his chair. 'You'll see him again.'

He smiles at me, but there's a sadness in his eyes and I realise how long it's been for him without my grandmother. 'You'll see Gran soon as well.'

'I know,' he says, finishing his tea. 'I always do, y'see. Just like you and Jason, there was never anyone else for me but her.'

Tears come to my eyes, but they aren't bitter. They are sweet, instead, the sweetness of love acknowledged. 'She's your soulmate.'

'She is,' he says, blowing a breath out. 'And I have Heaven all ready for her, when she's ready to join me.'

'You do?' I realise I haven't really thought about Pop's Heaven, spending all my time here or with Jason at the beach.

'Yep.' He grins. 'I'll take you there later, if you like. I think you'll enjoy it.'

'Later?'

'Yep.' He raises his eyebrows. 'Once we've had another cuppa.' He holds out his mug and I take it from him, standing up. There is warmth inside me, healing the torn edges from Jason leaving and I realise that this was what the Guardian was trying to tell me, when it said I wasn't alone.

'You're on,' I say, turning to go back inside. I'm looking forward to another cuppa, I realise. Plus maybe something to eat.

A little later we leave, stepping off the verandah and heading into the woods. I'm holding Pop's hand and it's just like when I was a child, letting him lead the way. We take a path through the branches and they open out to a wide lawn, a weatherboard house sitting shaded by gumtrees. I gasp, my hand coming to my mouth as I take in the yellow painted boards, the green trim around the windows.

It's Pop's old house.

My heart swells at the thought that this is his Heaven. I remember my grandmother, never wanting to leave the house they'd shared, and it's bittersweet that he seems to feel just the same way. A kookaburra calls, chattering laughter coming from the tall gums, eucalyptus scenting the air. The lacy ironwork on the verandah looks freshly painted, geraniums in pots bright against the faded paint colours. I remember rubbing the velvet soft leaves between my fingers, the pepper/sweet smell of the juice on my hands.

'Still looks good, doesn't it?' Pop has his hands on his hips, beaming and I slide my arm through his.

'It's just how I remember, when I was small. You know, Gran still lives there-' I stop, thinking that might not be the best thing to say. But he just squeezes my arm with his.

'Oh, I know, Katie. Where d'you think I go every night? C'mon, let's go in. I've got lemonade, freshly made.'

He winks at me and I laugh out loud, letting him pull me along the front path to the door. He opens the screen, wood frame painted the same faded green as the windows, then pushes the door open and we step inside.

And it's just as I remember it when I was small, though everything looks even newer. I let go of Pop and wander through the familiar rooms, breathing in the smells of pot pourri and beeswax polish, the clean lined fifties furniture shining as though it's just been delivered. My favourite painting is hanging on the dining room wall, above the long low buffet with the pull out bar, and when I see it I pause. It's of a forest, long lined trees against a blue sky, graphic shapes and colours and, as I see it again I realise how close it is to my own Heaven. That's pretty cool, hey?

I run over to the bar as well, looking back at Pop who grins and shakes his head as I pull open the drop down door, sliding the leaf patterned Perspex tray out from its hiding place. I used to love to do that when I was a kid, mixing 'drinks' for Pop while Grandma Jean held her breath and tried not to wince as her glass cocktail stirrers clinked against the glasses. Oh, it's all just the same! Then I leave my game and go with Pop into the kitchen and again, it's as I remember, yellow painted wooden cupboards, white counter top and an old fashioned radio, playing songs. Plants and a flower vase are on the windowsill above the sink, though the curtains are different, a Pop Art pattern of yellow and white stripes on a beige background. I sit down at the round table and chairs, my hands smoothing the yellow checked gingham and I remember sitting here with Grandma Jean as she told me how she couldn't bear to leave. I guess Pop felt the same way. I smile delightedly at him as he opens the fridge and pulls out a jug of frosted lemonade. He reaches for two tall glasses from the cupboard and fills them, ice cubes clinking and my mouth waters, just like it did when I was a kid and he made me the same drink. He brings the glasses over to the table and sits down opposite me, his smile wide as he passes one of the glasses to me.

'So what d'you think of my Heaven?' He smiles at me and takes a long drink. I do the same, closing my eyes as the sour sweet familiar taste fills my mouth and runs down my throat, cool and refreshing.

'I think it's perfect,' I say, once I've finished my mouthful, putting the glass down. 'It's just like how I remember.'

'Well, it's almost right,' he says, looking thoughtful and I look at him and wonder. He can ask for anything, right? So what's missing? I get an inkling of what that might be but, as I do so, Pop gets to his feet

'We need some music, I think,' he says, his voice sounding a little rougher than usual. He goes and flicks the switch on the old silver radio and the kitchen is filled with music, a cheesy eighties pop beat that I remember I loved. He comes and sits down again, holding out his hand across the table and I take it, smiling at the memory of how it feels.

'It's perfect,' I say again and he nods.

'Well, it's familiar, I guess.' He gets that wistful look again, and fixes me with his faded blue eyes. 'It's here where I had my happiest times, Katie, when we were first married, when your mother came along and then you, dancing fairy girl.' He lets go of my hand and stands up before coming around the table. 'One more dance, for old time's sake?'

I stand up, laughing again, not feeling silly or self-conscious, not feeling anything except love as we dance on the shiny linoleum, letting him swing me around as the torn edges inside me soften, Jason a pure bright memory of love. I know I'll see him again one day, can feel it just under my breastbone and I hold onto it like a hand curving around a flame, keeping it bright so he knows me when we meet again.

The days pass by, calm, the nights turning like a wheel towards sunrise. It's how I've made my Heaven, so it feels normal to me. I guess if I wanted to I could have sunshine constantly, or rain, if I wished for it. But something in me needs sleep, or the appearance of it, waking each day in my quilts and pillows to get up alone.

I make myself tea, often something to eat, then wander through my closet to my little shower room where I stand in the steamy water for as long as I feel like it, emerging to dry myself on a fluffy towel, put on another comfy set of pyjamas and while the day away.

Pop joins me, most days, sitting with a cup of smoky coffee, puffing on his pipe while I sip my tea, both of us content to just be. We talk of life, of family and love, the words weaving rich tapestries that seem to dance through my Heaven, winding like a cocoon around me, keeping me calm.

Jason isn't here, but I am. And I can deal with it, for now.

But one morning I wake with the sound of waves in my ears, and realise I haven't been back to Jason's Heaven since, well, since he left. After all, why would I? I'm in my own Heaven now. Even when Jason was here I didn't go anywhere, other than the beach. For that's the whole nature of Heaven, you see. Once you're there, you don't really want to be anywhere else.

But today is different. The hiss of water stays with me, like the sound you hear when you hold a shell to your ear, and I feel as though I need to go and visit, one last time. So I walk to the very edge of my woods, pushing through the trees that grow thicker here, their branches interlacing like a fence around my world.

Strange.

When Jason was here we had a way through, a gap opening out onto the sandy dunes, the forest becoming seagrass, bushy clumps waving in the wind from the ocean. But, try as I might, I can't find it at first, coming up against first one tree then another, glimpsing other worlds through the branches, but not the one I seek.

Right.

I stop and step back, closing my eyes and seeing if I can reach out with my mind. For this is how I get back to my Heaven, when I visit my family. I hold the image in my mind and it pulls me back, as though we're connected by a long glittering thread. A bit like how, when I was first dead and didn't know what was happening, I just had to think about a place and I was there.

So I think about Jason's Heaven now. I picture the shack and the whales and the shimmering sky. The two chairs and the soft bed, piled high with cushions the colours of driftwood and the ocean. I shape it and taste it in my mind, visualising the way the stars curved above us like a dome, lighting our nights.

And I can feel it. The thread is faint, the glitter gone, but I think I have it. I take a step forward, then another, not opening my eyes, following the thread. I feel the softness of leaves against my face, the resistance of a springy branch as I take another step, then another. The ground underfoot changes, my feet slipping as earth changes to something more fluid. I open my eyes.

And I am there.

But it's not the same. I secure the idea of my own Heaven in my mind, but I don't look back. Instead, I keep going forward. The dunes are still there, the sea lying blue beyond. But there are no rolling breakers, no crashing waves sculpting stone and flinging shells. The water is calm, lapping quietly at the shore, the colour midway between blue and grey. As is the sky. The sun isn't out, but it's not raining either – clouds hang there, not really moving. I venture further into the dunes, looking out to see if whales are passing by, listening for their hoots and bellows.

But there's nothing.

It's strangely quiet, nothing except the faint hiss of wind across the sand, the quiet lapping of water on the shore. No sea birds calling, nothing. And then I see it.

The cabin. I stop for a moment, my head tilting to one side. It looks... faded. I mean, it always had soft colours, driftwood walls bleached grey by the ocean. But when you got up close you could see the colours still in the wood, tan and grey and blue and brown, all twirled together. But now it just looks a uniform grey, blending in with the sand and the sky and the sea.

As I move closer I can see that some of the decking timbers have come loose, and our two chairs hold only piles of sand, dried grasses caught in tumbleweeds around the legs. I catch my breath, remembering sitting there with Jason on our first night together, enjoying the warmth of tea, of his presence, of knowing I wasn't alone any more.

Like I say, strong emotion doesn't play so much in Heaven. But this is still difficult to see.

As I get closer there is a creaking sound, and I see the door on the side has come loose, hanging by a hinge and swaying, the wood rubbing against the doorframe, a dark space beyond. I don't want to look inside. I know what I'll find there. More sand, more dead grass, the bed where we spent so many hours now tumbled and grey, the fireplace cold. I'd rather remember it how it was, a haven from the world and everything in it, a place to love and heal and be loved.

Things are a bit blurry now, and I stop, rubbing my eyes. Perhaps I shouldn't have come at all. I don't know why I did, really. Something hard is under my foot and I look down to see a stone, half covered by the shifting sands. I bend to pick it up. It's rough, pale like the sand. And it's in the shape of a heart. As I hold it in my fingers it starts to crumble, the faint breeze taking it away. And I realise that this place is nothing without Jason to bring it to life.

It's time to go.

I turn and start back across the dunes, holding the thread of my own Heaven in my mind, spooling it within me as I move towards it. And I can see it now, a wall of green, startlingly bright against this world of blue and grey.

When I reach the trees I stop and turn for one last look. The cabin is no longer visible, as though it's already been swallowed by the dunes, and the sea remains eerily calm. I close my eyes and remember it how it was. Then I step through the trees.

Later, I curl up in bed, hugging my pillow the way I did the night after Jason left. And I no longer hear the sound of waves.

Time To Go

It's another perfect morning. Birds are singing and I can hear the faint ripple of water nearby, pale light coming in through the long windows, striping my bedcovers, warm across my bare skin. I stay in bed a while longer, enjoying the feel of soft linen, the perfect warmth when you don't want to get up, nor do you have to. You might think it would get boring, just sleeping and waking and whiling the days away, but then it's my Heaven, not yours. Every day feels as though I'm waking at the start of a holiday, endless potential hanging in the air. There is no stress or guilt or need, none of the things which made me so restless when I was alive. Here is calm, orderly, a sweetness of familiarity blended with the thought that I can go anywhere, do anything, whenever I want.

    I get up eventually and go into the closet, running my hand along the soft clothing hanging there, colours like ice cream and beach stones and mist rippling under my fingers as I decide which one I feel like wearing. My 'death outfit', as I like to call it, has its own little section – skirt, cardigan and camisole all hung together, my shoes neatly placed underneath (I think I may have left my underwear at the beach). I can't bring myself to wear it again, not yet. It's not that it scares me or makes me upset, it's more that it doesn't feel like it's the right time, as though it's had its moment.

Once dressed I wander out into the woods, still holding my mug of tea. It's a beautiful day, but that's Heaven for you. I tried changing the leaves the other day, brilliant hues of red and yellow and orange, like a postcard of autumn. But it didn't feel right and so I changed it back, returning to eternal spring.

When I reach the river I sit by my pool, my hand trailing on the water making silver ripples. I set my mug down and lean forward a little, waiting for the water to settle so I can see my reflection, shadowy against the pale sand. Then I breathe out.

'Mum.'

The water clouds over, then clears and I see Mum walking through a car park, feet in pewter slides, smart white trousers with a patterned blouse, her coloured scarf blowing in the breeze. She brushes her hair out of her eyes and I frown, noting the tightness around her mouth, the furrow between her brows.

I don't recognise where she is at first, then I see the glossy leaves and sliding glass doors. She's at the hospital. It's the same one where Ellie gave birth, where I saw a woman's soul snatched into darkness. But why is Mum there?

A Thousand Rooms

'Hey, Katie.'

I look up and see Pop standing there, smiling at me. I hadn't heard him approach, but he can move pretty quietly when he wants to.

'Hey, Pop,' I say, standing up. 'I just saw Mum and-'

'It's time.'

I look at him, confused. Am I being reassigned? But then he starts to change, his features growing younger and younger until he is the handsome young man I only know from photographs and all at once I get it. It's time for Grandma Jean to join us.

'Oh, Pop,' I say, a lump in my throat, so happy for him.

He holds out his hand. 'You need to come too, Katie, she'll want to see you.'

'Are you sure?'

'Surer than anything,' he says, and when he grins I see my Pop again, rather than this dark haired young man, all the world in his blue eyes. He moves his hand, and all at once there's a flower in it, a pink rose. 'They were always her favourites,' he says, in answer to my questioning look. 'Shall we?'

I nod, overcome for a moment. Then, something doesn't seem right. 'Wait for me,' I say, starting to run back to the cabin. I rush inside, breathless with it all, heading straight for the closet.

My death outfit. It's time. Besides, I'm basically wearing pyjamas and this is my grandmother, for God's sake. I know she'll be happy if I look nice. And yes, I know I'm being completely ridiculous, but you know how you *know* something, deep inside? This is how this feels.

So while I'm thinking this I'm putting my clothes back on. They feel a bit strange at first, buttons and waistbands and buckled shoes constricting after the loose comfort of my glam lounge wear. But it's the right thing to do.

I do up the last buckle and race outside again, slipping a little in my heels. I run the short way back to the pool and see Pop there, kneeling on the flat stone. When he hears me coming he looks up.

'We need to go, Katie.'

I nod, coming to take his hand as he stands. Then we fall together.

We end up in a corridor. It's the hospital, just as I'd seen.

'What's happened?' I clutch Pop's hand. 'I mean, she was fine, last time I saw her…' I trail off. It's still strange, that this young man is my Pop. But his voice is the same, not so gravelly but with the familiar inflections I've always known.

'She fell,' he said. 'In the garden. She bumped her head, couldn't get up. She was there for twelve hours or more. I was with her, the whole time.'

'You were?' I draw in a breath. 'Oh.' I can see in his face that it was hard for him. He nods, his lips pressing together.

'She loved her garden,' I go on, trying to inject a positive. 'I mean, of all the places…' God, that's stupid. But it seems to work. He smiles at me.

'She did. Always happy, among the flowers.' He brings the rose to his nose, his eyes closing as he sniffs the

A Thousand Rooms

velvety petals. He opens his eyes, blue and bright as stars. 'She's ready.'

I chew my lips, frowning. This is going to be weird. *Weirder than tagging along with dead people, Katie?* Yes, weirder than that. I didn't know any of them, you see. But I can't think about it any more, as Pop pulls me forward and through the door into the hospital room.

Oh, poor Gran.

As we enter the room the lights flicker for a moment, and Mum looks up. She's been crying, her eyes red, looking smaller without her usual mascara. She's holding Gran's hand. Gran is so pale, nasty purple bruising running from her temple down the side of her face, standing out like thunderclouds against her translucent skin. She's hooked up to wires and drips and machines, green lights measuring her breaths as they wind down towards the end.

For she is on her way to us. I can see the glow starting, the golden glitter around her frail form under the white cotton blanket. Pop lets go of me and goes over to her, his hand covering her free hand.

'I'm here,' he says, smiling at her with such love my eyes prickle.

At the same moment Mum says it too. 'I'm here. It's okay, Mum. You can go now, if you want.' Her voice quavers, but doesn't break, and I can see her whole body is tense, though her hand on Gran's is gentle.

And, as though it's a signal, Gran takes in a breath, slowly, her chest rising. Then, it slowly deflates. The glow around her increases, just like the golden glitter surrounding the young couple making love, as their child came to join them. This time it is the light of leaving, of Gran's soul moving on. And I see her face start to change, the features becoming younger and younger. She looks like Mum, I realise with surprise, then like Ellie. But her hair is shorter, bobbed and curled. Her eyes open, which is strange, for they stay closed on the figure in the bed. Mum has bent over, weeping, gold and grey sparkles twining around her, the cord that connected her to Gran breaking free as Gran sits up.

'John,' she says, smiling, her heart in her eyes.

'Jean.' He pulls her up and into his arms, the gleam around them increasing as they embrace. She spots me, over Pop's shoulder.

'Katie! Oh, my darling girl.' She lets go of Pop and comes over to me and hugs me and oh, it's just as it always was, the scent of roses all around her, powdery and sweet. I'm overflowing with happiness at it all. Despite Mum's sadness, despite all that has happened, this is a moment of purest joy.

We join hands, the three of us, Gran in between us both as we soar up through the night sky, beyond the stars. It's beautiful. This time it's Pop and I taking someone with us, rather than me tagging along, unseen and unwanted. It feels more right than just about anything, and I hear her laughter as we ascend.

When we land, it's in Pop's heaven. Or so I think. It's just the same, the old house under shady gums, geraniums by the front door. But Gran lets go of my hand and turns

to Pop, saying, 'What do you think?'
He tilts his head, frowning. 'What do you mean, love? This is Heaven.'
'It is. Just how I've always dreamed it would be. Us, together again, like we were when we were first married.'
Pop looks at me and I shrug, raising my eyebrows. Though I think I see what's happened here, and it's pretty cool.
'Shall we all go inside?' says Gran, starting up the path, half turning as she walks to add, 'there should be-'
'Lemonade in the fridge?' Pop laughs out loud. I think he's just realised it too. Gran stops, turning around fully, hands on her hips.
'What's going on?' she says, though she's smiling too, joy beaming out of her face. Her dress is pretty cool too, floral with a full skirt, soft cotton blowing in the eucalypt scented breeze.
'Well, my love, seems as though your idea of Heaven is the same as mine.'
Pop goes up to her, putting his arm around her waist and taking her other hand, twirling her around on the path as she finally gets it and starts laughing, her head going back, honey brown curls bobbing.
'There will be a Guardian along soon,' says Pop, smiling at her.
'A Guardian…?'
'Oh, I have so much to tell you,' he says, kissing her. They dance up to the verandah, and it's so romantic, Pop scooping her ups in his arms as he pulls the door open with one hand.

Hmm. Think I might leave them to it.

'I'll be back later,' I call, as they go through the door.

I hear Gran call out, 'See you soon.'

I head the other way, taking the thread back to my Heaven, dancing a little as I wander along the path dappled with light and shade. I turn back for one last look just before I pass through, and I think I can hear music, the kitchen curtains blowing in the open window. I smile, heart full.

Later, I sit on my verandah, tea in hand as I watch the trees dance endlessly in the warm breeze. I've changed out of my death outfit and am back in my comfy pyjamas, soft slippers on my feet. I'm feeling, not exactly sad, but just, sort of, done. As though a small shift has taken place, somewhere inside me. I sip my tea and think about it, wriggling my toes in my slippers. Then I remember. Jason's Guardian, the one who took him away, had told me there was one more thing I needed to do before I could be with him again.

Had I just done it?

I frown, wondering if that's the case. If me being here to meet Gran had been the last thing on the cosmic Katie To-Do list. Then I consider the implications, taking a deep breath in and out. What would it mean, to be born again? To no longer be... Katie? I mean, I know it's happened before – Jason had told me, and then I'd remembered, fragments of other lives playing like old films in my mind. So I guess it will be okay. It just seems to be a completely weird thought, the idea of becoming someone else. I drink some more of my tea. But I can't deny that I want to see Jason again. In fact, the thought of a life with him fills me with a fizzing sort of joy that seems to burn away all my doubts.

I put my tea down. Right. If I am done, if I have to leave soon, I should probably check in with my family. You know, one last time. I tense, expecting a tug under my breastbone, the pain of being apart from them returning. But all I get is... peace. As though that little shift inside me has made all the difference.

I look up as Pop and Gran appear, moving through the woodland, hand in hand. They're both a bit breathless when they arrive.

'Hello,' I call, standing up.

'Oh, you're still here,' says Gran, panting a little as she hops up onto the deck. 'I'm so glad, my dear.'

'Here?' I say, as she pulls me into a hug. 'Where else would I be-' There's a sizzling zap noise and a silver figure lands in the clearing. 'Oh.'

Oh shit.

It's happening. Guess there's no time for me to visit the pool for one last look. Now Pop has me in a hug and I can feel a tugging sensation starting under my breastbone as I hold onto him one last time, eyes closed, breathing in tobacco and sunshine. Then I let go.

'You can come here whenever you like,' I say, rubbing at my chest, my mouth twisting. I know they won't, though. They have their own Heaven. I turn to Dezariel, a flicker of excitement starting within me despite my apprehension.

'Is it time?' I ask. As if in answer, the tug comes so strong I gasp, bending a little.

'It is,' says Dezariel, reaching out one long silver finger to touch me under the breastbone. The pain lessens. There is a smile on the beautiful silver face, peace in the endless eyes. 'It is time for re-assignment.'

I nod. There's a question I need to ask, of course.

'Will he – is he there? He was born, wasn't he?'

'He was, and he is waiting for you.' The silver smile deepens. 'This will be a good life. Simple and full of happiness. Are you ready?'

Am I ready? I turn, looking at my woodland abode, the house where I've been so happy, my grandparents standing together, hand in hand on the wooden verandah. I look up at the trees, blossom swirling on the breeze, the earth brown and good beneath my feet.

And I think back to my life, remembering the blessings, the love, all that I was. I think of Mum and Dad and Ellie, of David and little Charlotte, of Sarah and Pete, of Jeremy and even old Velvet Boom Darryl, my life a string of beautiful pictures, all the way back to my childhood. And beyond. I see India, full of light and colour, silks and satins in an eighteenth century palace, a knight riding through dark woods, a lady at his side. All of it comes together in a tapestry of great beauty, a story woven through the centuries.

A story yet unfinished.

'I'm ready,' I say, gathering it all to me, holding it to my heart. I take Dezariel's hand, and smile.

Then I let go.

I see it slip away, Heaven receding from me, my grandparents raising their hands in farewell, Dezariel's silver smile the last thing I see before I turn towards the earth once more.

Blue ocean streams beneath me, lines of foaming water breaking on a strip of golden beach fringed with dense palms, houses made of wood with pointed roofs. There's a glow in one of the houses, and I know that's where I'm supposed to be.

And I am there.

Reborn

I am upset. In fact, I'm devastated. Yuda has thrown my new necklace, the one my mama gave me for my birthday last week, up into a palm tree. And now it hangs there, dangling from a leafy spike high on the trunk, coloured beads glinting gold in the sunlight coming through the rustling green leaves. I scream when he does it, running to the tree and jumping up, my hands stretched up as if I can make my arms longer just by wishing it, my bare brown feet kicking up dust as I land, jumping and sobbing until I am out of breath and can't do any more. I shoot Yuda an injured look as I sink to the ground, my head hanging, black hair in my face. I can see he is sorry, but he doesn't want to say it, his bluster gone. But everything goes blurry and I start to cry, my loss hurting me so much.

I am ten, and my mama had made a big deal about giving me the necklace, that I was old enough to have something so pretty and precious. I had felt so grown up in my new clothes, walking across the dirt square at the centre of our village, the ladies reclining on the covered platform smiling and calling to me, the hot sun and ocean's roar constant in my life. But now I will have to tell mama I've lost my necklace – I can't tell her what really happened. Yuda would get a beating and he always takes it out on me, after.

Then I hear another pair of feet running. They come to a stop in front of me, the toes almost touching the bright material of my skirt, the skin as brown and dusty as my own. A gentle hand touches my shoulder.

'Hey, what's wrong?'

I look up to see Wira, his face full of concern. I love Wira. He has always been there for me, since I can remember. The other day he told me his dream, his idea to build a surfing camp for tourists, right here on our beach. I looked at him in surprise then out at the rolling waves, white foam against brilliant blue and it was almost like I could see him riding the waves, dressed in black, his hair sleek against his head. I grinned at him.

'It sounds good.' He smiled then looked down, his hands tracing patterns in the sand as he spoke, not looking at me.

'Maybe, you know, you could help me?'

I was thrilled. Of course I would help him. It's what we do for each other; whenever either of us needs someone, we are there. Just like today. It's as though he knows when I need him. I look up to the tree and point, my tears starting again and he turns his head and spots the necklace.

'Oh, is that all?' He grins at me, teeth white against his nut-brown skin. Then he makes a run at the palm tree, climbing up to where my necklace hangs and unhooking it. He makes it look so easy, but he is nearly two years older than me, old enough to work picking the coconuts that bring income to our village. I scream again, jumping to my feet, but this time it's in joy. He slides back down the tree and comes over, acting all cool, like it's nothing, what he just did, but I can see the joy in his eyes.

Silver grey eyes.

That's what he has, unusual in our village though not unheard of. My mama said once that we've had many visitors to these shores, but I don't know what that means. Anyway, I think they are beautiful.

He holds out my necklace and I take it, blushing, all at once feeling shy. I put it around my neck and look down, my foot scuffing in the dust. Then I look up to see him still holding out his hand.

'You want to go to the beach, look for shells? I have a little time, before my father comes back.'

I blush again and he is smiling at me. I take his hand and I feel safe. I am home.

A short note:

Valhalla, I realise, has an accepted canon of belief around it. When it became apparent that Katie would be visiting the hall of warriors, I did research whether or not she would be allowed to enter. My research indicated that no women, other than Valkyries, were allowed entry into Odin's hall, and that half the chosen dead went there, with the other half being sent to Folkvangr, or Freya's Meadow. According to researcher Britt-Mari Näsström, 'as a receiver of the dead her [Freyja's] abode is also open for women who have suffered a noble death.'

(Näsström, Britt-Mari (1999). "Freyja - The Trivalent Goddess" as collected in Sand, Reenberg Erik. Sørensen, Jørgen Podemann (1999). *Comparative Studies in History of Religions: Their Aim, Scope and Validity*. Museum Tusculanum Press.)

Based upon the above reference, I decided to take slight creative license, making Valhalla for men and Folkvangr for women – whether this is actually the case, I suppose none of us will know until we get there.

ACKNOWLEDGMENTS

I have to thank Esther Newton for her editing insights, and Rich Jones at Turning Rebellion for the beautiful cover design. Thanks also to my wonderful beta readers, Loretta, Kelly, Angelika, Louise T, Ali and Louise A for all your wise feedback, to bloggers far and wide for their generosity, to my family and friends for their love and support, and to my beloved Marcus and Isabelle – I could not do with without you.

And I'd like to thank you too, dear reader. If you enjoyed reading A Thousand Rooms, please leave me a review or star rating – you can find me on Goodreads and Amazon.

Thank you for coming on this journey with me.

Other books by Helen Jones:

The Ambeth Chronicles

Oak and Mist
No Quarter
Hills and Valleys

When Alma disappears between two trees at her local park, she finds a whole new world.

Ambeth.

A place where gardens weave a spell around a stone palace, near to a pounding sea. Where Dark and Light struggle to control the Balance, a struggle that threatens the human world too.

And they are waiting for her…

BOOK FOUR, *UNDER STONE*, COMING SOON

ABOUT THE AUTHOR

Helen Jones was born in the UK, but then spent many years living in Canada and Australia before returning to England several years ago. She has worked as a freelance writer for the past ten years, runs her own blog and has contributed guest posts to others, including the Bloomsbury Writers & Artists site. When she's not writing, she likes to walk, paint and study karate (when housework and family life permit!) She's now working on several other novels unrelated to Ambeth, enjoying the chance to explore other fantasy worlds. She lives in Hertfordshire with her husband and daughter and spends her days writing, thinking, cleaning and counting cats on the way to school.

Blog: http://www.journeytoambeth.com

Facebook: Author Helen Jones

Twitter: @AuthorHelenJ

Amazon: https://www.amazon.com/author/helenjones

A Thousand Rooms

Printed in Germany
by Amazon Distribution
GmbH, Leipzig